FEELING BALLSY

A LOVE IS AWKWARD NOVEL

BECK ERIXSON

Aegir Haven, LLC

Published by Aegir Haven, LLC

ISBN 979-8-9875998-4-6 (Paperback)
ISBN 979-8-9875998-5-3 (Hardback)
ISBN 979-8-9875998-3-9 (ebook)

Editor: Kristen Weber, www.kristenweber.com
Copy Editor and Proofreader: Maria Tureaud, authormariatureaud.com
Cover Art: Melody Jeffries Design, www.melodyjeffriesdesign.com

DEDICATION

For the ones who know love is awkward and wonderful.
Those who value their friendships wholeheartedly.
And, for those who fell for their best friend.

CHAPTER ONE

R EAD HER BODY LANGUAGE and hold the line. Just like in every other game.

A hard clap of my thick gloves smacks the stale air while I bend my knees. *Shit.* I'm the last person who should be in goal to block this.

I glance at the opposing team's striker. They chose her to take this penalty because of her speed, her power, and the fact she's got the best shots in the league.

I'm not ready.

The striker's toe digs into the dark green turf, hips pivoting at the last second. My eyes widen as the laces of her indoor cleats lick the soccer ball.

My heart—and I—leap left, riding the high of competitive adrenaline, cutting through the air like a confused gazelle as I careen toward the wrong goal post. The neon pink ball curves right, past my toes, and I don't have a prayer to stop it from going in the net. My body slams flat against the turf, launching tiny black rubber beads from the base of the fake grass into the air. The referee blows a whistle and the scoreboard changes to award the other team the goal.

Thank goodness for hip padding. I roll to my back as the buzzer sounds on the adjacent field, and two bright bulbs glare down at me from the white aluminum dome ceiling.

We lose. Again. A deep breath pulls one of the tiny beads up my nose, and I cough up a lung 'til the little brat finds its way back out onto the ground where it belongs.

Penalties to determine the winner of a tie game are exhausting. This place needs to not book the fields so tight so we can have extra time added like the outdoor games. *Why do people even agree to play on my team?* My reputation as the worst keeper in the league precedes me, but playing a field position would be worse—I'm not a big runner.

Get up. Go shake hands, and wallow later. Screw the wallow, just hand me something frothy, and give me laughs with my teammates. The benefit of being in a beer league like this one is *most* players don't actually care who wins or loses. No one on this team is a pro. We're a mix of scientists, lawyers, and a VP of I-don't-know-what at a bank. There's even a professor. Wednesday match days are a guaranteed escape each week to blow off steam and chill with friends. To erase the far cry of the fantastical advertising world I'd imagined myself in when I took my marketing analyst courses. Rather than soaking in the world of creativity, most of my work life revolves around spreadsheets and occasional meetings.

A few of the Bees competed in college, but these days we all play for camaraderie and our new, quirky, extended family. *Still* … a win now and then would be nice.

I plaster a smile on my face and wipe off the combination of rubber beads and sweat. With a grumble, I hop up and scope the field. My teammates smile and laugh with one another.

"You did great!" Margaret jogs over, with her jet-black curls bouncing; her sunny disposition matching the yellow shine of the Bees' jersey. By day, she's a CPA for some big accounting firm in the city, and at night ensures the ball stays as far away from me as possible. "You can't stop a rocket shot every time." She pats my back and pushes me to the handshake line.

Perspiration-soaked synthetic leather smears across my lips as I rip open the glove straps with my teeth before pulling them off. I stick out my tongue and gag from the taste. Not my finest moment.

I walk the line, shaking hands with the winners. Margaret waves me down to the flap and I follow the team over to the bench. The dome scoops the blow of whistles and obnoxious buzzers high into the arched roof. Industrial fans overhead circulate the stink of sweat, blood, and body odor across two full indoor fields.

I step through the small pathway between the black netting and grab my bag, concentrating to not trip over the slack in the mesh, but thick, frizzy brown hair and a yellow jersey block the path. "Good game, Keep."

I missed though.

I pull at the bulk of my padded sleeves to squeeze past another teammate.

"Head up, Keep." Rose lathers white menthol on her ankle. "Damn that smarts." She's a high-powered attorney who occasionally works from the bench, but hasn't missed a game since joining. She's responsible for, and quite good at, getting the ball to the other team's goal.

My heart squeezes. *Stop trying to lift me up.*

"We'll get 'em next time, Keep." Another player pats my shoulder.

Keep smiling. I'll bench myself next game.

Their efforts to shake my cloud of failure are sweet, but I'm still the one who missed in the end. The loss is on me. I squeeze onto the corner of the bench, and push my bag down. Nate's signature black peacoat falls to the ground, spreading a thick smile across my face. *He's a keeper too, he'll get it.*

A glance around the field yields no sign of him and the sinking in my stomach draws away my smile. The flit of hope that he stayed to watch me evaporates like droplets of sweat. I pull my hair down and shake it out to reset all that frizz into a ponytail high off my neck.

A quick sniff of my jersey and my eyes cross. I peel it off and shove it deep into my bag. I tug on a warm-up jacket over a hunter green sports bra and damp skin. I don't mind that we lost, but I do mind the idea that I've let my friends down. Even if I'm the only one who thinks that. I've seen them win before, and their excitement. I love when I can help give them those feelings.

"Man, when you dive, you dive," the unmistakable taunting of my best friend's voice cuts through my frustration. After fifteen years of friendship, he instinctively knows when to poke at me. How we're friends has always been a matter of balance. He's the loud one.

Good days, bad days, whatever. Hawk has a way of making everyone around him laugh and feel important. In high school he was popular, a sculpted soccer jock and two years older. I like to remind him of the older part. Our friends all got married or had kids, and our once-large circle grew smaller and smaller until we became the remaining, single, survivors. Well, us, and whoever we're dating or seeing at any given point in time. We've always had very different views on dating. I'm the serial monogamist, and he, well, he's a serial dater.

We've kept our friendship close by maintaining our routines each year and joining things like this league. And this league was his idea, despite my lack of soccer skills. He gave me two options: soccer, or ballroom dancing. I chose soccer.

A smirk sketches across my face, and I lean into the corner. "You got a game next?" Where did he come from? Whatever, company is company.

The bench dips down, and Hawk brushes his finger against the side of my neck, fixing my collar.

"I'd hug you, but you smell." Hawk leans away and waves a hand in front of his nose.

"Man, are compliments like this why you kill it with the ladies?" I open my arms for a hug.

He shakes his head, claps his hands, and leans toward the net. I don't blame him. I'm pretty rank right now, and I'd have done the same. No one enjoys getting sweat stamps.

The next teams are busy warming up on the pitch.

I grab his bottle of water, gulp it down, and catch him giving Margaret's backside a once-over. "Hey! Stop scoping."

"Too late." He glances back at me with a wide grin and waves his phone.

He got her number? "Damn it." I chuck the water bottle back to him. "Stop dating everyone on my team."

"Stop finding intelligent and athletic women to play soccer with." He waves to Margaret. "Besides, it's just a phone number—for now."

I shake my head. Please, not Margaret. If he fights with her or hurts her heart, I'm in danger of losing another player. Beer leagues, at least this one, are magnets for hormones and hookups. Which might be why Hawk was so interested in the league. Mr. Scientific keeps a smiley face rating system, and even a color-coding system for evaluating acts performed on, or with, dates in his calendar. The entire calendar looks like an impressive rainbow by the end of each month.

The whistle blows and the next game starts.

"When's your game, Mr. Horny?"

He faces me with a raised eyebrow and places a finger over his lips. "Shh. Don't blow my shot."

"No worries there, sir." I laugh and lift my arm to block a ball from hitting my face through the net. *That* I block. Why can't I do that in goal?

"Game after this. We're playing Nate." He slides off his sandals, a bold footwear choice for October in New Jersey, and pulls his bag out from under the bench. "Staying to watch me beat your boyfriend?"

Where the hell *is* Nate? "He drove tonight, so yes." I crack my knuckles atop the wood bench. "I'm here 'til he drives us home."

Hawk rubs his palms on his jeans and leans forward. "Good. Make sure you yell loud enough for me to hear when I score on him."

I giggle. Things I have to keep inside include yelling if Hawk scores tonight. "You're playing in those?" I point to his jeans.

He pops the collar of his leather jacket and brushes back his hair. "Yes, then I'm going to sing *Greased Lightning* and slide on my knees across the field." He tilts his head and dips his shoulders. "*Then* I'm going to sleep with Margaret."

Fucker. "Have you seen Nate?" I pull my sneakers on and drop my indoor shoes into the bag, trying to feign not caring.

Nate's keys and phone slide off the bench to the ground. Chewing the inside of my cheek, I glance down at the keys with a tiny shot of disappointment that, once again, *they're* here instead of him.

Hawk elbows me and points to the door. "He's playing on the other pitch."

He missed my shitty game. Nate doesn't take losing well, which means Hawk will crank up the volume if Nate lets any balls in.

Hawk's hand slaps the side of the bench. "You played well. Get out of your head."

The player on the field has no one near her and charges the goal on a breakaway. My chest and stomach tighten as she winds up her leg to take a shot on goal. *POP*. The keeper's hands go up and punch the ball straight into the air, and she catches it tight on the way down. She barrels with a clenched jaw past the other team's player and screams at *her* team. My chest and stomach relax.

"Great job, Keep," I scream. Cheering for the other goalies is second nature. We all feel the frustration intensely when a ball goes into goal. "Woo!"

"Number twelve was robbed. Her team was all over the place." Hawk gestures to the field.

"The keeper should've leveled her for stepping in the goal box. That's a cocky play. Take the shot from farther out." I watch as the players effortlessly glide up and down the field.

"Man, you play dirty," Hawk says.

"Night, Elin." Margaret's voice cuts through our exchange from across the field. She waves at us as she heads to the door.

That wave isn't for me.

Hawk waves at her, and she disappears out the door. He tilts his head back and swivels in my direction as a grin tugs his lips.

"Don't fuck Margaret over." I turn my attention back to the pitch. "She's sweet and a good player."

He wags his eyebrows. "I intend to take her for a date and see what happens. Scout's honor." His knuckles rap on the bench.

Great. That's what he said last time he dated someone on my team. Where he sticks his body parts is up to him, but I got a ball to the face from the last teammate he "dated." "What are you going to do if one of the ghosts of your past talks to her about you?"

"It'll be fine." His tone shifts to hushed astonishment. "Besides, women don't talk about those things."

Ha. Wrong. Come get a beer after the next game.

"Right—" I zip the jacket up to my nose. "I can describe your penis in full detail without ever having seen it."

A glance at his wide eyes and dropped jaw draws a smirk.

"Prove it," he says.

"I know where you have a freckle. This is what happens when you use my team like a dating website." I feign a shiver. "I learn what your penis looks like."

His cheeks flush red, and he stares ahead at the game.

"Cat got your tongue?" I glance over at the doorway. Where is Nate?

The buzzer sounds for halftime. Hawk stands and removes his belt before I can turn to offer him privacy.

"I thought you knew what it looked like already?" he says. "Relax, would you? I've got shorts on."

I avert my glance to the pitch in time to catch Nate entering the field, barreling up the center with his arms tucked in. Sweat flies off his face as he jogs the last few feet to defend the goal I couldn't. He blows a kiss and waves. I give a small wave back and catch Hawk sliding his shorts over maroon boxer briefs.

"You liar!" I pull up the side of my jacket, covering my peripheral vision.

Hawk hikes his shorts, tugs down on his jersey, and smacks his abs. He's barely shorter than Nate, but in a much more compressed package.

"I'm going to go take some shots on Dolph." Hawk gives two thumbs-up and grips the netting to find the field entrance.

They get ten minutes to pummel each other before the game resumes, while everyone else uses the time to practice.

"Woot! Come on, Nate!" I clap.

If I call him Dolph, it'll be an issue. That's Hawk's pet-name for him, not mine, and it isn't a term of endearment. On occasion, instead of calling me "Keep" like my teammates, or using my actual name, he calls me Wildflower. My nickname from him dates from well before I met Nate. Hawk's team lines up six balls preparing to take open shots. *Come on, Nate. Plant your feet, arms wide, watch for tells.*

Hawk winds up for the first shot. The ball blasts toward the upper corner pocket, and I lean in. Nate jumps up and catches the ball with ease. Hawk turns to me, winks, and opens his arms wide.

"He's a house," Hawk mouths.

Fair. Nate's not built like any other soccer goalie I've seen. He's the opposite of lanky and has the build of a linebacker with agile feet. He's good—he knows it too. Getting him off a soccer pitch, or away from a ball, is nearly impossible.

One of Nate's teammates lines up for a shot, and the floor about shakes when Nate punches it. He points to his teammate and rolls the ball back out with a challenge for a faster shot. He sticks out his wide tongue and shakes it with a, "Baaa."

Hawk lines up a shot, points to me and then to Nate. His leg lifts to blast the ball, but instead he pushes it up the field with his head down.

Shit. I brace my stomach on a sharp inhale, watching as Nate dives at Hawk's feet to stop the advance. Hawk skims it over Nate's body and winks at me, catching the ball on his toes, and gently taps it over the goal line. Nate slams his fist on the ground and takes the goal line again. I exhale and shake my head, garnering a tiny wave from Hawk. There's no blood, but Nate's face is red, and he's fixated on the ball. Hawk is in his head.

The buzzer goes off and the men exit the field before the second half begins. Hawk slides onto the bench next to me, and Nate slides in on the other side, leaving me stuck between their egos and dislike of each other.

"Did you see my goal?" Hawk gloats.

I nod and offer a kind eye-roll.

"Everyone gets a lucky shot now and then." Nate kisses my cheek with no emotion, no accidental brush of an eyelash on the skin or spark of heat. He doesn't even really look at me when his dry lips stab down. He waves his hands for Hawk to slide down and make space.

"Amazing how the simplest of plays still catches you off guard." Hawk smirks and slides over.

The bench dips as Nate sits close to me. The sweat from his arm leaves a mark across the back of my shoulders while he pulls me close. *Sweat stamp.*

"Guess we'll see how it goes during our match," Nate says. "Wouldn't be the first time I've beaten you to something."

Six years ago they were on the same team. Hawk never said why he left, but it wasn't long after Nate and I started dating five years ago. I lean forward to drop the sweaty arm from my back, and hope the tension in the air resolves during their game.

The scent of testosterone is thick.

Hawk looks down at his phone and clicks away texts while the game resumes for the second half.

"Hey, sorry I missed your game. The orange team needed a goalie." Nate kisses my forehead. "I knew you wouldn't mind. How d'you do?"

"She did great," Hawk says, still clicking away on his phone.

I did *great*? I showed up, rooted for my friends, and let six balls cross the line tonight. Nate wouldn't be talking to anyone right now if he let six balls in, and he'd have me running drills to help me improve if he saw the penalty shots. But Hawk knows I need a cheerleader right now, and he'll always be a better cheerleader than my boyfriend.

Chapter Two

MY STOMACH RUMBLES AS a toasty pepperoni pizza comes out fresh from the oven and is placed into the glass display. The pizzeria's wooden booth only helps me slide lower with each glance at the door. He's only a little late. The fresh vegetable lasagna I had started cooking before his calls can finish baking when I get home. Dinner at home together is, once again, not happening. This is the third Thursday in a row Nate's picked up extra games. The league needs to recruit more players.

At least we'll get a little time before he rushes off to the indoor arena, and I can eat pizza.

The bells on the door chime, and the man behind the counter waves, sending my focus and a flit of hope to the entrance. Nate stands tall in his pea coat, fresh shiny gel slicking his hair to the side, and his sexy upper lip curls while he shakes hands with the owner. I sigh, sit tall, and wave him over to our booth. He gives me a cold kiss on the cheek, looking past me to the glass display. Routine stale kisses sink my heart, but every relationship has difficulties.

Not every kiss sends those flutters of magic across my chest or arms. Then again, we've never really had that same spark most couples do—us dating was unplanned. There was no real courting, or flirting.

When we met, I was at the field a lot to help the women's league during a down-slide in team registrations thanks to a baby/marriage boom, and he offered to help with my garbage goal keeping skills. We hung out so much it led to being physical, and suddenly we were in a relationship. One year led to two, to five, and I keep searching for the spark I know deep down doesn't exist for us. But it's like neither of us knows what to do at this point. Our lives are so intertwined in so many ways, sometimes I wonder if we are a habit, or if love always turns into cold kisses and congealed cheese.

The amber pendant above highlights the confidence entrenched in his body.

"Hey! Hope you weren't waiting too long." He squeezes between the back of the booth and the bolted down table, grabs the menu and places it to the side. His chin dips low and narrows his focus on me. "You okay? I'm not even getting a full smile."

His knuckle graces my cheek and I offer a half-smile. Tonight's stay-in date night is a bust, and even though I'll finish cooking the lasagna later, it won't taste the same tomorrow.

I shake my head and brush my hand against his, searching for a tingle or a spark. *Nothing.*

He leans back and squirms in the booth to pull his jacket off.

"Your arms are too big," I joke, and make a muscle.

He kisses his arm and bites his lower lip. "Best muscles for hugging with."

Ah, yes, hugging. His arms were once easy to get lost in when they were around me, pulling tight. Now they typically have his phone or a ball in them.

"I ordered a plain pie. I know you've gotta get to the field." The ice bobs in the plastic cup, shifting the straw while I stare down. "Whose team are you playing for tonight?"

"Matti's. Their goalie tore his bicep." He rubs at his arm. "Nightmare situation, really."

My stomach churns. Bicep tears are awful and only take a slight wrong turn, overthrow, or hit and rip to end someone's time on the field. I stick my tongue out mid-gag. Injuries happen, but focusing on or hearing about them and the recovery is awful. Crunching numbers at work doesn't involve touching needles or blood—I'd never make it in the medical field. The league and my team help decompress the monotony—and sedentary—atmosphere of scanning numbers for patterns and projections, but the fear of injury looms each time I take a strong hit. Nate plays for some of the same reasons, to escape the repetition of stamping insurance forms based on results from a software program and a manual. He gets the bonus of living out some of his best memories from college. We've all taken a hit at least once on the field, where the crowd grows still as the room waits for a fallen player to get up and be okay.

"Yeah, so he'll be out for a while." He looks over at the server. "Thanks, Buddy."

I whisper low as the server leaves the table. "That's not his name."

Nate shrugs. "You're so literal." He pulls his phone out and scrolls for a while. His eyebrows lift when he looks up. "Your Blues won today."

We don't play or banter well together like Hawk and I do, unless it's about sports. But Nate can be goofy when he chooses.

"Good, did they beat your team?" I raise an eyebrow. Truth be told, I don't follow professional soccer as closely as he does. My Blues are an easy team to root for, and give me a team to talk about when he gets deep in the weeds with the pro sport fanatics.

"They play each other Saturday." He grabs at his glass and tosses the straw on the table. Ice shifts, sending bubbles up the cup with each gulp of his water. The Reds are loud, flashy, and every other week, one of them is getting in trouble. A fact burned into my skull from hours and hours of sports highlights blasting from the basement at all times.

"Want to have friends over Saturday?" I grab a slice of pie, fold it, and watch the oil drip onto my plate. "I'll make a bunch of snacks." He'll still be jumping up and down, yelling at the television and ignoring me 'til there's a good play, but I'll have friends there and time with him off the field.

"I was hoping you'd ask." His face lights up and he smiles. "I'll invite the team over. We'll make a day of it."

"Sounds good." I take a bite.

"Invite your team too. It'll be like a college mixer." He winks.

"Can they bring their other halves so they don't feel like offerings of fresh meat?"

"Absolutely." He takes a big bite of his slice and grabs for the cheese stretch before it hits the plate.

"And Hawk?"

He nods several times, grabs a napkin to wipe grease from the cleft in his chin, and gives a solid eye-roll with a crooked smirk.

"Balls are going to fly through your hands tonight." I laugh and nod my chin up at him.

He crosses his eyes and sticks out his tongue. A familiar wave of normal rushes over my body and erases the nag of doubt in my stomach.

"Today's Thursday. When are we shopping?" I sit back in the booth and eye his jacket.

"Text me a list and I'll go after the game tonight." He bats his big damn eyelashes. "Or, since you aren't doing anything tonight, maybe you could get the groceries, or we can go together after my game."

"You smell rank after playing. No one is going to want you in their grocery store." My smile shifts to a smirk. "I'm fine to get the groceries and hang out at home instead. My fingers are still sore from playing last night." I extend my pizza greased hands to show my pale fingers.

He grabs them, and his warm lips press against their tips, offering much better kisses. Warmer, and not obligatory or routine.

"Damn charmer." I press my lips tight together. "How much time we got left?" *Please, skip the match and stay with me, we can get groceries together and plan for Saturday. Maybe watch the movie I queued up for tonight.*

Nate glances at the clock over the door. "Crap." He snatches the napkin from the table and dabs the oil from his face. "I've got to go." He looks down at my hands, then back up to my face. "I'll wait 'til you finish your pizza."

He leans forward on his elbows and grabs for his cup of water while his attention darts between the slice and the clock. So much for being patient.

"It's okay if you have to go. I'll research some recipes and think about what to do to ensure the Blues win this weekend." *Please let them destroy his team this weekend. Though, then he'll stay mopey 'til the Irish league comes on.*

He stands, adjusts his jacket, and leans forward to plant a greasy kiss on my lips. "See you tonight."

I nod, and take another bite of pizza, smiling past the cold edges. Nate offers a wave to the owner on his way out the door. With a familiar look of pity, the server comes and sits with me, kicking up his feet in the booth. Eating alone here isn't an option, it's not the family way. But my Italian is garbage, so like last Thursday and the one before, our common ground is watching the cooking channel while he keeps me company until either I'm done eating or another customer arrives.

CHAPTER THREE

CLEANING AND PREPPING FOR today started on Thursday night, immediately after my non-dinner with Nate. The pre-match starts at one o'clock, which should've given me enough time to set up for the party with our teammates. Leave it to me to be behind like usual—the barbecue chicken, bread, and beer-laden sausage and peppers all need to finish cooking. Placing the tables and cleaning up the basement took longer than planned.

"Hey! Have you seen my jersey?" Nate stands at the base of the stairs, holding a towel to his hips, reeking of Old Spice and balm. "I checked the laundry—"

I shake my head, and do my best to ignore his defined triceps. "Is it in your disgusting game bag?"

One too many sweat-drenched jerseys, left too long for my liking—mixed with the constant smell of mildew when he forgets to throw them in the wash fast enough—is the reason he does the laundry. Between the mold and the entrenched smell of raw musk, his gear bag makes me want to vomit.

The overhead lights shine against the drops of water clinging to the few hairs on his chest. I walk over and set my hands on either side of his hips, biting my lower lip. My fingers walk up the sides of his abs and his free hand presses against my back. The palms of my hands press across his upper back and I glance up at him.

He kisses the side of my neck, and a sad tingle of long forgotten flutters scatter down my body. My lips part and his cover mine, accepting the invitation to glide his tongue over mine. He pulls away, and grazes his lips against my forehead before releasing me.

Rejection is coming. Dry spells happen in relationships, but this one is never ending. I get it though. Where I should feel excitement and desire, I don't. But I try to search for it inside me. My fingers glide down his sides, and he brushes a piece of my hair back.

"We don't have time—do you want them to walk in on us?"

He's never lasted long enough in bed to politely answer this question.

Nate's always in a rush for something. He scans across the room. "There it is." He gives one more flutter-less kiss to my cheek and walks to the bar to grab his shirt.

My reflection in the framed jerseys on the wall offers a well of emptiness. I could dress up, or maybe make more effort than a ponytail. Try makeup. But that's not who we were when we met. He likes that I'm rough and tough—at least he did.

"What do you think?" I gesture to the dish filled with Swedish meatballs, an assortment of finger foods and loads of carbs spread across card tables around the room. If nothing else, I know how to feed people.

"Smells great." He throws his towel on top of the bar to pull on shorts. "My friends would be fine with bags of chips and beers."

"Eh. I figure people will be here awhile—everyone's gotta eat." I nod to the backyard. "The pop-up goals are up for a quick scrimmage if there are any takers."

He flicks the elastic on his shorts, and his warm hand slides into my back pocket. "Cool."

Cool. I set the room while he slept, showered—probably jerked off—and messed around on his phone, and I get a cool. Seems equal.

He shakes his head and clinks glasses. "Do you need to get changed?"

I glance down. Wasn't planning on it—jeans and a black dress shirt seem appropriate for company.

With a nod, I run up the basement stairs to the main floor.

The doorbell rings before I can grab clothes or a shower. He still wouldn't have lasted as long as it took for the first visitor to arrive.

I reach for the handle and a loud side-fist bang says hello from the other side. "Patience!"

Which one is he? Forward, defender?

"Hey, Elin." A gust of wind whips his auburn hair to the side. He raises an eyebrow and a flash of glacial blue draws me in. "I'm Thad." I paste a smile on my face and open the door. He leans down to kiss my cheek in the same way someone would kiss a sister.

Another hand reaches out and knocks on the door frame. Ah, Hawk and Margaret. Did they arrive together? I back up to make space for all three to enter the tiny living room. Thad takes off his hat and nods to the white-washed custom bookshelf.

"Why didn't you come in through the downstairs back door?" I gesture to the back of the house.

Hawk shrugs. "I hate the steep steps to get down there. Plus, I saw Thad and figured I'd try this way."

"Who's the reader?" Thad scans across the books and photos while he hugs tight to a plate of cheese chunks.

Hawk takes the plate from Thad and walks to me with his hands out. "I brought these for you."

Thad rubs the side of his face. Hawk's rollicking personality is well known in the league. Only very few people see the softness inside.

"I told you to bring something!" Margaret raises her hand to her forehead and nods her head back. "Ugh." She flashes her perfect smile, reaches into her bag, pulls out a gold box fitted with a red ribbon, and hands it to me. "Thankfully, I have manners."

"She only likes my mom's cooking." Hawk gestures his hand to the side. "I'll bring Mom next time."

"Please do, she's a sweetheart." His mom can also calm him with a single eyebrow, a trick I'd like to learn.

I take a quick sniff of the gorgeous dark chocolates and color-ful array of cheese. Do I have to share this with everyone? That's the polite thing, right? "Thad and Margaret, you didn't have to. Nate's downstairs if you want to watch the game."

Thad waves his hand across the room. "There's no TV in here."

I nod. "True. There's a huge one downstairs." No television on the main floor is the minor concession Nate made when I'd moved in last year.

He bought the place two years ago but wanted to live in it for a year by himself. This made sense at the time. With three years in and no talk of marriage, living together was a test run, but I think it was a way to stall any talk about the future be it good or bad. We don't hate each other, we coexist in relationship purgatory because neither of us wants to admit it isn't working.

Thad clicks his tongue and offers a half-drawn smile. His hand hovers over the philosophy books flanked by biographies of Marcia Ball, Norah Jones, Fats Domino, and Dr. John. A beam of possible enchantment joins his finger as it slides down the spine of Fats Domino.

"Can I take your jacket?" I smile and pluck a leaf off the collar of his thick brown corduroy jacket, letting it glide to the worn hardwood. "Ah, yeah. I guess I don't have much need for some of those anymore."

"Nah, they're great." Thad takes a step back and the floor creaks. "I'm not the only music nerd at the party." He offers a chuckle.

Hawk pats my shoulder. "Don't worry. You're still queen nerd."

I give him a soft elbow and nod to the stairs. Hawk takes Thad's jacket and tosses it into the master bedroom. I cringe when Margaret peeks into the room, hoping she doesn't notice only my side of the bed has wrinkles. Nate's side is smooth because he rarely sleeps there. Instead, he falls asleep on the big couch in the basement, watching sports highlights almost every night, and I get the queen bed all to myself.

The railing shakes from the speakers below as we descend the narrow staircase to the finished basement with walls the color of an exploded frog.

Margaret takes one end of the shuffleboard table against the wall and motions for Hawk to come join.

"Holy shit! Is this thing regulation?" Hawk's excitement to poke my ribs feels like a hot rod jabbing at my core.

"Yup. I call her, *Not A Vacation*."

Margaret waves me over.

I grit my teeth and offer a half-smile. "Can I get you guys drinks?"

"I got 'em!" Hawk wanders off behind the bar.

"Did you two drive together?" I fidget with the unraveling hem on my shirt. It's not like he didn't tell me his intentions. I don't like this sinking feeling that by the time he's done with her, no amount of mending will keep her and I friends in the long run. I'll be blamed or asked to pick a side.

Margaret pushes a blue puck up the board and claps when it lands on the "three." "Yeah, it was sweet. We were texting, and he offered to carpool so I could have a drink."

Sweet is one word for it. "Yeah, he's a great guy." *Trying to get in your pants.*

Hawk saunters over, hands her an IPA, and slides a red puck up the board. His puck bounces Margaret's blue one into the no scoring zone. His arm shoots high in victory and Margaret puffs out her lower lip.

Dumb, Hawk. Come on. Though, the dumber he is now, maybe I'll be able to salvage a friendship with her if they're super short term.

Hawk leans in and pokes her bottle, then wraps his soda arm over her shoulder, pumping his free fist into the air. I shake my head and wander to the overstuffed leather couch where Nate is busy talking to his boss, a few coworkers, and a mess of newly arrived teammates who came in through the always-open-enter-or-exit-whenever back door. I grab a chip and take in the increasing volume of chatter in the basement and the number of plates stacked with food. Nate gives a wink and blows a kiss in my direction with a small wave.

At least he knows I'm here.

Nate gestures to the framed jersey of a small Irish team on the back wall. His coulda-shoulda-woulda claim to fame on how close he was to the pros. "I was out on the pitch with my dad and we were kicking around. This old guy was watching us, and he walked over and offered me a tryout." Nate touches his hand to his heart and glances at the jersey. "But we were leaving in a few days and ..."

I groan inside. Once upon a time, I believed him. If he'd wanted it badly, he could've made it happen. Now I know it's nothing more than a small local team jersey that he fluffs like it's a top tier league and he's more talk than ambition.

"Honest. I still have the letter and everything." Nate stands proud with his feet wide and hips square to the goal on the television. "Man—life would be so different right now—eh, Elin? I'd have been traded up, up, up. The coach said talent oozed from me."

"We'd have never met." Lights from the too-big-for-the-wall-television scrape at my skull. Not a soul in here believes him, we know how the clubs work, but there's also no point in calling him out or saying he wouldn't have made it to any of the big paying leagues.

"Nah. Something always brings two people together when they're meant to be, babe."

I nod and turn to fix the chips escaping their glass bowl, inevitably crushing some while little flirts and sparks ignite across the room between Hawk and Margaret. If they make it six months, I'll have a screaming and distressed teammate. From there, she'll either leave the league or find a new team. Six months is a long time for Hawk, he's usually in and out faster. If they last less than two maybe three weeks, we can grab a drink. I can listen to how much she's sad and then we can go back to pre-Hawk interactions. A clearing throat draws my attention, and I jump back as Hawk stands mere inches away with two empty plates. My heart decides now is the time to beat hard, muffling the chuckles and conversations around us, leaving me in our small glass friendship bubble while the rest of the world moves on its own.

"Hungry?" I ask.

"It wasn't all me!" He nods his head back at the table. "They're animals I tell you. Animals!"

I glance over at Margaret, and she found Liv. Now they're both busy smack-talking Nate's teammates around the table.

Thad places a quarter on the edge of the shuffleboard.

"Table's open." Hawk pushes the quarter off the table. "How about Elin and I, versus you and Margaret?"

What are you up to? I raise an eyebrow.

He grins, focusing on Margaret. I've seen this pre-play dance before with other members of my team. He's calculating his move.

His pinky taps mine, calling me in as his wingman. Crap. I'm not doing this to her.

He kicks my foot under the table, and I kick his back. His glance down at me includes a half-bitten lip of frustration. Too bad his half-cocked smile locks back on Margaret. He's going to move forward with or without me.

"This place needs a puppy." He glides the blue puck up the light brown wood.

I roll my eyes. Not the *puppy* move. Granted, I've seen it work way too many times. It's a standard play for him.

"Oh, I love dogs!" Margaret takes his place at the table and sends the red puck up, bouncing his to the sand on the side.

Nice! Ugh, wait. Those are my points too!

"I have the cutest dog ever." Hawk lays the bait.

With a quiet huff, I softly push the blue puck up the wood, and it lands short.

"I've got a ton of pictures of Curie in my phone." He punches keys, and the vibration of Margaret's phone on the board shakes my puck closer to the points area.

Margaret quickly grabs it, swipes the screen, her forehead raises high as she taps Thad's arm. "She's so cute!"

Emotional connection success. He honestly should teach classes. This is a slight pivot from his normal tactic, but he already had her number.

"Hey, we should take a group photo." Hawk waves Margaret, Thad, and I in. Hawk wraps his arm over Margaret's shoulder and holds the phone out. His warm palm slides against mine to tug me closer. A bright flash blinds me, and he releases my hand to play with the phone screen. "I sent one of the group to all of us, and one of Margaret and I with you two cropped out."

I open my phone and the image he sent includes a smiley face with its tongue sticking out over my face, and a smiley face with hearts over the eyes on Thad's face. Smooth.

Margaret touches his shoulder and runs her fingers down his arm, mixing it with a sweet laugh as she looks at the photo in her phone. His dance worked. His barely needed efforts have her wrapped up in his outward personality.

Thad gives the board a once over, then pushes his puck up the table. It smacks into mine, and I land on a point.

More teammates arrive and the basement feels smaller than usual. I glance around the room for Nate but he's busy chatting with his boss next to the jersey still. The noise grows thick. I need air.

There's never anyone upstairs in the kitchen during these parties. I slowly head up the creaky steps to avoid shaking the television. The first floor of this open ranch is a glorious escape from the crowded basement. Opening the side door creates a breeze tunnel when the front is open, and the temperature drops at least ten degrees. The volume of noise from downstairs is dull, and as quickly as the overwhelming feeling came on, it's gone again.

I open the oven and remove fresh pepperoni pizza, bread, and a tray of barbeque chicken.

"Hand over the chicken and no one gets hurt." Hawk puts his hands out and stares down at the tray.

"Well, okay." I offer the tray fresh from the oven. "Your hands will suffer."

A high-pitched, playful yelp releases from his mouth. "How dare!" He kisses his fingers. "These are magic. Magic, I tell you."

I roll my eyes playfully and place the tray on top of the oven to cool. "You had your hands out."

"Why isn't Dolph helping you?" Hawk helps himself to a tray from the upper cabinet with a grunt as he stretches high.

His ass draws my focus mid-reach, and I nearly slice my finger instead of the heavenly bread. Hawk must've broken out the perfect-butt jeans for Margaret. We found them on a shopping trip a few years ago, for when he wanted to impress a woman he liked. He still wears them early on in a relationship before switching to comfy athletic clothes. According to him, his best feature is his bubble butt. Which isn't bad, but the dimples he gets when he smiles are better than his ass.

"His team's downstairs. I don't want to disturb him," I reply. "Why aren't *you* downstairs?"

Hawk tilts his chin down and looks at me. His entire body sways like he's studying my face. He holds the tray like a soccer ball—elbows wide, and pointed to the side—then widens his stance.

He raises his voice for his signature fake Nate impression. "The man kept nodding and offered me a tryout right then." His foot swish kicks at the air like a bad jazz move, before he runs a lap around the tiny kitchen like Fred Flintstone, and I choke on a giggle.

"Cut it out." I shoot a finger to my mouth with a shush, and glance at the basement stairs. "Grab another tray?"

"So you can check out my ass again?" Hawk turns and shakes his butt. "Admit it, it's glorious in these jeans."

"I'm immune to your ass." I swallow back the flush in my cheeks, and tug a tray from the lower cabinet to hand up to him. "Can you and your butt bring these downstairs?"

Laughter radiates up from the basement, and a cheer from my team trumpets from below.

"Sounds like the Blues scored." I waggle my eyebrows and nod for him to follow.

He clears his throat and adjusts his hood, revealing a silver collar below the zip up.

Since when does he wear collared shirts? This isn't how he dresses, not for hanging out to watch a game.

Hawk flashes a cheeky smile, takes a tray from my hands, and bounds down the stairs to rejoin the party.

My thick hair drops into the chicken with each steep step down. Sucking in my stomach isn't helping a lack of coordination holding all this food. The tray wobbles in my hands, and my feet spring to a quick step. At the base of the staircase, Hawk turns from the shuffleboard in time to catch the tray and offers a hand for balance.

His wide palm presses against my back and he stares deep into my soul, holding me suspended from certain injury for one second too many. The ends of my hair catch in his watch and when I go to straighten, I jerk my head back, releasing a tiny yelp.

Thad and Liv work to detangle his watch from my hair while I turn redder and redder from the horror of this moment.

Right, what was I doing? I place my hands on my hips and glance around the room. "Where's the rest of my team?"

"Out back." Thad points to the basement door but his gaze is set on the smorgasbord of food options. "I'm a little embarrassed by my cheese in relation to this amazing spread."

"Never be embarrassed by cheese."

He shakes his head and clasps his hands together. "Liv informed me you don't put toothpicks in Brie."

"Liv's a force." I purse my lips to stifle a laugh. "She's right. But maybe you'll start a trend?" Probably not.

Liv helped steal Rose from the men's league a few weeks ago, making her the newest recruit on the Bees. Liv can be persuasive. Her years spent practically living at the bank she works for, except for game days, paid off. She's a VP with a direct, blunt, and dirty mouth.

"Man, I suck." Thad pops another meatball in his mouth and turns his attention back to the game.

"Who are you rooting for?" I ask.

"Go Blue."

"Correct answer." I turn to go outside to join my team.

They've made themselves comfortable in the backyard.

Rose throws her arms up high. "Keep!"

I smile and bounce down the cracked concrete steps to the half-soccer field we've set up in the back. A few of Nate's teammates are outside with mine, passing and juggling balls high in the air to one another. I smile and raise my hand to signal for a pass. A glance up at the porch and Thad, Hawk, and Nate are standing on top sipping beer and chatting. His boss and coworkers are nowhere to be seen, which isn't too much of a surprise considering none of them really play or follow soccer. Nate tips his beer out and smiles. I wave him to come join and he shakes his head to disappear back to the television.

Thad taps a ball that hooks wildly from our field, and bounces off the neighbor's overgrown tree yard back to ours. The lake in the distance sparkles with pinks and lavenders through the naked branches.

"Head's, Keep!" I catch a shot and roll it deep into the yard for the first taker.

Being outside, stumbling over uneven grass as twilight hits, and laughing with my friends, makes me happy. I'll stay out here 'til full dark, my team distracting me from the emptiness of the house. Once they leave there won't be anyone here to help me push away the growing void in my soul.

CHAPTER FOUR

STODGY, LOW-END CATERING IN the bleak middle school-styled cafeteria at work is not my idea of a relaxing moment. HR seems to think company-wide social gathering events at least once a quarter help the different divisions bond and network. They're wrong. People stick to their tiny clusters, shove food in their mouths, and head back to their desks before the icebreaker games—with prizes like $5 gift cards to the in-house coffee shop—start. These events put too much pressure on me to perform, to be "on," and to not drop food on myself or trip over air. As it is, my leg won't stop shaking while I lean against a pillar and stare off at the empty doorway.

The only positive to these events is that Hawk works here too, and we can roll our eyes together. He claims he had nothing to do with my getting the interview here. But, after the beautiful woman in HR asked if he was single—not even a week after I was hired, as if she and I were besties—I doubt the claim. I've barely seen him since he drove Margaret over for the match party a few weeks ago. Texts, absolutely, but he's busy doing whatever it is he does in the early part of courting someone. Which means I'm home most nights rereading one of the dozens of books on the shelf while Nate is either at work or practicing at the field house. I did sneak out one night to the local musician's café to attend an open mic night when I knew both Nate and Hawk were busy.

Hawk arrives with his cluster of scientists in the dank lit room, and relief hushes the anxious tap of my foot. His hair is styled over with a side shave, exposing his industrial bar piercing and black studs in his lower lobes. Jewelry and the denim nail polish he has on are easy tells that he hasn't been in the lab all day. The lab coat is for show. He stands in stark contrast to the balding and white-haired, mainly men, around him. The scientists' crisp white coats are always eye-catching. A glance around the room yields my division huddled at a table, with an empty chair held for me, in their jeans and half-decent tops with smart blazers instead of suits. Suits are reserved for the sales teams or temps trying to make solid impressions.

I shake hands with the new HR rep, side-eye Hawk, and excuse myself to go to the bathroom.

"I forgot to lock the lab." He says loud enough for it to hush the room. He's not smooth at *all*. Then again, he probably didn't mean to be.

After veering away from the bathrooms and the lab, Hawk and I head to the car and speed to the high-end sushi buffet, an indulgent twenty minutes from work. Sneaking out of the company party for our own long lunch is brilliant. I've missed him, but this is normal whenever one of us starts a relationship. The other adjusts and we move forward.

The bright lights of the restaurant, and clanging of plates from the backroom, join with knives smacking sharply against cutting boards. Fresh fish. Fresh salad. Fresh everything in abundance, begging for my plate to overflow and satisfy my watering mouth.

The server's quick usher to our usual table is a sure-fire sign we come here together too much. It only gets more awkward when one of us comes at night with our family, or me with Nate, and Hawk on a date. Our usual spot is the perfect distance to avoid any breeze from the door, has a direct line of approach to the multiple, gargantuan, stations of food, and back far enough to not get constantly bumped by overwhelmed newbies shuffling back and forth in a daze.

"What's eating you?" Hawk asks with a raised brow. "You've been quiet since we left work."

I stare off at the drink menu as if my regular order suddenly won't involve a jasmine iced tea.

"You can talk to me about Nate." He clears his throat and flips the menu. "Jasmine iced tea."

"What's the point? It's the same conversation over and over." I sigh. I should enjoy that I'm out and finally seeing Hawk, but instead, my heart squeezes at the mention of Nate.

Hawk leans back in his chair and places his palms on the table. The fingers on his right hand raise high, and if I don't answer him, he'll use the table as a drum kit until I do.

"Okay, okay." I touch my forehead and shake my head. "No drums."

He lifts his hand high and runs his fingers through his hair. "Deal."

"Am I hideous? Unattractive? Not someone to run and have a quickie with before everyone comes over?" The words rush from my lips, painting his cheeks pink.

A grunt scrapes the back of his throat and he leans forward. "Those are all ridiculous questions and I refuse to answer them. I need context, and are we really going to talk about sex? I thought we didn't do that." A sparkle from the light above hits his eye as he shifts in his seat. "What's ... not eating you?"

A deep, embarrassed laugh shakes my shoulders. "He was weird at the party. He's been weird overall lately. It's like each time I try to be sexy, or sweet, or intimate, I'm shot down and left feeling stupid."

Hawk stares at the table, ripping a napkin to pieces. "Can we never say Nate and intimate, or talk about the two of you having sex? I prefer to picture him without a penis."

"Do I get to keep my vagina?" I shake my head. "Fair. Things have never been simple with him. I see other relationships and I don't get it."

"You never know what's happening in someone else's relationship though. You don't know what's real or fake unless they come out and tell the truth. How often do people let you know the mess behind the curtain?" His potent gaze drifts up, locking with mine. "Let's think about this. You opted to date a guy dumped by his fiancée like, the weekend after she left."

Hawk's eyebrow twitches high. "If you knew the mess behind the curtain, would you have gone out with him?"

"No—well, kind of. We went to innocently kick a ball around." Why is he always right? "Things evolved—"

"No, he saw an opportunity and took it." He leans in with an evil grin. "I was there for the beginning. I've been here the whole time. Dolph's an almost-middle-aged frat boy who won't grow up. But you're Ms. Loyal, giving chance after chance even when the guy is a douche who deserves none of your time."

I roll my eyes high into my skull. "People can kick a ball around and have it be nothing. You and I do it all the time."

"True, and not. First time we did it, I thought you were hot."

My heart hits a forceful beat and I struggle to swallow down the lump in my throat. "New topic please." The enormous goldfish in the tank on the back wall stares at me as if he knows how many years it took for me to suppress the idea of Hawk and I being anything more than best friends.

I point my pinky at the man standing with an empty plate, staring at the stations. He's lost. First timers have no routine or understanding of how to grab a dish off the moat.

"How long do you think it'll take that guy to figure it out?" I ask, mumbling around a mouth full of salmon.

"No." He narrows his brows, and bops the table with his index finger.

I hate when he gets like this. He won't let this go.

"He treats you like shit and you keep going back."

Great, it's "be frank and have a lecture" time. Time to shove in more sushi and fake a smile.

His wooden chopsticks clink down on the ceramic plate. "I'm not wrong. All he does is play soccer and hit on your teammates. He offers them lessons when you're not around." He crosses his arms and leans back.

My ears and temples throb. I drop my chopsticks on the table and push away my plate. Avoiding the conversation is useless.

"If it were me coming home late, sleeping on the couch downstairs, falling asleep watching soccer with my dick in my hand—or not having dinner with a girlfriend—you'd yell at me."

"He's happier on the field."

"He's a guy stuck in his glory days thinking he's some fantastic pro. He's not. Dolph's a sad dude in his late thirties without much ambition."

"How's it going with Margaret?" A pressure at the bridge of my nose intensifies which does nothing to push away the burn in my nostrils. I know the list of issues, and I won't get through lunch without crying if I focus on them right now.

"Deflection—but I'll answer." He chews a bite of rice, swallows it, and crosses his arms. "Can't get mad." He raises an eyebrow.

"I promise nothing." I clear my throat and the clamp on my lungs releases. "Are you being you, or are you trying this time?"

He lifts a hand to his chest, leans back, and gapes, comically. "I'm always a perfect gentleman. How dare." He laughs and his focus drops to the glass of water between us. "You need to know he was texting her. And trying to get her to kick around with him."

My heart sinks. Liar. No. Staring back blankly is the best answer I can muster.

His gaze rises to meet mine, almost pleading for me to listen. "She showed me the texts." He rests his fingers on the table and tilts his head. "Did you not want me to tell you? Are you going to ask him about it?"

Liar. Liar. The tinges of concern in his voice aren't settling the urge to rip the phone from my pocket and call Nate. I'd never really do it. Searching too deep could reveal what I've been suspecting. And Nate would say it's innocent, he's being a good friend. I'd have to believe him, because I want to believe the person I've dated for so long—despite my growing reservations.

I press a palm to my chest to calm my heart. "He probably wanted to kick around." Without me. What the hell?

He looks down and shakes his head. "You weren't invited. She asked, then he said no." He glances up catching my gaze. "She likes you, and thinks he's a douche. Dolph the douche."

With a stiff breath in, my nostrils flare. There's no evidence. Hear-say yes. Not that I don't believe Hawk—it's Nate thinking he's helping my team get stronger. Nate likes to play soccer all the time. I like to play music, or bake, or go to a museum. There are days I want to go for a hike without having to worry if the ball will fall down the ravine. Go for a bike ride, anything really. But every day is soccer for Nate. I love my teammates, and the atmosphere, but sitting my ass on an unforgiving bench seven days a week to shout and cheer gets exhausting. Soccer was more fun when it was only a night or two for Hawk and I, rather than an all-consuming activity.

Nate could sit all day on the bleachers. Yelling at the ref, the field, everyone, before pointing out ways they could improve next time. His offer to kick the ball might be to help Margaret play better for my team, and therefore be for me. Margaret's my defender after all—she's there to keep the ball from the box.

"How's your food?" Hawk jerks his chin at my plate.

The tears forming in the corners of my eyes must've prompted a topic change and softer tone. "Are you two ever going to get along?"

He coughs into a napkin and raises his eyebrows. "We were. But then he hit on the person I'm seeing—while dating you. I'd be a dick to be like, hey buddy, let's go kick around while I pretend you didn't try to hurt people I care about."

The server clears his throat as ice clunks into our glasses with a refill. "All good?"

"Splendid." I smile at the server.

Water spits onto the table as the pitcher lifts high. He dabs at the droplets, and rushes off.

I stare down at the glass as the ice shifts to a more comfortable position. "What if—"

"Uh huh," Hawk says. "What if, what?"

"It'd be helpful if you let me finish."

"I always let a woman finish. It's only polite."

My cheeks flush. "Good for Margaret."

"She wouldn't know yet." He tilts his chin down and waggles his eyebrows.

His crude humor comes strongest when he's stuck. When he wants to protect someone from the truth, or thinks he's inching too close to feelings.

He has "tells." Like tapping his fingers, flicking his ear from back to front when he's pulling back on sharing something heavy, and crude little jabs. I have the Hawk Handbook down fairly well. Very little surprises me at this point.

I can't imagine what he'd say mine are. Tears welling, being careless on the field, tripping over my own feet, or going through absurd amounts of flour when I'm stressed. There was one night, before I met Nate, I'd broken up with my super-sweet-but-not-right-for-me college boyfriend because we didn't click anymore. He deserved to find the person who made him happiest. I baked until all the flour in the apartment was gone, and then cried into the empty bag.

I texted Hawk and asked if he had flour. Instead, he shoved me in his car and we drove around for hours listening to horrible music until I talked. He insisted that when I'm with the right person, life gets easier and more fun, and for a split second I thought maybe he was that person for me. Then he started sleeping with *his* college ex again and I pushed the what-if thoughts far from my mind. Two weeks later, my college ex ended up meeting the love of his life and they're married with a kid now.

"What if—what would you do if—" There's no way to ask this. "Do you ever feel unsettled and you can't put your finger on why?"

"I can put my finger on why." He jiggles the ice in his glass, and takes a big swallow. "I can smack an entire hand down on a buzzer with blinking lights to explain why."

I playfully roll my eyes, leaving the whites showing a second too long, knowing he'll groan with disgust.

"Charming." He chews on the ice. "Are you happy?"

"I'm in my head and it's making my brain throb trying to answer that question for myself." The air is drying my contacts, and I keep blinking to keep them in.

"Fair, but you living in your head is how you have your job."

True. I get paid to analyze everything over and over. At least I found a good way to put my ability to use. Give me all the facts and I'll dice them a hundred ways possible and come up with a ton of scenarios. I do the same thing on the field. Track the players to the ball, watch their feet, and react after analyzing. The problem on the field is knowing when to stop analyzing and take action. Other players can turn off their heads and react on instinct. That's got to be so freeing.

Hawk stacks the empty plates high on the table.

He seems extra fidgety.

"I need more food!"

"Why are you yelling?" I slide down in my seat too far and hide below the lacquer tabletop wishing it had a tablecloth. A shrimp's head stares back, judging me, from the floor of the next table over.

He crouches low. "Why do you let stupid shit embarrass you?" Hawk runs a hand through his hair and stands. "Come on, before they think you're giving me a blowie under there."

I cross my arms and shake my head. "I live here now."

"Fine." He crawls under the table to sit across from me. "This is great. If we had a tablecloth, it'd be a full-blown fort."

Well, now, we both look stupid. He leans forward and puts his head in his hands. "Think this will become a trend?"

Tears pool in the corner of my eyes as a laugh draws up. "Absolute trend in the making."

"I usually only end up under one of these when I'm drinking." He looks up and traces his finger along the underside of the table. "Hmm ... missing a few screws here."

The table could collapse? My heart beats fast and I shift my gaze left toward freedom. Too bad everyone will see me if I get up.

"I'll go first." Hawk lurches out from under the table and grazes his toe across the wood base. He stands and brushes off his pants. "Coast is clear." He crouches, reaching out a hand to me.

I grab it begrudgingly and my body braces for the table to fall on me. He tugs my hand and my contorted legs fail me. I push up too fast to gain balance and bang the back of my head on the underside of the table. Water, iced tea, sushi, and all the sauces knock to the floor. Jumping backwards proves useless as a never-ending cascade of liquid and food creates a mini moat next to the black chairs.

Hawk bends over and wheezes between each chuckle.

I can never, ever come back here. I glance around, and other guests are covering their mouths, staring, offering thumbs-up, and looks of pity. My chest tightens and my inability to poof out of a place is a strong hindrance in moments like this.

"Ready, Wildflower?" Hawk bends down and picks up the chucks of ice and wasted fish scattered across the floor, plunking them one by one into a glass.

Our server rushes over like a white knight with lightning-fast speed, prepared with a stack of napkins and a bucket.

Without thinking, I grab the bucket and drag it to the table.

The poor server waves his hands for me to sit and takes the bucket. Water rains off the edge of the table covering my jeans, and the heat in my tomato face grows like fire.

Hawk passes him a stack of twenties and keeps laughing. He walks over and squeezes my shoulders as the evidence of the floor debacle is gone. "See, we can come back again."

I glance at the far corner. Can we escape through the kitchen?

"Man, I'm so sorry I bumped the table," Hawk says loudly enough to cross the restaurant.

My shoulders fall, and I cringe. "Thank you," I mouth to him.

Nate would've been so embarrassed and I'd be crying. We'd never be able to come back. My gaze drops to the floor and I follow Hawk's footsteps sloshing across the rug to the exit.

Chapter Five

THE TICK-TICK-TICK TO THE holidays goes faster every year. Friendsgiving, the week before Thanksgiving, is our small team ritual each year. A chance to get together and pig out, where the central focus isn't whistles, balls, or beer. Okay, there might be beer. Balls dependent on definition, and whistles at actors and actresses when we start the movie marathon at the end of the night. Either way, we end up eating too much and rolling around on the rug in the living room of Erika's townhouse. She's one of the most senior players on the Bees and started two years before me. Not only is she an incredible player, she also cooks like a chef at a top restaurant in New York. Everyone here will end up grabbing for one more bite of dessert with their grubby hands until we all pass out. Too bad each time I touch my face, gentle whiffs of dead fish make me gag three days after trying to scrape it up from the restaurant floor. There's no hunger rumble in my stomach today.

"Throw the cheese on the counter." Erika waves at the overflowing smorgasbord of options.

I look at the table, frowning as I glance at my measly offering of baked brie with a homemade lingonberry jam. This plate is small compared to everything else, but once Nate let me know he wasn't coming, I almost canceled to sulk at home.

Erika peers up into the living room mid-chop. "That's not Nate." She looks back to me and raises the knife and an eyebrow.

I look behind me. "Hawk?"

He's on the couch, sitting next to her wife and gesturing at the television.

I turn back to Erika. "Yeah. I figure most people know him already, so it wouldn't be too weird. He's like part Bee from how many games he attends anyway."

Coming alone wasn't an option—especially with all this knife swinging. I'd already sent a plus one, which in this circle means, grab a body, and bring them because there's enough food for everyone to eat five times over. Giving my friends and teammates an opportunity to open fire on Nate's lack of presence, while sorting everything from the restaurant with Hawk, is too much to navigate when the purpose of today is food and fun. Hawk brings happy to most situations.

She waves the knife as she checks out the living room, shrugs, and goes back to murdering carrots. "I like him for you." I love her, but her tone is always set to too loud. She once told me it had to do with growing up with too many siblings and needing to be heard.

"I'm still with Nate." Nate, who is out playing soccer with his friends because a match was more important. I take a step to the side. "You're going to slice someone."

With each chop, the bottom of her blue floral dress waves back at the counter. "Come on, I want a formal introduction." She laughs, puts the knife down, and wipes off her hands with a dishrag.

"You see him at the field."

"Not the same thing." She shakes her head and grabs my hand, practically dragging me to the living room.

"Okay, official introductions. Hawk, this is Erika. Erika, meet Hawk." I gesture around the packed living room to the couples on the floor whose names I don't know, and a variety of current teammates piled into couches and chairs. "Hawk, the team you know, and—everyone else."

Hawk smiles and waves.

Erika gives him a once-over with a hand on her hip, and nods. "Drink?"

His lips part, and he rubs his jaw. "Water'd be great. If you point me—"

"Kitchen. Help yourself, like you would at home." With a short, tight wave, she calls her wife over and drags her off to the kitchen.

"They're talking about me, aren't they?" Hawk smirks.

"Absolutely." I take a seat on the overstuffed maroon cushion next to him. "Better go get your water."

"Don't abandon me here." He pats my thigh, and with a squeeze, leaves for the kitchen.

Ariana elbows me and takes a long sip of her drink. "Uh, he's cute in non-soccer clothes."

Yes, and he is very aware. There's a reason women ask me about him all the time. He exudes confidence in his broad shoulders and thick brown *look-at-me* hair that takes more time to style than I ever take for my own.

"Is he with Margaret now?" Ariana glances at him and his form-fit charcoal sweater up and down. Her blonde bubbly personality and heart remain forever set on matchmaker. She's a Bee with a love of love who comes to cheer at most games, but can't play thanks to a back injury.

Good question. He hasn't confirmed anything, but then again, I haven't asked for details and he tries to play it cool on the pitch when he's with a player in the league.

"They seem to like each other, but I don't know many details I can share." I grab for the carrots on the coffee table in hopes the crunch will eliminate questions about Hawk or Nate.

"Have you two ever hooked up or dated?" Rose adjusts her purple flowing shirt and sinks into the far end of the sofa.

Blinking is not an answer, but it's the simplest one I can offer while I pause. "We've never dated, and I can confidently say I've only heard graphic rumors about his penis. Happy to draw a sketch if you'd like." Man, I need a water.

Ariana's attention is on the kitchen. "What's his story? Is he divorced? Have a job? Is he a serial killer?"

I plant my feet on the tan carpet. Shouldn't they direct these questions at him and not me? "He's not a serial killer. But I'd assume serial killers wouldn't advertise it if they were. He's single, never married. He works for—"

Hawk stands in front of me, beaming like he ate a pile of chocolates when no one was looking, and hands me a glass of water. "I'm a scientist. I studied bio in school and now I try to set things on fire for research purposes, at the same place she plays with spreadsheets. I enjoy soccer, movies, and making Elin's face turn a bright shade of red." He raises an eyebrow and waves me to move down the couch. With a mini hip-bump he pushes space between me and Ariana.

"I enjoy puppies, long walks on the beach, and meeting new people." He turns to Ariana, crosses his legs, and tilts his head blocking my view. "And you?"

Hawk's ability to be comfortable with everyone is a personality trait I wish I had. He walks into a room and people gravitate to talk to him.

I sigh, stand, and head back to the kitchen with Erika. Her wife, Amanda, is busy leaning over the stove stirring a pot of gravy and humming happily.

"Can I help with anything?" I ask.

"You can go put food in your mouth." Erika places her knife down, gives the lettuce a break from being slaughtered, and hands me a plate. "Can you fill the chips?"

"He seems nice." Amanda says.

"Looks like Ariana and Rose think so too." Erika points her chin to the living room.

I pour the chips into the wooden bowl on the counter. "He's got his eyes on Margaret right now." The team approval is great, albeit weird considering the small bits they do know about him from life on the pitch. "Speaking of, where is she?"

Erika stabs her knife into a piece of salmon. "Working. She said she'd get here in time for the movie marathon."

Rose sits comfortably in my seat, deep in conversation with Ariana. I catch Hawk glancing at me through the pass-through and wave. He reciprocates, smiles, and lifts his cocky chin when he leans back into the overstuffed couch. Ariana and Rose laugh back and forth while Hawk nods, smiles, and moves his mouth now and then.

"Dinner," Erika shouts, using her wooden spoon to give the cap of the metal pot a single loud smack.

I wander into the living room and pull Hawk off the couch. "Pace yourself. I've made rookie mistakes before. This isn't real dinner yet, it's like holidays at your mom's, but even more food. The courses keep coming."

"I've trained for years for this." He pats his rumbling belly and walks us to the kitchen. "There can't possibly be that much food."

Hawk groans and holds his stomach. "Just let me die on the couch." He flops vertically over the cushions with a graceless thud. Leaving Erika's to bring him home to his mom's was smart. Despite the warning, he was under-prepared for the amount of food and didn't pace himself. Amateur. He stared out the car window, a greenish tinge in his cheeks the entire way. At least he made it to the den, or man cave as he prefers to call it. With a quick flick of the wrong switch, the gas fireplace kicks on and I smack my forehead.

"Oh, ambiance." His half-chuckle groan serves him right

"You're supposed to walk when you overeat, not lay down."

He waves away the comment, and places a hand on his stomach.

I'm not sure how well he'll do tonight, taking care of his mom. I understand him enough to know he'll pull himself together and manage. He always does. That's why he moved home, to help her maintain appointments and the house as her Parkinson's progresses. She doesn't need him most of the time, but he likes being here to help when she does.

I flick the next switch and the lights on the far half of the room near the sliding glass doors turn on.

"You could've said no to Erika, you know. You didn't have to keep eating everything in front of you." I toss a pillow at him and it bounces to the floor.

"Listen, when a woman offers me something to eat, I take it." He opens his eyes a crack and lifts his eyebrows.

Gross. "I don't think anyone wants you eating anything else today. One more bite and you'll puke." There's a strong visual. He'd be more likely to fall asleep putting in a solid effort than actually puking in their laps. "Give me your pants."

"Oh! No pants party?" Hawk tucks his legs up and his stomach lets out an awful gurgle. His fingers give up fidgeting with the top button and fall to the side of the couch in defeat. "Just cut them off me. Scissors are in the drawer—use caution with the blades." He grimaces and forces a pained smile. "I don't need a second circumcision."

"How about a Prince Albert?" I grin, and make fake cuts with two of my fingers.

He cocks his head up from the couch, and a look of playful panic dances across his face. "No scissors for you." His head crashes back to the worn cushion. "You can go home. I'm fine."

"You're not fine." I disappear into his childhood bedroom and pull a pair of crumpled gym shorts from his bed. I walk back into the den and do a double take. His pants are off and he's butt up, showing off a pair of gray boxer-briefs with magenta smiley faces on each butt cheek.

"You can go back and leave me here to die." He waves me off and shuts his eyes. His hands grope the back of the couch near the crocheted blanket.

I flip his burgundy shorts over and slide them up his ankles. "You could help here."

He puffs out his lip and hugs the pillow as he lifts his hips up. I use caution to ensure not touching anything I shouldn't, and hike up the shorts. His hips slam back down onto the cushion and his stomach grows soft. My left hand is wedged between the cushion and his hip. With a yank, nothing changes. Instead, he pushes his hip down harder to trap my hand.

"Funny. I need those fingers by Wednesday." With another tug, I free my fingers from under him without toppling to the floor.

"Thanks," he says, mumbling into his superhero pillowcase.

With a quick pull, I lift the blanket into the air let it drape across him. I can watch movies while he sleeps. The movie marathon is my favorite part of Friendsgiving, but Hawk wanted to get home—for easy bathroom access. He said I could stay, but there was no way he could comfortably drive. The rug on the floor offers a comfortable place to sit, and I pull my phone out.

There's already a slew of texts waiting for replies.

Rose: *Come back and watch movies when he wakes up.*

Hawk groans on the creaky couch.

To Rose: *I don't think he's going to wake up. Erika killed him with food.*

Erika: *I like him. I made you plates of leftovers to pick up later.*

Eye-roll straight up to the god of antacids. Of course she did.

To Erika: *You may have broken his pants. :'-D*

The phone offers an extended vibration in my palm.

Three messages pop up. Shouldn't they be busy with dessert?

Erika: *YOU should break his pants.*

My cheeks flush.

To Erika: *I thank you for thinking of me for that unique responsibility, but no thanks.*

Rose: *Important question. Do you still have pants on?*

Are they sitting next to each other? I click on the television and flip through movie options before settling for a Meg Ryan romcom. He can't complain when he's sleeping.

Erika: *Tell him sweatpants next year. More room, less restriction.*

A gentle tap on my shoulder draws my attention back to Hawk.

"You okay?" I ask.

He nods. "I got you to put my shorts on."

An exasperated sigh escapes my lips. "Do you need something for your stomach?" I clear my throat. His eyes are still droopy.

"You've got mail." He nods his chin to my phone, referencing the movie on the television.

I look over at the TV screen, then down at my phone. More messages.

Nate: *We won! I joined another game after and we won!*

I don't care about the win. He ditched me for soccer and now Hawk's curled up on the couch.

To Nate: *Great! I'm at Hawk's. He didn't survive Erika's so I'm hanging out to make sure he's okay.*

The phone glows with an instant response.

Nate: *Have fun. I'm going out with the guys to celebrate. I'll see you late-late.*

Late-late? A cold rush layers itself under my skin. A new message vibrates through while I close the last one from Nate.

Hawk: *You're too good for him.*

I turn to face Hawk and his eyelids are hovering, pretending to be shut. No need to get into another discussion like lunch the other day. Besides, he'll be snoring soon enough and I can enjoy Tom Hanks and Meg Ryan. "Do you need water?"

No answer. It would probably be better if he succumbs to sleep, and lets his body take care of the mess in his stomach.

I punch out a message to Rose: *Which movie are you on?*

From Erika: *Everyone is in pajamas and under blankets. We miss you!*

Hawk lets out a short sigh, and rubs at his cheek like a dreaming puppy.

From Rose: *They started two at the same time. I don't know which screen to focus on. Delicious Tom Hanks and Meg Ryan everywhere! Help! It's sheer chaos!*

Oh, man. Her head's going to blow. That's too much to focus on at once for anyone, let alone poor, distractible Rose.

To Rose: *Put on headphones. You've got this.*

To Rose: *I'm on YGM.*

The purple blinking dot on my phone flashes.

From Rose: *You're brilliant. Let's do this!*

I rest my head against the cushion in front of Hawk's stomach and pull a spare blanket from a basket beneath the side-table to get comfy. There's nothing but an empty house to go home to as usual.

CHAPTER SIX

S HOPPING THE SUNDAY BEFORE Thanksgiving to skip
the mass hordes of people is a ritual Hawk and I have
partaken in for at least twelve years now. His stomach recovered from last weekend's Friendsgiving, despite his attempt
to sneak in more turkey once he woke up.

"You're going to make us late." Hawk messes his hair
while resetting his knit gray slouch hat. His black pleather
gloves grip at the worn gray steering-wheel while he bounces
up and down like an impatient child.

I flash a smile with little enthusiasm. Fall is switching to
winter way too fast, and naked trees wait for snow to clothe
them. Beautiful snow to hide the barren gloom of leafless
fall.

This year it's a struggle to get psyched up for holiday shopping, but he's had years where he's struggled too. His worst
was the year they diagnosed his mom with Parkinson's a week
before Thanksgiving, and I found him at his condo, sitting in
the dark, drinking chocolate milk straight from the half-gallon
jug. Mainly, the reason for this outing is to spend time together
before the chaos of the holidays, with family, and possible sig-

nificant others, kicking into full gear. Essentially, it's *our* annual holiday.

"How can there be a "late" if there's no set arrival?" I ask.

"Science. All the parking spots are gone by 10:05." His answer for everything. Science.

There's no science here. Mr. Punctuality wants to arrive at the same time each year.

I suppose this is what I look forward to most during the holiday. Shopping for Margaret will be fun. He likes to go all out when he's trying to woo a person. Woo is *his* word, not mine.

We're once again at different ends of the dating spectrum. While he's ramping up toward dating, I'm half-single. This morning I woke up and realized I'm once again alone for breakfast. I rationalized in my head for an hour as I cracked an entire carton of organic brown eggs onto the griddle and let them cook beyond well done. The steam from the burning eggs did its best to show me all the good times we have, and how Nate's not really a horrible person. The last egg spurted grease on my hand, snapping me out of my daydream. I've absolutely hit that moment in the relationship when it's over, but have no idea how to end things.

Nate is horrible for me. I'm stuck. And the house smells like charred farts.

"Think we'll see Santa?" Hawk pulls two waters from his bag. "Hydrate."

"You realize we have plenty of time." I wave my hand across the half-empty mall parking lot.

He tugs my sleeve and whines. "Come on, where's your holiday spirit?"

At home, wallowing in single for the holidays. Almost single, sort-of.

Hawk skips ahead as we enter the mall and pulls my arm up to the entryway. The scent of the holiday smacks our faces with warm cranberry and mulling cider. Cheery music fills the hallway, and a smile draws across my face. It's nearly impossible to be mopey when Springsteen is letting you know Santa Claus is coming.

"See, there it is." Hawk lets go of my sleeve and then knuckles my arm gently. "Where to Miss Claus?" He saunters in, motioning his arms wide.

I laugh. "Who's first on your list?"

Hawk's not giving in to my funk.

He pulls out his phone and hits a few buttons before settling on a hidden notes list. "Second is my mom."

"So, Margaret, your mom, and your grandma?" I raise an eyebrow. "Anyone else?"

He nods. "All my little cousins."

Ah! I love the littles. The littles now range from two to seventeen. The older ones no longer think we're cool, but I look forward to seeing them—I suppose it'll be Margaret and not me this year. My heart sinks. I'll miss the tiny ones too, the ones who only now understand Santa. Plans change. People change.

"Are you getting anything for Dolph?" he asks.

I give a weak shrug. "Something small."

Last year I shelled out over a grand on tickets to see the Irish pop band he loves, and his black peacoat. In exchange, he gave me a broken, possibly used, bread maker with rosemary breadcrumbs caked to the bottom. Money or used wasn't the issue, the lying it was brand new was an issue. The stock I put into finding the right gift and then being lied to put a dampener on Christmas. Maybe if he hadn't also bought a spa day gift for his boss, I'd have been less upset. Secret Santa he claimed. I've never seen a company have a cap so high for a boss.

For a gift this year, I set up a boudoir shoot for next weekend a few months ago to take pictures for Nate. A silly, holiday image where I can cover the bits I don't like with a sled or a reindeer. After the party, lunch with Hawk and Friendsgiving, I'm even less confident about the shoot. Plus, he doesn't seem interested in me physically anymore. Pictures with a Rudolph nose or antlers won't change his lack of interest level. And I don't want to be crushed if he's not over the moon about the images.

"Earth to Elin." Hawk waves a hand in front of my face.

Shoot. I dazed out. Weren't we walking?

"Dolph, your mom, and your cousins?" He taps his foot. "Did you not prepare for the best shopping day of the year?"

"The Sunday before Thanksgiving?"

"Yes!" He screeches.

I stifle a laugh. "You do know most people start the day after Thanksgiving, right? Creepy Santa isn't even on his throne yet."

"Tradition." He throws a hand on his hip and the other high in the air.

I grab his hand before he can start dancing. "Okay. Before this gets embarrassing, let's go."

He skips ahead and nods at the body lotion store. "You know the drill." He hands me his wallet.

"You're a grown man, buy it yourself." I hand him back his wallet, point at the store, and grab a basket.

"Are you and your girlfriend looking for anything in particular?" The wide-eyed saleswoman asks.

Always with the assumptions. Girlfriend isn't bad. Older sister from the sales lady last year, now that one was plain rude.

He pulls a blank scent card from her stack. "I want to pick something out for me." He grabs for the handle on the basket and pulls it from my fingers.

I'm unnecessary at this point. The saleswoman's face lights up and she waves him toward the woodsy scented lotions. I have a good thirty minutes before he leads her back to the white lotion with silver sparkles. He'll tell her he likes glitter, then rattle off a long list of things to make her laugh.

Nate would never come in here. Not for himself, and certainly not for me. He'd be down in the baseball card shop trying to figure out which card to splurge on next. His investment for his future. I pick up two bottles of snow scented lotion, and a hand sanitizer, to add to the pile of gifts for him to give his mom and aunts.

When I glance over, the saleswoman is putting lotion on the side of her hand for Hawk to smell. I roll my eyes and push the bottles to the cashier. This is going to be a long day.

"Anything else?" The cashier asks.

I point to the oak scented travel lotion and add it to the pile. The lady rings me up and throws a stack of coupons I'll never use into the bag. The point of coming on a Sunday is to avoid the holiday rush—thousands upon thousands of people traipsing through the corridors, touching everything in sight.

I grab the bag and head toward Hawk, tapping him on the shoulder as he mulls over the glacier sparkle lotion bottles. If nothing else, he's predictable. The woman who greeted us waves a tiny finger wave as we exit the store.

Hawk makes grabby fingers for the bag. "What'd you get?"

"A bottle for your mom's stocking. A bottle of the same lotion I saw in Margaret's soccer bag, and something small for *one* of your billion cousins."

"Is this oak?" he asks.

Shoot. I nod and bite the inside of my lower lip.

"How'd you know I was out?" He opens the bottle and takes a deep sniff.

I shrug. So much for using the bottle of lotion as a small bow on whatever bigger gift I find for him. Back to square one.

"I'm famished." He rubs his belly and points his chin toward the smell of greasy mall food.

"We've barely started shopping." I point at him. "You're stalling."

He places a hand over his chest and releases a long sigh.

"I swear your insides are going to fall out at some point." I laugh and stick my tongue out in a half-gag.

"That's an awful visual." He skips ahead to order from the small white kiosk in the aisle. "We'll take a jalapeño pretzel and a box of mini cinnamon sugar pretzels."

"It's too early for this much grease." My stomach rumbles at the delicious, buttery goodness wafting from the station.

"I know! The water is so unhealthy." He waves off my wallet, hands me the jalapeño pretzel and crinkles his nose. "How do you eat those things?"

I shrug. "I like spicy."

"Like me!" He shouts out with wide open arms.

I cringe and curl my body tight to disappear. "You're so loud."

"Who cares?" He gestures around the mall. "No one here is going to remember enough to judge. You should try being loud for once—off the field." He smirks and nods at me.

I glance around. No one is staring, at least not in an obvious way. "I'm good." Drawing attention to myself is horrifying. My stomach twists with the line of what-ifs. What if people think I'm an idiot? What if I scare someone, interrupt them? I don't need noticing.

He stops walking and stares into my eyes. "Come on. Shake it off." His voice is full of warmth and sinister undertones, making me question why I subject myself to this each year. "Da-shing through the maaalll!" He belts out with an open stance, and a wider grin.

I slouch, attempting to become one with the polished white tiles. The sound of his voice echoes through the hallway and my insides are refusing to transform into a puddle and disappear. A tug on my jacket joins the last note of, *open sleigh*. My cheeks are hot, there's not a single pillar to block his stage performance.

He puts an arm over my shoulder, pops another pretzel bite, and points to the jewelry store. "Let's go, cherry cheeks." He lets out a high, wicked laugh to punctuate his performance.

Is spontaneous combustion too much to ask for?

Hawk pokes at my arm. "Can we do it?"

"No." The half-single me is not in the mood for hope, or tormenting a poor saleswoman into thinking she's helping choose my dream ring. Dream *anything* shiny, really. The twist in my stomach reverses course and swaps sides while Hawk leans over the glass.

His demeanor is calmer and more focused while he checks out the stones and metals with a slight frown. He cares about what he picks for the holiday. Choosing requires concentration, planning, and me. His fingertips drop to the metal edging on the case, and he sways as he studies each piece.

I track his gaze. "Amethyst got your tongue?" He has decent taste. The ornate filigree on the earrings in the case is so perfectly symmetrical that his math brain is likely doing back-flips.

"Are they pretty?" he asks, his tone calm and soft.

Not my style. "Yeah, they're pretty."

"Is it too much?" He crouches lower to get a better view from the front of the case and tugs my arm to join him.

He really likes her then.

I shake my head. "Nah. If you feel like it's good, then it's good." At least he makes the effort.

I straighten, and wave over the salesperson who's busy pretending to not eye us. She walks over, her hair in a perfect, wide-swept bun, a bright smile across her face, and thick strands of rose gold necklaces on display against her form-fitting black dress. Without so much as a wobble from her four-inch black heels, she glides to us and pulls out the array of amethyst earrings.

"These arrived just in time for the holiday. They're great with everything." She focuses on me. "Even jeans."

I look down at my comfortable worn jeans and will myself to ignore the judgment. At least there aren't rips in them today. I glance to Hawk's hands, and he's inspecting the earrings like he has any idea what he's looking for.

"Is it too easy?" He stares at the stones and chews on his lower lip.

"I can hold them up on you, sir." The saleswoman offers in a cheery tone as she glances at his pierced ears. You can take your balls out."

He and I snort-laugh in unison. Look down. Don't laugh in her face.

I glance up and her tiny hand is covering her mouth, her cheeks bright red.

Tears well from laughing, and I point to my lobes. "Your earrings. Take the soccer ball studs out."

"I'd strongly prefer to not take my balls out in the middle of the mall, thank you very much. It's unsanitary." He runs a hand over his face and half-swallows laugh. "I appreciate the offer. Such great service they have here." He taps his fingers on the glass.

"Miss, can you hold them up for him?" I ask.

Hawk raises a brow.

"Not your balls, Hawk." I bite back my lower lip, pulling back a chuckle.

"Please, hold them near your ears." He points to the earrings and stares at me with puppy dog eyes.

I wish the saleswoman would share her magically regained composure with me.

"I'm good."

"You hate them." He pouts a lip out.

"They aren't my style." I run my hand across the back of my ear and highlight the simple sun hoop that cuts through the center cartilage and the basic silver studs running down each clustered piercing in my ear.

He removes my emerald wide-brim fedora, tugs my now messy hair back, and holds the package up to my ear. The saleswoman places the hat on the counter for him and slides the mirror over.

The gorgeous earrings sparkle back at me. They don't fit—not for me. They're elegant and soft. More suited for someone who drinks wine and exudes grace. The number of bruises from falls, or absorbed hits from a soccer ball just doesn't mesh with delicate.

"They're pretty." I place the earrings on the counter and slowly turn to face him. "You done good."

His soft lips form a hesitant smile demanding attention. A flash of unexpected flutters scrambles from my chest through my fingertips.

He stares at me blankly.

I avert my gaze to the other sparkling objects and walk to the far counter. Amethyst, Margaret's birthstone. Ornate and delicate for the woman who, despite all the hits she takes on the field, *never* has a bruise on her. She goes from soccer cleats to a flirty short dress in under five minutes, looking flawless. Sweat sparkles on her while I look like a wet, grumpy bunny.

"She's going to like 'em, right?" Hawk asks, standing at the counter with his debit card outstretched.

"Of course." Who wouldn't? "How many holes does she have? Should we look at a pair of studs to go with them?" I turn to look at him.

His eyebrows furrow. He draws the debit card back and shakes his head. Stress exudes from the contortion of skin on his forehead and his face goes pale.

"You look like you're going to hurl." Bad pretzel?

He taps the card on the counter and rolls his neck. "I don't know if she has pierced ears."

I blink blankly at him. "Why are we shopping for earrings?"

He runs a hand over the back of his neck and the light reflects off the titanium industrial in his upper ear. "I—don't all women have their ears pierced?"

I shake my head. Oh, Hawk. "Do you have a picture you can check?"

He pulls out his phone and scrolls through pictures. One after the other he swipes through photos where her gorgeous black hair falls in front of her ears. She beams positive energy. Energy that's good for him and his slightly twisted soul. Maybe he won't screw this one up. *One* of us should be in a healthy relationship.

Hawk clicks off the screen and shoves his phone in his pocket with a heavy sigh. I look down at the cascade of sparkles in the case, searching fast for an out. The necklaces are simple, but I've never seen her wear a necklace before.

The saleswoman clears her throat. I glance back over and Hawk is rubbing the back of his hand with a pensive expression on his face.

"I'll take the amethyst necklace instead." His tone is steady, confident. "Worst case, between now and then, I check her ears. If they're pierced, I'll return the necklace and get the earrings" He lifts his card to the saleswoman and taps on the counter.

I nod and smile. Margaret's lucky. She holds his interest in a way I haven't seen before. I glance back down at the rows of glistening diamond rings and shake my head.

Hawk gives a silly grin. "Not too late to try them on." He takes my hand and goes down on one knee. "Come on."

I tug him up while the brows of an older woman waiting for the saleswoman escape into her wig. Sorry ma'am, it's not what you think. Embarrassment slaps at my chest while the lady mouths, *so cute*, at us. My pulse pushes into a dance and the room feels like it's smaller. I snatch my hat off the counter and put it back on, hoping to shield my flush from any onlookers.

Hawk stands, grinning at my scowl, and shimmies the bag in his hand.

"If you want to land Margaret, maybe you don't fake propose to people in a store." How is this one of his favorite things to do to me?

He clicks his foot on the marbled tile and victory-dances to the hallway. "Who's next on the list?"

No one. Because I don't want to buy for Nate right now. "Bookstore?" My voice cracks at the end.

He nods and tugs on my coat. With quick steps, we arrive at the bookstore, ready to get lost in the stacks, and read through ridiculous titles together with dramatic inflection—Nate finds this stupid. Then again, getting him in a bookstore requires a lot of shoving. Maybe there's a book on baseball cards he'd like.

Hawk shoves a book in front of my nose. "Over the Edge." He reads off the title. "Without looking, what's it about?"

"Olympic ice skater discovers the world is flat and almost falls off the ice." I force a smile past my heavy cheeks.

He nods. "Yup, not even close."

"Marshmallow Dreams." I read with a half-enthusiastic tone. The holiday music is no longer working to lift my mood.

"Oh, that's easy." He lifts his chin high and pokes at my arm. "A woman owns a marshmallow bakery, and her dreams become dashed when prince charming brings the rose chocolate. He missed the memo. Dark chocolate is better."

"Close." I let out a chuckle and rotate the book toward him on the shelf. "Which flavor marshmallows are best for invoking dreams?"

"That can't be real." Hawk grabs the book off the shelf. "This entire book is about a man who lives in a marshmallow land and eats different parts of the land to invoke different dreams? How does something like this even get published?" He shoves the book back on the shelf.

"Sounds heavenly to me." I raise my eyebrows and head to the biography section to search for anything new on soccer players from Europe. Simple. Impersonal but personal, and something Nate will use as a doorstop.

CHAPTER SEVEN

Tonight is Friday, not Wednesday, which means I'm at the field house for Nate's game. He's too busy cracking his neck and checking the door for players to notice my arrival. He promised date night at the diner between his games tonight, and I need time with him to talk outside of the field house.

"Can you grab my phone? I left it in the car." Nate yells across the field when he finally sees me.

His team is three players down and he's pacing back and forth. Looks like no one wants to play the night after Thanksgiving.

"Yeah, no problem!" Good. Maybe there's an extra sweatshirt in there, this place is freezing. I understand the players get hot, but my spectator ass is ice.

"Grab my other cleats too. These hurt!"

I nod and grab his peacoat, throwing it on over my jacket. I'm swimming in it, and look like I stole a grownup's coat, but it's warm and smells like his woody cologne. If there's one thing he's decent at other than soccer, it's picking a fantastic cologne.

The door opens and wind whips icy rain at my face with a slash. I raise my arms to shield my face and squint into the darkness to search for his car. Oh thank goodness, it's close by.

I shove my hand in his coat pocket and unlock it. I grab the handle and tumble into the musty car, slamming the door shut behind me.

The frosty air fills my lungs and fog puffs out from my nose. *Phone. Phone. Phone.*

Where the hell is it? The tiny blue light flashes at me like a beacon under his driver's seat. Success.

I open the phone and enter 2-4-0-1, the jersey numbers of Howard and Scurry, two of my favorite goalies. Nate's knowledge of technology was limited so I helped set up his phone. He doesn't think the numbers are as awesome as I do, but he still hasn't changed them. I click to the messages to see who's coming.

1. Tony is out. His kid is sick.

2. Chet has car trouble and needs a ride.

3. Mark is out. He worked late each night this week and his wife wants some time with him.

Good for you, Mark. Get off the field for a night.

4. August: *Thanks for agreeing to come to fix my window tonight.*

August is his boss. Why is Nate fixing his boss's window super late tonight? My stomach knots. He said we were going to the diner and then he has another game ... when is he going to her house?

5. August: *I still can't believe you got out of that stupid friends-thanks thing she has with her team to come over and help christen my sheets. Either-way, a bet is a bet and I'm wearing your jersey tonight. See you super soon. XOX*

I choke on a deep inhale and my heart pounds painfully like it's going to explode. If I could vomit all over his car right now, I would. Asshole. Fucking mother, fucking asshole. I slam his phone to the ground and step on it. My chest grows tight and hot anger shoots through my fingertips. He lied. It's all right there, and stupid me wanted to believe he was playing soccer most nights of the week. I'm an idiot.

My stomach churns violently and I'm doing the best I can to fight a scream. Five years wasted. I can get in my car and leave, or go back inside and handle his ass now.

I snatch his extra cleats, and his now pancaked phone, and march back into the building. Anger prickles at my skin, burning like tiny needles. He lied about Friendsgiving.

He lied. He fucking *lied*.

I'm here for him. Again. Cheering him on. And he's swapping shirts with his antique boss and blowing the dust off her bits. I can't get him to even paint a room, and he's out unsticking her windows while I eat at home alone most nights.

She can have him. His nasty snoring. His stank ass self that sweats way more than any one person should be able to. Rage seethes through my nerves in a manner separating me from rational thought. Now isn't the time to think clearly or make excuses. To believe the lies, to believe it's all in my head.

I march onto the field and chuck his cleats from half-court along with his phone at his head. "You fucking bastard. You are a fucking, fucking, asshole." Spit flies from my mouth with each word. Tears stream down my face and my heart squeezes tight. The room is blurry. The lights are bright, so bright. Heat lamps above my head urge my rage to heighten and encourage me to pass out on the turf and embarrass myself. Not today. I can get out of here, head held high.

Nate shrugs at me, looks down, and lifts a hand to his ear. Liar. He heard me. The entire field heard me.

He pulls a ball from the net and kicks it to the far side of the field.

"That's it? You're going to shoot from goal and not talk to me?" My focus on his form grows hazy. He doesn't have the balls to even come dispute this or to see why I'm upset. Soccer is more important. A lifeless ball is more important than the last five years.

Of course it is. I straighten my arms at my sides, and my fingers flex outward. With a dig of my toe in the turf, I about-face and head to the door. Thad comes running and stops in front of me, blocking the path.

"You okay?" Thad puts his sweaty hand on my arm. He dips his head low enough to be level with the pool of tears streaming down each cheek. "Come on, let's go to the water fountain."

I shake my head and take a step to the side, heading to the lobby alone. Thad walks silently next to me and pauses in the hallway while I lean against the wall and slink down. The anger in my nerves rises like steam from my pours.

Thad lifts his finger and disappears. I'm an embarrassment to myself right now. A shriveled, crying mess on the floor while whistles blow and balls get punted back and forth.

I'm stuck. If I go home, it's his house. What am I even? The roommate? The girlfriend when it's convenient? Most girlfriends get time, attention, sex. If I looked like a soccer ball, he'd want to fuck me.

Thad hands me a water and slinks down the wall to sit at my side with a sigh. I can feel his pity. If I look up, he'll see how weak I am. Stupid, emotional, and weak. I'm allowed to be emotional. I'm allowed to cry, to scream, to express myself.

"You don't have to sit with me," I whisper. "You have a game."

"You're upset. How can I leave you out here upset? It's just a game." He crinkles a cup in his hands. "Besides, with me out here, there aren't enough players for today. People are more important than a plastic trophy."

I cough to clear the tightness in my throat. The air is cooler in the hallway, and the lights aren't buzzing as loud out here. My vision clears, but my head throbs.

"How bad did I embarrass myself?" I ask.

"Not at all." He pats the floor. "Do you want to sit in a chair?"

I shake my head. The floor is fine. Inviting. I can't fall off the floor.

"Floor it is then." He opens a bottle of water and refills my cup.

"You should be in there," I say. Why does he even care? He's Nate's friend.

"I'm captain. I can sit out here and enjoy the cool air."

A deep breath in fills my lungs, and clears the remaining tightness from my chest.

"If you were one of my little sisters—I'd kill him." He rests his head against the wall. "He's okay to hang out with. But, man, I'd beat the stupid out of someone if they treated my sisters the way he treats you."

The smile working to cross my face quickly reverts to a frown. They knew. They had to have all known about Nate and not said anything. Come, eat the food, hang out, don't mention he has a side piece. My arms are heavy, numb, and want to merge into the floor. In the background, I hear Nate's weird game bird calls that are meant to communicate his intentions with the team.

Whoop! *Ball.*

Whoop! *He's open.*

Whoop! *Fake-out with a toothy grin at his opponent.*

He's not coming to check on me. My heart slows and the weight of my chest pulls my shoulders forward, clearing a path for the tears to fall from my face to the worn blue rug. Dread seeps into my skin and weighs heavy on my head with the awful night to come at the house.

There won't be a Thad or a Hawk. It'll be another forever night of sparring with words and indecisions. Relentless, silence, and avoidance. Either way, my body wants to sleep on the scratchy floor here, which isn't an option.

Self-worth. I'm important, and life is too short to accept a relationship neither of us is fully in. He's out with his penis, and I'm out with my mind. He's not the first person I call when I'm excited or when I accomplish something great. Those calls go to my best friend or my teammates.

I pull my phone from my pocket and send a text.

To Hawk: *I need you.*

CHAPTER EIGHT

WIPING THE TEARS FROM my face is pointless. The front of my jacket is soaked from the ride between the field house and here. After Thad went back to the field to cancel his game, I sat in the parking lot crying hysterically. Hawk and I exchanged a firestorm of text messages which led me to stand outside the giant red door of my best friend's house with shaking shoulders.

Tonight solidified the need to pull the plug on this spiraling world that is Nate and I, and unfortunately, all I could muster to text Nate before taking off in my car was, "I need a break." The words were right there to end everything, but I realized I'd be homeless. My teammates all tie to the pitch, to him. Suddenly the best I could come up with was "break." I'm a blubbering, cowardly moron, and far from the strong captain my teammates flag me as. I raise my hand to knock on the thick wooden door, but it swings wide before my knuckles make contact.

"Elin!" His mother is sweet. Kind. And has no idea what to make of me as concern crosses her face. Years of me coming to this house, and I don't think I've ever looked like such a disheveled train-wreck.

"You okay, honey?" Her tone drops low. "Did Hawk do this?"

I shake my head and laugh. My fists rub at the tears from my already-red eyes, and offer a smile at her warm presence. She's a bonus in my life thanks to my friendship with her son. Occasionally, we even sneak in brunches, and she brings a to-go box home for him. He screeches and stomps and is grateful for time to himself, while I'm grateful for her ever-gentle company. She's someone I'd be friends with even if she wasn't his mom. Christmas six years ago, after a few too many sips from several wine glasses, she let me know her son was a sweet idiot but never filled in why. She then fell asleep on the couch with a big smile on her face.

"Where you off to?" I ask.

"Florida with my girlfriends for two and a half weeks." She lets out a tiny squeal. "No more treatments for right now—and I picked up some work down there."

"Nursing?"

"Yup." She waves me inside and shuts the cold behind us. "I'm loading up the camper tonight and heading out." Her pale brown eyes scan the worry on my face. "You're as bad as my son. I'm not driving and I'll be home for Christmas. It's only a week-long contract." She wraps her arm around me and kisses my cheek. "Promise."

Her amber, shoulder length hair bobs as she slowly takes the short flight of steps from the landing of the split level down to Hawk's section of the house. Her hand shakes as she fights for grip on the white painted rail, and hesitation jiggles her knee as she takes a sip of air at the last step.

Curie's wide, wiggly, bulldog butt comes barreling off the couch and she sniffs the side of my leg 'til I crouch down and oblige her request for scratches. This sweet girl isn't taking no for an answer.

"Hawk!" His mother taps on the door to his bedroom. "Hawk put some pants on. Elin is here!" She raises a finger to her lips and emotes a silent giggle.

I chuckle, and throw an arm over her with a hug. She's standing taller than my last visit. Her frail complexion disguised with makeup and sheer determination to defy the doctor's diagnosis.

"Take on the world, meet some handsome men, and bring home a step-dad for Hawk."

"Hey! Don't encourage her!" Hawk opens his door and stands in the doorway, sporting a pair of jeans and brown sneakers.

His mom points at his chest and back to his face. "Forget something?"

"Oh yeah! Thanks, it's cold out." Hawk disappears back to his room.

She shakes her head. "I swear he does this stuff on purpose."

Oh, he does. He absolutely does.

Hawk appears in the doorway wearing a knit viking-style hat, complete with red beard, and lifts his elbow high. "Ready to go?"

"Go put on a shirt." I wrap my arm across my stomach and glance at his mom.

"He wonders why women don't take him seriously." She turns and heads back to the stairs. Her shoulders twitch before she lifts her knee high.

Hawk slams on a thick hoodie and thrusts his hands out to steady his mother on the steps.

"I can do this on my own." She shoos him off the front door landing area of the split-level.

His face drops and he barrels to the bottom of the upper set of stairs, ready to catch her wobbling self. Her footsteps shuffle above and dampen as she cuts across to the upper kitchen and small beeps come from the microwave buttons. Hawk stares up at the living room in silence.

I tap on his back. His body jolts up and he shakes his head.

"Wanna walk?" This is reality. Not the crap with Nate, but my best friend slowly crumbling while he watches his mother deteriorate.

The jokes, hyper personality, all of it—masking the crap he never lets people really see. Difference being, I was here before he built those guards to protect himself.

I touch my head against his shoulder and push past him to the door. "Got a leash?"

"Ooh. It's going to be that kind of night, huh?" His voice rises back to full, and a smile slides up the right side of his face. "I like it."

He gestures to the shelf behind the door and before he can tap his leg twice, Curie snuggles in at his knee. I pull down the chain leash and click my tongue against the roof of my mouth twice, calling her up to the landing. Her playful butt bounds up the steps, and she turns in excited circles, making it a struggle to clasp the leash.

Hawk grabs for a scarf.

"Are you really going to wear that?" I ask.

He nods. "It's for snowboarding."

"We're walking up back streets." There's no way I'm going to let someone see us together while he wears this odd hat. If imploding were a possibility, I'd take it rather than letting my chest twist. Nothing embarrasses him.

Hawk takes the leash and opens the door. The icy breeze knocks at both of us and Curie sits, refusing to go outside.

Smart girl. I shiver and pull my coat up higher.

He tugs the beard down. "Want the hat?"

I shake my head. Yes—for warmth, but he's not getting that thing on me.

Curie whines and reluctantly joins us outside as we cut across the lawn onto the dark, tree-lined street. Whistles blow in the distance at our old high school. The players must be freezing. *I'm* freezing.

I walk closer to Hawk, and the red yarn in the beard bounces as his strides get longer. The jingle of the leash matches the pep in Curie's step as we cut across the empty street to wind through the development. The black pavement and tree branches glisten as streetlights illuminate the thin layer of settling frost.

Fog rolls from my nose with each exhale, leaving a trail of our intertwined breaths as we trudge forward.

"How's she doing?" I ask.

He shrugs. "That's not why we're walking."

I bite down on my tongue. True.

"She's fine, though. Getting stronger, I think." His head dips low as the wind whips.

"Are you going to go back to your condo while she's in Florida?" I ask.

He needs his space again. A place where her pictures aren't everywhere and he's not constantly worried.

Hawk shakes his head. "I can't." He stops walking and looks over at me. "You need the condo."

"Stupid soccer telephone chain. Half the league probably knows what happened on the pitch already." I shake my head. "I'll figure something else out. It's only for a bit."

We walk further from the house to the other side of the almost vacant mall to the jungle of condos. Curie trudges forward in the lead across the slick metal bridge with her tongue out, panting happily. Hawk jingles the keys in his pocket and nods toward the steps.

"Have you been here since I remodeled?" he asks.

I shake my head and stare up. He's had a tenant in the place since moving into his mom's to help offset her medical costs and help her around the house. He says he hasn't rented to anyone in the past few months because finding someone this time of year isn't easy. I think it's because he wants to move back in when his mom takes her trips, which I'm now preventing him from doing.

Curie takes his wave up the steps as a special message for her, and bounds to the front door. With an impatient whine, she rocks back and forth, patiently watching the keys sway.

We cross the threshold. Freshly painted white walls accent soapstone countertops, and various throw rugs cover the dark hardwood floors. Plastic, itching for peeling, shields the brand-new stainless-steel appliances.

The table from his grandmother's house sits in the open dining room that connects to the rest of the area.

His keys clink on the marble counter. "I'm not going to get a tenant 'til well after New Year's. And, I've got to be home for mom."

I glance over at him as the tears well. "I can get a place of my own—or go to a cousin's—a hotel or something." My heart twists.

Even in a shit-show relationship, this isn't how you're supposed to spend a holiday. I'm alone.

"It's just going to sit here. Mom's coming back for Christmas and everyone's coming over." He reaches out and rubs my shoulder in comfort with his thumb. "Join us at Mom's house."

I stare at the blank walls. He lowers his hand and my arm grows heavy. With a single nod, I reluctantly slide the keys off the counter and grip them in my trembling hands.

"You don't have to tell me what's going on—but this whole moving out, separate holidays thing—" He runs a hand across the back of his hat and his attention drops to the floor. "You love Christmas."

Curie's wet nose nuzzles against my leg in a search for attention or a treat hidden in a cabinet.

I exaggerate a shrug. "It's only for a few weeks?" I don't want to be at Nate's alone for Christmas. One of us must pull the cord at some point and stop making excuses, but for now, we'll call it a break. Until one of us has the guts to admit it's not a break.

Hawk opens his arms and hugs me, and his hand gently strokes my back. Not crying isn't happening. My tears christen the rug below and my shoulders shake with deep sobs.

"You'll come over." He pulls back and kisses the top of my head. "Mom will kill me if you don't."

I wipe the tears from my cheeks with my coat sleeve. "Well, we don't need murder for Christmas."

CHAPTER NINE

STEWING IN FRUSTRATION, WHILE entering the season meant for joy, isn't fun for anyone. The messages from his boss were the final straw. I didn't sleep much at the condo last night, not for a lack of trying. I haven't slept well in the weeks since I started staying there. I'm not taking a break—I'm done. After tonight, I'll finally have Christmas and New Year's Eve with someone who wants to be with me in the new year—me.

The light green reading couch across from the oversize bookcase offers the easiest spot to sit and wait for Nate to be done with his eons-long shower. I fidget with a zipper on my overstuffed backpack. Being in his house unsettles my nerves.

Maybe I should wait for him with a soda. No. Caffeine is not the best idea. My legs are already jittering against the creaky spot in the wooden floor, centered in front of the couch. I can shake the pictures if I bounce my feet right. Off-angle pictures bug me more than him, and I'd never be able to concentrate.

This is ridiculous. My heart thumps in my throat.

Five years is enough time to know there really isn't a future. But we did so much work together on this place. Putting down new floors, pulling down mirrored walls, and painting every room. We made it ours—even though it was never meant to be mine. I should've taken the fact that two years ago he chose it without me, paid for it himself, and didn't put my name on a bill as a sign.

I never looked for bailout signs. Instead, I focused on the glimmers of maybe. Hours of watching too many romcoms made me think we could be the *it couple* behind closed doors. He'd have some kind of magical moment where he looks at me and sees the person he wants to spend his life with. We could be the mediocre king and queen of the pitch, and host constant parties for our friends. Only, I don't see him as the person I want to spend my life with.

Now the only sign that's left is finally forcing him to confront the text messages from his boss. I should've left him then, but the rage of emotions inside me fogged my brain and rational words became difficult to form. Plus, five years.

I need to stop with excuses. Vomit rises in my throat and I press a hand to my chest to stop it from coming the rest of the way up.

Christmas is in a few days. Dragging this through couples holidays is cruel. Couples holidays force the world to believe everything is glittering and perfect. Christmas Eve, Christmas Day, New Year's Eve, Valentines, heck let's add St. Patrick's Day because this is Jersey, after all. He can be with her, and I'll survive alone.

I didn't take note of any neon signs pointing toward the proverbial exit when I should have. Nate can keep the curtains and rods that he almost killed himself trying to put up. The memory of him struggling to use a drill, while holding tight to a flat surface like a spider, can stay right here in this house.

This ranch was *his* dream. He'd made it out of Philly and could take care of himself. The day of closing, he was full of excitement and awe. The keys were *his*. We packed up *his* garden apartment, and a group of guys going door-to-door talking about Jesus were more than happy to help us pack the truck. They were sweet. Packing for strangers in August wearing full suits must've blown. But they remained cheerful the whole time—never once asking if we wanted a brochure.

A glance across the bookcase, and over to the spare bedroom where my life exists, reveals what little I really have. I own nothing in *our* bedroom. The closet is his, which is okay because I took over the second bedroom with my clothes and just about everything else. The dining table is mine. Unusable after he lied about putting a table saw on it and the antique wood splintered with the weight. It'll get fixed.

The knot in my stomach isn't going away. He plays soccer constantly, and I told him I didn't want soccer to be my whole life and wanted to do other fun things too. I gave in to spend time with him. His time on the field is still increasing, and I spend the majority of my time with the Bees, Hawk, or alone. There's evidence. Actual evidence this will never work. Though, I never expected primary source documentation.

I refuse to sit through a family Christmas to help him avoid the slew of questions he'll get as to why I'm not there. The misery needs to end for both of us. If he wanted me, he'd be present. He wants a soccer ball with a vagina, not a girlfriend, a partner, and certainly not me.

No fighting. I'll calmly explain it's over and if he argues or cries—he's going to cry.

He cries every time. Tears and pain crackling low in my throat are from the habit of him—not from loving him. We grew apart long before the sex stopped, before the arguments and the damaged feelings. We were the nauseating couple when we started. Now, the thought of his lips on mine makes me nauseous. They're tainted with another woman's lip-gloss and old lady floral perfume. An image refusing to get out of my mind, and one I won't tolerate.

Soccer, and stubbornness not to fail like our parents did at relationships, are all that bind us anymore. The door to the bathroom turns and steam pours forward as Nate enters the sitting room.

I look at his crystal blue eyes through a clear veil. "I'm done," blurts out without hesitation, releasing the tension from my head.

This is the right move.

He stares back at me.

Say something.

"So throw out your plate." He lifts his arm out to grab a bottle of water off the table.

I have no paper plate, no food. No desire to continue this mess about to unfurl.

"No. I'm moving out. For good."

The TV blaring downstairs goes quiet as he flicks the hallway switch.

"You're going to embarrass me like this? I have a game tonight. How do I explain why you're not there? What about Thad's party on New Year's Eve?" He stares at me. "I figured you wanted time to cool off, but come on, this is us. We fight and get back together."

"You made a choice to exit the relationship as soon as you cheated, only you forgot to tell me we were done."

Tears form. I can do this. Keep pushing forward, today is long overdue.

"You've been cheating with Hawk, haven't you?" His hands flex and the veins on his arms bulge. "I see how he looks at you. He thinks I'm dirt, always calling me stupid names like Dolph."

"None of this is about Hawk. Stop trying to blame me to excuse what you've done. You cheated. I didn't. That's what you can explain to Thad at the New Year's Eve party. Though, I'm pretty sure he and your entire team heard it well on the field already." I shake my head. He cheats and assumes I'm cheating too—deflection is great.

Nate pulls on a pullover too tight for his biceps, and it gets caught high on his chest. "How is it going to look when I show up alone?"

"Like I have a backbone and standards." I shake my head.

He yanks the gray zip-up cardigan, splitting the sleeve open wide, and tosses it to the ground. He takes a few jerking steps back and smacks the back of his head intentionally on the side of the press wood cabinets. The dishes clack, and his skin squeaks while he crumbles to the floor. Mounds of tears fall from his cheeks and he raises a hand.

He sniffs back a bubble of snot, and I gag. *I. Hate. Snot.* He's getting really dressed up for a basic game tonight.

I get up and take the space next to him with a view of the front door. "You care too much about image. You don't want a girlfriend, you want the image that comes with being part of a couple."

The floor shifts while he stands and shuffles to the bedroom, leaving me on the frigid wood planks.

He walks out wearing a button-down, an inch too small for his neck. The one he insisted he could fit into. He'll show me, until the damn button snaps off, taking out an eye.

"You'll be back." He lengthens his neck, straining to clasp the upper buttons. "We fight. You come back."

I shake my head and whisper. "I'm not coming back."

He clears his throat and glowers at me with a half-smile. "I'll tell them you're sick."

"Tell them we broke up." Suppressing the desire to scream isn't easy. Yelling solves nothing—we've yelled, screamed, and we're still here. This isn't what I want in a relationship. We're two only children who don't know how to deal with one another anymore.

Nate swipes his keys from the counter and stomps to the door. "I'm not telling them, because I know you."

"*I'll* tell them." I whip out my phone. "Who do I message first?"

"No one. Give it another week or two, take a breath and we'll go to Thad's together."

"I'm not going to Thad's. I'm not starting the New Year with someone who won't be part of my life anymore!"

Oh. Shit. I said it. I press my thumb into the soft spot below the knuckle on my third finger and apply pressure with hope to drain the anxiety and panic that's taking hold of my nerves. Should I be crying? My eyes sting, but tears don't fall.

He turns and slams his arm against the wall in the narrow hallway. He's mumbling.

"I'd think you'd be happy to go play soccer seven days a week, multiple games a day." Calmness washes over me where disdain should be.

Five years is over.

I blink, staring ahead. The front door slams shut and my shoulders jump. His engine roars in the driveway and his tires scream at me while he peels out.

He left. I glance over to the bedroom doorway and his brown shoes sit perfectly in line, waiting to be slipped on. The idiot left without shoes. He left without his gear bag for his game.

A shiver goes down my back. He's someone else's nightmare now.

CHAPTER TEN

THE TINY WHITE LIGHTS on the balsam tabletop tree twinkle a pinch of holiday into the dim condo. Enough to make me not look like a *full* sad-sack while I non-stop check my phone for signs of life from anyone. A few lit red paper stars in the windows, and it *almost* looks like this isn't the darkest Christmas Eve I've ever had. The easier path would be telling my family I wasn't coming tonight for our big traditional party because I broke up with Nate and need to not answer all their questions. I told them I didn't feel great, so I was staying home. I didn't lie, I just intentionally left out why. Nate seems to be taking it well, considering we've held radio silence since I ended things. In my family, being alone for Christmas makes people throw side-eye, try to set you up with morons, and sprinkle blue glitter of pity over the single person.

I don't want pity glitter.

But the beautiful sparkle of fresh falling snow creating ambiance for one isn't helping my mood. I should be destroyed that our relationship ended with him cheating, but honestly, I think we were both looking for a way out. I'm relieved despite the small numbness in me that slumps my shoulders.

Sweatpants and a tattered tank-top are a stark contrast to the beautiful black jumpsuit with gold flecks I wore last year. I was sassy and glam. Happy. Well, not happy, but blissfully stupid, believing things would improve.

I've got to snap out of it. I don't want Nate, but my entire life has shifted and the uncomfortable unknown hits in cruel ways at holiday time. Glancing across the practically bare apartment squeezes my heart.

Apple cream pie for dinner will help. I've never really liked Christmas Eve dinner. People shove all those heavy fancy foods down their throats, when what everyone *really* wants is a thick piece of pie.

Hawk's mom makes great pie.

I pull the caramel goodness from the counter. Pie with—no ice cream. I could go get ice cream ... or just suffer without—in case a stray family member of mine is out searching for the same.

I cut a third of the circle and slap it on a plate, drowning it in a heavy dose of whipped cream. With a grab of the lighter from the drawer, I slink to the table.

Why am I miserable if this is what I wanted? Because, it's not what I want. No one wants to be cheated on. If I tell Hawk, he'll get upset that I didn't tell him the minute it happened. When my teammates found out what happened on the pitch and why I was throwing his extra shoes, they sent me virtual hugs and told me he's an ass. I don't need any help or reminders right now. I just want cream.

The chair creaks as I crash my weight into the rigid seat.

I flick up the flame on the lighter and press it to each of the four wicks on the chime candle. Heat rises, and gold angels turn, chiming happily across the quiet apartment. The whipped cream slides off the pie and smacks to the floor, splattering a path to the door.

I tap my foot, sigh, and shove my fork deep into the pie before leaving it on the table. Still no messages on my phone. No happy pictures of people celebrating, or saying hi, or screaming about wanting to escape their families.

I rip my tank top off, opting to skip the extra six feet to the kitchen for a towel, and mop up the splattered dairy. My knees hit the floor and keys jingle in the door, drawing my gaze up as it swings wide open. In a rush, I throw the cream laden tank-top back on, smearing it through my hair and across my face, looking like a one-year-old enjoying their first smash cake.

"Damn it," I smear chunks of cream off my cheek. "A little warning!"

Hawk throws the keys on the sideboard and stares at me, before bursting out laughing. There's no rescuing this situation.

"What in the—?" His eyebrows rise to right below his hairline and his lips part.

I rush to the kitchen and grab for paper towels to cover the mess on my shirt. "Sexy, right?" If nothing else, I ooze in ways that make men run for the hills. "You're interrupting my classy dinner."

The top of the pie slides with the fork from the plate down to the floor.

Don't look at it. The chimes of the angels pick up speed.

He laughs louder and points. "I need a favor—" His eyes linger on my stomach.

What is he—crap. I tug down the side of my shirt, covering my bra and belly, and clear my throat.

He shakes his head and looks up. "I need a *big* favor."

"I dunno. I've got a very hot date with some angels." I drop the paper towels, covering the evidence across the floor.

"They sing beautifully." He wets a dishcloth and dabs it across my face and hair. "Man, you're covered—"

I hold up a finger at him. "Don't say it."

"You've got to be sticky." He snickers before tossing the towel and rag into the laundry closet. "Go shower and I'll grab you some clothes."

"Why am I showering? I'm not going anywhere." With a less than sexy wipe of the drool forming, I gesture to the pie. "I'm set."

Hawk frowns and turns the water on before pulling me into the bathroom. The door closes behind him and I strip down to rid my hair of the sugar wash coating my hair.

"Shouldn't you be with your mom?" I shout over the water.

"What?" The door cracks open.

"Shut the door!" I pull the curtain closed tight.

"I can't see you. I don't have x-ray vision." His voice squeaks at me. "Your nakedness is safe. Except for those cameras I've hidden."

The washcloth I fling smacks him, and he releases a shriek. "I'm leaving clothes on the toilet."

The door jingles as he shuts it, and a towel thumps to the floor.

Is it bad I'm relieved he's here? Minus the naked part and … minus the whipped cream.

The water cuts off with a turn of the handle and a thud inside the old pipes. I pull the towel up from the ground and look over at the toilet.

He's got to be kidding me. "What is this?" My voice lifts high enough to get a pound on the floor from the condo below.

"Oh, yeah." His fingers drum on the outside of the door. "I need you to wear that. Mom's waiting for us."

I walk out as I'm buckling the thick black belt around the velvet red pants. Hawk shakes his head, loosens the belt, and stuffs a pillow in the top.

The back of his hand graces my collarbone and my head swirls as I stare at him, dazed from the simple touch. I pat at the pillow belly for a good minute. What the hell?

His cheeks flush. He stares at my chest, and tugs down the top, clasping the top button, hiding my cleavage. "Santa, your rack is huge in this."

"Well, this Santa has boobs, no beard, and long hair." I slam my hand down the jacket to adjust the restriction in my chest. "Why aren't you or Margaret doing this?"

"Ha. Santa boobies." Hawk grins, brushing his fingers across the redness lingering on his cheeks. "Margaret and I aren't together."

I raise my eyebrows and pull back from him. "Define "aren't together," please." Slowly, I slide the scrunchie off my wrist and sweep up my wet hair. Instead of intelligently saying to him, *neither are Nate and I*, I let the opportunity go. This is about him and Margaret, and he doesn't need my Nate drama. Not yet.

He shakes his head. "Aren't doing anything other than being platonic friends. You still have your teammate."

"I'm sorry. Is there anything I can do to help?" A small part of me is relieved. Their relationship was so short I'm selfishly hoping she and I will stay friends and she'll remain on the Bees.

I tug up the pants. Despite never actually having verbalized agreeing, I really have no excuses or anywhere to be. Maybe I can sneak out a better dessert in my sack when I leave.

"You're the best!" Hawk claps his hands and gives my cheek a kiss. "The little ones will know it's me."

"They'll know me too."

He fastens a beard to my face and pulls a hat on. "Nope. They think you're coming tomorrow for Christmas Day."

My heart fills with warmth from either this disgusting jacket or the fact he didn't tell his mom why I'm at the condo. My hands clasp either side of my belly. "Ho. Ho. Ho."

He gives four quick puffs to blow the candles out, slowing the angels to a halt.

I trip across the mat as he tugs me outside. "I'm only doing this for her pie."

Nutcrackers line the hallway of Hawk's mom's house, and fake garland wraps around each banister. Balsam candles turn the house into the inside of a forest, and the blue and white lights wrapped around the Christmas tree next to the living room fireplace twinkle in invitation. Hawk's mom laughs as I stand in the front doorway, far from where the kids can see. I open my arms out and she rushes forward with a full hug.

She swats at me with a dish towel. "You should've told me Nate had to work."

So that's what he told her.

The floor squeaks with encouragement as she takes each step to the main living room.

Hawk raises an eyebrow and slides his arm around his sweet Nonnina's shoulder.

"You're the best, love." Nonnina winks and rushes with quicksteps to the tree, ready to see the action.

"I've got something for you for after," Hawk whispers.

I raise an eyebrow at him. "You got a kink for Santa?" My hand rests on his shoulder and I shake my head. "You sick, sick man."

He flashes his teeth and bites his tongue with a smile pressing his cheeks high.

I nod and pull jingle bells from the Santa sack. "Show time?"

Nonnina's voice calls as she walks up the stairs to the living room. "Do you guys hear that? What do you think it can be?"

I clasp my hands. Don't screw this up. Do not destroy the holiday for the littles.

Hawk bounds up the steps and gives out a large huff at the top of the landing. "You'll never believe it! Can you believe it? I think I heard someone come crashing down the chimney when I was in the potty!"

That's lovely. Santa comes crashing through while he's taking a pee. Hawk should be thankful that Santa isn't murderous.

Nervous flutters scamper across my body. The kids are going to know. I'm too "familiar" for this. My voice, my eyes, all of it. Santa puking in a gift bag better be allowed.

Santa is sad, confused, and single.

"Ho, ho!" a tiny toddler voice screeches across the house.

"Santa!" another voice whispers with thick excitement.

Man, they're going to be disappointed. Keep smiling.

"Ho, ho, ho." *What am I doing?* I jingle the bells and thunk my weight down with each step. "Ho, ho, ho."

Sparkles from his mom's silver tree cut across the room, cascading rainbows across the pale pink walls. The glitter of the tinsel crinkles as ornaments spin, and little wooden reindeer clips hang onto the lower branches for dear life. This year's holiday craft, no doubt. The room is packed with Occhipinti family members. His older relatives are stuffed onto the couch, while the ones nearest in age to Hawk and I are on chairs. Sprawled across the floor are the younger ones, spanning in age from two to seventeen. There are a few people I don't recognize, but their get-togethers are notorious for inviting as many people as they can fit into the house. I'm pretty sure his mom invited her dental hygienist once.

"Ho, ho! Sit. Down." The two-year-old tugs me to the green leather wingback.

"Hey Santa, you need a drink?" Hawk clasps his hands in front of his chin.

"I'd love something. The wind from the sleigh really dries out the mouth."

A two-year-old tugs at the leg of my pants.

"Milk?" I ask.

Hawk's mom waves a hand at me. "Oh, I made you a special drink, Santa."

She places a crystal glass, filled with a dark thick liquid and giant snowflake ice cube, on the credenza next to a stack of fresh ginger snaps. I smile under the scratchy beard. She knew I'd come. Hawk doesn't like the dark ginger snaps, but I do.

I clear my throat and drop my voice again. "I have an important question. Has anyone seen my list? I had it around here somewhere."

The toddler taps on the pocket just above my breast, landing on my bra strap. I bite my tongue and lift the toddler onto my lap. *Keep pretending.*

I pull a receipt from the pocket, and the little girl pretends to read it.

"I dunno. I see names on both sides. Naughty and nice. Which do you think Uncle Hawk is?"

"Naughty," Nonnina, his mother, and the bashful little girl peeking from the side of the tree say together.

"Naughty? Huh." I crinkle the receipt and throw it in the bag of gifts. "I suppose you've all been checking my list. 'Cause, I'd have to agree with Nonnina." I grin to his grandmother and the lights from the tree sparkle in her beautiful caramel eyes. I'm one of a handful who call her Nonnina rather than Nonna, or grandmother. Hawk said it once in front of me and I liked it. She's not *my* grandmother, but she treats me like family when I see her. Nonnina is a tiny woman who possesses a huge heart, like Hawk.

Hawk presses a hand over his chest and drops his jaw in playful astonishment. "Me? Naughty? How dare. I'm always on the nice list."

I grab for a sip of the brown liquid and the warm spices burn at my throat, causing me to choke.

"Ho, ho, ho." Two-year-olds yell everything. Everything.

I nod and cover my mouth. "Yes! Santa likes it spicy." After several blinks, the burn sits in the back of my throat.

With two fingers, I wave the little girl in her crinoline dress over.

"Will you be my helper?" I ask, my voice hoarse and thick with alcohol.

She nods and pulls gifts from the bag, passing them without a care for who is on the tag. Her ring curls bounce up and down as she delivers the gifts like a good little elf, and returns to my side.

"Where's yours? Did you give them all out and skip yourself?" I ask, bopping the girl on the nose.

She nods, and sits at my side. I puff out my lip from beneath the beard.

Do. Not. Cry. I miss being as innocent as Hawk's niece. She's as excited as Hawk gets about Christmas. Either the magic of the season is getting to me or the burn of the alcohol lingering in my sinuses is making me teary.

Hawk's mother lifts her finger and pulls a gift from under the tree for the little girl. "Here Santa, there's one left. You dropped it off last night."

Oh, thank goodness.

I accept the gift from her hands, and the tag on top reads *Elin*. I throw her a nod, and hand it to the tiny sweetheart. She tears through the wrapping paper without a moment's hesitation.

Mrs. Occhipinti mouths: "Sorry!"

I shake my head and smirk as the little one pulls out a pro-level soccer ball way too big for herself.

"I get to be like Uncle Hawk!" She screeches, and runs through the house, kicking off the white, patent leather shoes.

A raging little girl hell-bent on breaking everything in the house with a ball, that requires barely a touch to fly, replaces the sweet little angel.

I throw my hands on the pillow. "Ho, ho, ho." The sack slings over my shoulder and I head to the stairs with a wave.

"Where are you going?" the little girl asks. "We're going to have dessert."

My stomach rumbles, urging me to go sit at the table.

"Santa's got to go deliver more gifts." I take a step down. Hawk follows closely behind.

"Boobies," the toddler says.

I pull back a laugh and the dread treading over my chest.

"Santa boobies." An innocent giggle comes out as she smacks at my chest. "Boobies." Her curious little face buries itself, looking for a nipple.

Sorry, sweetie, no milk is coming out of these for you. Time to high-tail it before there are too many questions. "Bye-bye" I wave and offer a nervous laugh. Her mom comes over and collects her, mouthing the word sorry.

"Bye-bye," she says.

I rush down the first set of steps, past the landing, and down the next set of steps to Hawk's area of the house. He meets me in the garage. I peel off the hat and beard and bend over laughing.

"Boobies." Tears streak down the sides of my red face. I'm a pathetic excuse for a Santa.

"The kid has a future." Hawk throws his arms in the air. He pulls a plate from the garage fridge. "For your services."

I glance down at the plate, pull my frown in, and smile back. The thought is sweet.

"Thanks." I pull the hat on to fight the wind whipping through the open doors to the long, dark driveway.

"Let me drive you home," Hawk says.

I shake my head. "You go enjoy Christmas Eve. I've got an enormous plate of food, and floor pie to get back to."

"I'm going to walk, the night is cold but beautiful." To clear my head, to figure out how tonight went from floor pie to Santa.

Hawk walks over and gives me a tight, warm hug. "Thanks for this."

The sour notes of the Christmas carols from upstairs fill the garage. I turn to walk up the driveway and Hawk follows.

"Borrow some clothes and come back inside." He takes my hand, and turns me to face him. An army of butterflies attack my stomach and nearly knock me over. His touch shouldn't do this to me.

"I think the kids will notice." I brush a finger down the side of his cheek and my pulse races. He studies my face, reading line by line from my hairline to my chin, as if he'll be quizzed later. Shit. I blink at him several times and take a step back. What did I do? I pull my hand away quickly and trudge up the hill of his driveway to head back to the condo.

"I'll text you later," he shouts.

His whole family is over. Tonight's not the night to tell him about Nate. I'll do it after the New Year. I smile, throw the sack over my shoulder, and take a big whiff of delicious ziti and shrimp while I head home. I need something stiff to help drown these butterflies and clear my head.

CHAPTER ELEVEN

T HE LIGHT FROM THE lamppost filters through the shades, warming my hand and highlighting the tear stains marked on the empty cannoli paper stuck to my cheek as I sulk, stomach down, on the couch. A sugar cream stupor is the perfect escape while I watch headlights cut out to the main road, likely taking off to go celebrate with people who love each other. I'm alone and it sucks. I'm a vagabond. Sitting in a condo that's not mine. Barely moved out of a house that's also not mine. Happy freakin' New Year's Eve.

Lucky for me, the bakery was open on my way to couch time. The look of horror on the cashier's face when I licked the cream in front of her was priceless. Her own fault, really. She was too perky when she handed me the box. She wished me a Happy New Year and declared that my friends would love them. Licking the next two and placing them in the box may be what rushed her off to the back super-fast. Like they've never had grumpy weirdos at the holidays before. Not grumpy, overwhelmed. The cream isn't a celebration, it's a cry for—what am I even doing?

I did it.

Woo—bleh. I wedge my hand between the cushion and my stomach. This desire to drown in sugar needs to pass.

I should be happy. Instead, I want to shove another cannoli in my mouth to keep my hands from grabbing the phone and betraying me. I want to tell Hawk I ended things with my ex, but at the same time I can't get Christmas Eve in his driveway out of my head.

The smart move is to lie low and avoid Thad's party. Once I hear fireworks outside, I'll follow the social protocol of texting everyone a Happy New Year, and pretend like things are fine. No home. No boyfriend. No real anything.

The refrigerator kicks on and I roll to a seated position, peeling off the wrapper.

Music. I need to celebrate this newfound freedom. The freedom currently mimicking a lead weight on my chest and arms. I did the right thing. I flick the phone open to find the music app, and there're two missed texts from Hawk.

Hawk: *Dude. Where are you?*

Hawk: *Oh shit! Call me.*

My stomach twists and my throat goes dry. I click the music app and let the glory of female anthems ring out across the room. Pushing up from the couch, I spin across the floor without abandon or care for anyone who can see my forced, fun dance party for one.

Tonight's an occasion to dance, cry, and avoid social interaction. With side-steps to the fridge, I put my phone on top to keep from undoing the night with a single text.

The music dictates my body as I throw my free arm high in the air, and sing to ABBA with a cannoli shoved half-way into my mouth. Keys jingle in the lock and the door flies open. I bite down on the sugary goodness and lock eyes with Hawk.

Oh!

At least my shirt's on this time.

His mouth drops wide as he shakes his head. With a smash, his keys slide from the credenza to the floor and he's still staring at my I'm-a-strong-worthy-woman moment.

"You've got—" He swipes a finger near the side of his eye. "What's with you and food?"

I blink rapidly and rub my shoulder against my face to clear the evidence. "Better?"

He nods, staring blankly, and Curie tugs him to the couch. Ooh. Maybe he'll leave her with me when he goes back out.

He flops onto the couch and leans back while she nuzzles his leg for scratches. "We were out for a walk."

"Liar. You're checking on me." I flop on the couch deep into the cushion, and the old springs thunk beneath my weight.

"Can't prove it." He shrugs. "And what are you wearing?"

Short answer is too-small, tattered, college cheer shorts and a black glitter tank top to be festive. "It's got sparkles."

"Get dressed and come out to the—" He ogles my snack. "Practicing?"

I pull the thick sugar pacifier from my mouth and lean forward, pulling my tongue in last.

"Practicing would be this way." I open my mouth wide, stare him in the eyes, shoving the shell inside and pull it back out. "I'm eating the frosting out."

Hawk blinks blankly in my direction. "Right." He clears his throat with a high laugh. "Okay, can you not? Because I'm getting wicked strange images and can't concentrate."

"Perhaps you should practice with a cannoli—do it for the team and women everywhere."

The music hits a high note.

"I'll have you know, I've never had complaints about my eating habits. This is a golden tongue I tell you." He sticks out his wide tongue with unnecessary authority.

I stare down at it. "Right. Why do men always think they are so glorious when, in fact, so many tongues are mediocre egg scramblers?"

"Golden." He wags his eyebrows. "Women are no different—everyone thinks *they* give the best blow job. From years of experience, I don't really care. I want suction, lubrication, intense friction, and minimal teeth."

We're officially in a game of chicken to creep each other out, and neither of us will give.

"Just don't draw blood." His shoulders shiver. "That's the worst."

My jaw drops and I shove the shell into my mouth and bite, crumbling the tip. "It's food. Stop being a sick fuck."

"Oh, come on. You're sitting in here eating cream on New Year's Eve, alone"

"Shouldn't you be at Thad's?" I elbow him and pass the box of cannoli.

He shakes his head and unzips his jacket. "Curie needed a walk, and not when I found out my best friend left out a *huge* detail of her life recently."

"What'd you hear?" I clear my throat and stare up at the popcorn ceiling.

His half-laugh, with a flex to his stomach, shakes the couch. "Apparently, you broke up with Nate before Christmas and never told me. I told you about Margaret, you should have told me about Nate, but I get why you didn't."

My heart beats in my ears. "It's hot in here."

"It's not hot." He nudges me with his elbow. "I'll leave it alone, but I needed to see if you were okay."

I look deep into his eyes, and his green-streaked-brown peepers look back at me like a pitiful, wide-eyed-puppy. The rush of anxiety and twisting embarrassment throughout my body lifts with a long breath. Not telling him what was happening was harder than breaking up with Nate.

"Can I stay here longer?" I look back to the window and lean my head on his shoulder.

He leans his ear against my head. "However long you need."

How long I'll need—forever? I need a place to live and to stand on my own. The warmth of being cuddled fills me, yet still my body can't completely relax. Us being single at the same time is a weird chapter for us and I'm not sure what it means. It may mean nothing.

"Get me a lease." I lift my head off his shoulder and flick his jeans with my fingers.

He rubs his thumb against his leg and stares off at the gray rug. "I'm not getting you a lease."

I push out a pout and tug at his buffalo-checked flannel. "Please? I don't want to be the sad girl you pity."

Hawk rubs his palms against his eyes, and clasps them between his legs. "I trust you. I don't need a lease."

If he trusts me, why isn't he looking at me?

"What if I turn this place into the orgy capital of the condo association and you get fined?"

"As if I hadn't already hedged my bets and slept with the head of the association." He belly-laughs and curls his body forward. "Yes. If you're planning on making this the orgy capital of the condo association, we might need a lease."

I laugh until tears stream down my face. "I'm paying you."

He turns his head and raises both eyebrows. "I don't need—"

"I need a place, and you need a tenant."

"I'm not going to win, am I?" His tongue clicks against the roof of his mouth, then runs over his front teeth.

I shake my head and nuzzle into his shoulder. "Thank you!"

"I have conditions." He harrumph's and twitches his shoulder. "First condition—if there's ever anything big like a break up, you call me immediately."

"Is this a condition for all your tenants?" I unapologetically lick the last bit of frosting off my palm. "You're a very involved landlord."

He pokes at the soft spot on my side, and a giggle erupts. My heart lightens, overcoming the unease of starting over. I poke him back and he screeches loud enough for Curie to pick up her head with a happy snort.

"Now look what you've done." I lean forward and scratch the dog's sweet spot, between the brown and white seam on her giant head. "Any more conditions?"

"Are you sure you're done with Nate?" He flicks at his ear and stares down at Curie, who is a puddle of mush in my hands.

I nod. "I should have listened sooner—I'm sorry."

Hawk checks his watch and then fidgets with his lower ear. "Midnight's in a half hour. It'll take too much time to drop her off and get to Thad's party for midnight."

I lean to give Curie a soft kiss on top of her head and sit back up. "Leave her here so you can make it."

"Ha." He shakes his head. "You would want to keep her, wouldn't you? She's my date for the night and where she goes, I go."

Lights streak up the quiet road, cutting through the dark trees beyond the over-lit lot.

My fingers press at my temple while the sugar surges through my body, wanting me to spin in the middle of the room and dance in circles 'til midnight hits. Screw it—if he's staying, he can dance. I stand and bow to him, raise my hand, and tug him to the center of the room.

"I can't—can't—" he stands and the black leash thunks to the floor.

"If you're staying, you're dancing." I lift my arms high, like a drunken ballerina, and spin around myself.

His arms bend below his chin and he does his best to flail, embracing the she-power music.

The music cuts out, and we both stop dancing and stare at each other as the countdown on the app ticks away.

Ten. Nine. Eight. His hands raise out to grab mine and a tiny flutter sweeps over me. This doesn't feel like friendship right now, it's different.

Seven. Six. Five. My lips part and I stare at his full red lips. The heartbeat blasting in my ears blocks out the rest of the room. We'll still be friends in the New Year, and it's a simple kiss. It's not wrong to have someone to kiss at midnight.

Four. Three. Two. This is my best friend and I'm not ruining a friendship over a kiss at midnight. My lips are dry. I press them back together and force a half-smile.

One. Hawk squeezes my hands and pulls me in for a hug, lifting my feet off the ground in a large swing, sending a smile through my body as the air rushes around us.

We crash down to the floor and Curie comes scampering over to check on us with big licks on our cheeks. We roll apart on the rug, laughing. My midnight kiss is absolutely a being I want in my life next year: Curie.

"Happy New Year."

"Happy New Year."

My phone vibrates for three minutes straight, in a way that only happens when a big event happens in our soccer family.

Stillness settles over the room, and my heart steadies. I know I'm the topic of those texts, and I'm not ready to answer questions. Everything can wait 'til later. I lay back on the rug, with my arm over my head, and my fingertips brush against Curie's bristly coat.

Chapter Twelve

LIV'S GROUP TEXT CAME through to have a *welcome back to single life* get together after word spread on New Year's that I'd dropped the 260 pounds of unhappiness. She gave me an entire seven days to pull myself together, and that buffer cut down to three when the fieldhouse canceled our game tonight.

I have this weird suspicion that Rose, whose wavy red hair was set high in a viking-style braid before the game, has a set of wire cutters in the base of her bag somewhere. Her outfit is also suspicious. She never wears dresses on game days, and magically tonight she's sporting a deep purple sheath dress covered in black zippers with a pair of silver tights. But I'm not asking questions. As a team, we've withstood dating, engagements, weddings, divorces, babies, and are ready to drop everything to make sure we're all okay. They're the reason I lace my cleats each week, and the family Hawk helped me find.

The pub is nearly empty outside of our loud group. Sipping a foamy IPA doesn't alter the mass change raining down on my life. The condo is great, but not mine. Hawk is undercharging me, but at least he takes rent. I'm used to being the one to give others support. I'm comfortable there.

Fried pickles sit in the center of the table, their grease soaking into a napkin nestled in the metal basket, filled with multiple dipping sauces. The sauces all look the same 'til they hit the tongue, but after enough beers, there's really no difference. This grease trap is our third decimated basket of ceremonial pickles in less than an hour. Each satisfying crunch settles the growls of my stomach.

Black and white photos framed in orange, white, and green throughout the pub adorn the mahogany stained walls. Images of soccer players and hurlers as far as the eye can see stare back at us. Per typical, there are no women in any of them. Not even a single shot of a woman playing camogie.

I crunch down on another pickle.

"I'd like to propose a toast!" Liv raises her bottle high. "Elin Axelsson, and Elin's vagina, are officially free agents!"

Is this what we're cheering for? It's going to be a long night.

Rose playfully sighs and raises her glass to Liv. "To new penis."

Sliding under the table may be the only way out of this situation before it gets worse.

"I'm sorry, I have to ask. What on earth kept you with Nate?" Liv swipes foam from her lip with a firm thumb. "I hope he was …" She straightens her hands and widens her arms.

I shake my head and throw a peanut in my mouth. "Nope."

"You stayed with him and his loud mouth and he couldn't even spear you?" Liv shakes her head. "You need a transition penis."

I stare at her and blink. "What the hell is a transition penis?"

"No! She's fine." Ariana motions a circle over her lap. "Maybe her region needs a timeout."

"I guarantee, based on his mouth constantly flapping, he was not a great explorer." Rose takes a sip of whiskey. "You can tell." She holds up her thumb and forefinger, closing them in on one another.

The lights over the bar glow as green as the exploded frog-colored walls in his basement.

"We've all been there." Ariana bites a pretzel stick, scoping out the far side of the bar. "Why is it so quiet?"

"We're too late for the old crowd, and too early for the party animals," I say. "Everyone else our age is home with their families."

Rose sneers. "Don't screw the mood. This is a celebration!"

Liv leans over the bar from her high stool and waves down the bartender. She flashes a smile and gestures for shots.

I'm perfectly fine. Wonderfully fine. Okay, I'm lying. Pretending will only take me so far, and despite the fact I broke up with him, I feel like hot garbage. This isn't the first time I've ended a relationship, and the reality is Nate and I ended years ago. There's no reviving a cold corpse when the heart stops beating, no matter how many times the other person tries. Now we are down to loose ends, like my belongings being at his house with nowhere to go.

"She could sleep with the bartender. He's hot." Ariana slides her glass against the black wood table top. "Like a beefy mer-man."

"Uh—" So many questions on that one. "Do you mean Poseidon?"

"Tomato, to-mah-to." Ariana shrugs. "Who do I know who's single?"

With a slurp of melting ice at the base of her glass, Liv's shifts directly beneath the overhead light and a grin crawls across her face. "Kee-eee-arrr," bellows out in a low screech as she flaps her elbows at her sides.

I spit my drink into my hand and join the erupting laughs at the table.

"Was that a new mating call?" Ariana giggles.

"Let's hear you make a Hawk noise." Liv repeats the noise louder, staring down her nose at me with her elbows up. "KEE-EEE-ARRR."

Tears well and a chuckle wants to erupt from the ridiculous scrunch of her face. "No." I shake my head vigorously.

"Can *I*?" Liv smirks.

I shrug. Is it bad I want to shout, *no*? But I'm not sure why.

"Meh, he's off limits anyways." Ariana pouts and doesn't elaborate on her sentence. "Back to Poseidon."

Poseidon lines a row of shots across the center of the table and drops a stack of poker chips next to the pickles. Ariana pulls her shoulders back and her chest just about takes out his eye. We're never getting out of here tonight.

"Maybe I need to not date." That's an option, right?

Not dating is tempting. No need to clean hedges or shave legs. No need to stress out over every little sign I think is going one way, but will head in the opposite direction. The relief of not being worried about what the person thinks of me, my job, or my friends. Over-thinking each touch or statement flying from my mouth can take a back seat.

"Do you even know how to be single?" Rose doles the shots across the table.

"I've been single." Barely.

A sniff of lemon from the cloudy liquid in the shot glass cleanses my sinuses. I squint and brace my stomach for what's to come. Lemon drops.

"You've had back-ups." Rose lifts her fingers. "Two years. I've been single now, two years. Longest stretch."

"How many dates in two years?" Please let there be some hope out there.

"More than I can count on fingers and toes." Rose flicks back her deep red braids and raises the shot glass. "Welcome to single."

We raise glasses to the bronze ceiling before tossing them back. My eyes close as the vodka burns its way down my throat and chest. Poseidon's an ass for using cheap liquor. The glasses slam down on the table one after the other. Liv raises four fingers above her head with a chip tucked in the center.

Poseidon grins. "Same?"

"Bartender's choice." I shake a finger at him. "No dirty well vodka."

He touches his fingers to his chest and bows. His raven hair falls across his shoulders while he reaches up to grab a stronger vodka from the shelf. "I've got you."

"Yes!" Liv shimmies on the wobbly stool, nearly toppling to the sticky, dark wood floor. "Shit!" Her fingers clasp the round table top tight.

Ha. "Vodka got-cha?"

Liv shakes her head. "Poseidon's done fucked my nerves up." She waves a hand over her face.

I glance over my shoulder and concentrate on the bottles behind the bar. Twelve types of vodka, six kinds of rum, delicious amaretto, and a slew of whiskey bottles. The worn labels on the surrounding bottles are well out of my price range. A slight shift in my seat gives a full view of Poseidon.

He's not super attractive. Not even in dim light. His hair is long and wavy, he's average at best. There's no flicker in my heart to picture him naked on a bed, or out on a date. They can have him.

"Come on, talk to him." Rose taps the table.

"Meh." He's not my type.

"He doesn't check her boxes." Ariana pipes up. "She's got a lot of boxes."

I've dated guys who didn't check my boxes. None of those worked out, which begs the question: are my boxes "off?"

Poseidon lines up another round of shots. "Let me know if this one is better."

He takes the chip from Liv, kisses it, and drops it back on the table. She watches as he walks back to scrub down the bar.

"I'm going to say it. He does things to my nether regions without even a touch." She pushes the shots around the table, leaning far forward, offering Poseidon a full view of the back of her tight jeans. "Did you see how thick his fingers are? I wonder if he's thick everywhere?"

I laugh, and my disgusting pickle brine and vodka shot shoots up from the side of the glass, splashing across the table and onto my game jersey. *Crap.* I yank the napkin off the table and dab at the wet spot on my chest, only to make it worse.

"Yeah, you need to not wear that at bars." Ariana pats my back. "You'll learn. Boobs up, back arched, and flaunt what momma gave ya."

I blink at her. Nope. No one wants to see anything under this jersey.

"Promise me you won't let her nap too long before getting back out there," Ariana says in a tender tone, her silver shirt shimmers, ready to party.

Her? She didn't name my vagina, which is a positive, but wow.

"Give her a break. She's been single for a half-second." Liv comes to my defense. "She probably hasn't even had to replace a set of batteries yet."

Poseidon drops a round of drinks on the table and brushes his hand on Liv's shoulder.

"Batteries?" he asks.

Liv makes a jerking motion high into the air, looks up and shapes her mouth into a circle. Her shoulders jerk and she touches his chest. "Oh, yes!"

Poseidon's cheeks turn redder than the cherries on his station.

Liv looks across the table at me and smirks. "Batteries." She runs her fingers through her hair and taps his chest.

"Batteries. Okay then." He grabs the empty shot glasses off the table and shuffles back behind the bar without taking his eyes off Liv.

"Bet he can stir your next martini with a bigger straw." Rose flicks her tongue against the side of her cheek.

They are ridiculous. I clear my throat and take another sip of the martini.

"What are you so afraid of by being open?" Liv asks. "It's us. Let your freak flag fly."

My stomach twists. My flag's never been as open as theirs. Now, there's no one to help run me up a pole.

"Take off the jersey." Ariana says. "I need to see what we're working with."

Nope. "I'm fine." I sip at my empty glass, hoping to disappear into my drink.

"Do it. Do it. Do it." Liv taps at the table.

Screw it, it's the Bees and there's no one else here except the bartender, and it'll shush them. My nerves rush, accompanied by the confidence of several shots, two beers and a martini. I stand, slinging the jersey off. "Happy?" I take a full spin and take a bow.

Ariana yanks the jersey from me. "Yes, and no. You've got to get new bras if you're going to wear those tanks. Something pretty and comfy that pulls them up higher."

I grab my glass and bite at the red straw. "This is what I've got to work with." I throw my free hand on my hip and do a full circle of the high-top.

"That. That's what you need when you go out." Liv smacks my ass. "Confidence."

My left cheek stings and the right side is off balance.

"Confidence," she says.

Huh, that's some other person, not me. Where does one go to find confidence or unearth it after so many years of—the photo shoot. I'll finally reschedule the boudoir shoot. If I can do that, maybe I can have a minuscule amount of the confidence they have.

"I'll work on it." I grab my jersey, slamming it back on before my nipples cut holes in the glass.

I should text Hawk to get home. No, this is not a state he needs to see me in. When I pull out my phone the buttons are blurry. I do my best to make out the car service app and punch in the address to the condo. Ten minutes and another shot later, Hawk rolls up to pick me up. I squint at the screen and see that

I hit the wrong button. That I'd in fact simply texted him his own address. Hawk grins the entire drive home.

CHAPTER THIRTEEN

THE OLD CITY NEIGHBORHOOD of Center City in Philly vibrates with sounds and energy. The vibe here is absolutely not the same as New York City, where I feel rushed and can get lost in my own thoughts. In New York, I can walk for hours without a single interaction unless I initiate it, and this isn't what I want today. Not to mention my overall lame excuse for taking a three hour drive this morning to get cherry flavored Italian ice, and a pretzel. It's ten-thirty on Saturday morning. There are parts of Philly city still waking up. There are also people, like me, who likely never fell deep asleep last night.

"I need a coffee." Hawk yawns and takes off his red beard hat. He replaces it with a hunter green slouch beanie and grabs the handmade burnt orange scarf Nonnina made.

When we step out of the car I walk over and help him wrap the scarf carefully over his fleece lined leather jacket. Our eyes lock, and his pupils dilate. I'm instantly hyper aware of every ounce of my body. He pulls a pair of gunmetal rimmed sunglasses from his pocket and puts them on to 'block the wind.' He reaches out to gently free the end of my ponytail from beneath my thick brown stockyards jacket. A warmth fills my cheeks. Goosebumps climb my arms and I'm not sure if it's from the wind, or this strange unknown of us both being simultaneously single. I don't think it's the wind, because the Berber lining of my coat is practically making me sweat.

Hawk has always been the person who, when I start a sentence with *"do you want to,"* the answer is almost always yes. So this morning, after staring at the ceiling in the eerie quiet of the condo for an hour, I drove to his mom's house at six for a "do you want to ..." day. When I pulled up, he was outside, sitting on the front steps, drinking a coffee wearing the crochet beard hat with a fuzzy gray house coat. I'd honestly thought he'd still be asleep, but I'm not the only one with a lot on my mind and in need of a distraction. It took him thirty minutes to get dressed, take care of the dog, and we were on the road for an "adventure day," as he prefers to call them. Only, he opted to drive, and I took ownership of the radio to prepare us for the day ahead. The radio rules for today are that the artist or group had to have either been born in, or discovered in, Philadelphia. Songs with Philadelphia or Philly in them are also permissible.

We walk up the sidewalk and purchase two coffees from a cart on Walnut Street. The steam lifts—fogging his sunglasses. Hawk takes them off and hands them to me. I slide them on top of my head until he wants them back, or until the sun becomes too much for my own eyes.

The sidewalk transitions into uneven cobblestone pulling me back in time to the 1700s. The buildings around us are grand as we sip coffee and explore.

Hawk stops. "Do you think Ben Franklin slept with half the women in this city while he was here?"

"Yes. But I don't think that's part of the tours." I blow at the steam. "We're surrounded by gorgeous buildings, and you want to know who Ben Franklin slept with."

"I was thinking about sex." He shrugs.

I swallow. "You're always thinking about sex."

"Not true." His mouth parts. "Right now, I'm wondering why on earth you want Italian ice on a forty-degree day."

I shift my weight and look away. We both know I don't want Italian ice.

"Do you think Ben Franklin or any of those guys had sex on the Liberty Bell? Maybe that's why it cracked."

"I absolutely think that's how the Liberty Bell actually cracked." I playfully elbow him. "It would be nice, if just for once, people were honest about it. It's a much better story. Silly prude historians."

He grabs my hand, our gloves keep our palms from touching, and he tugs me up the street. "Come on. I want to go see the historical sex bell."

"Maybe they actually rang it each time a virgin lost their ..." I don't know how to finish the sentence, and unintentionally leave my lips parted as the sentence trails off.

"Wings? Pants? No, that's not historically accurate." He opens his arms for security at the bell to wand him. "Petticoats? Cat. Must be their cat. So many cats were lost due to Franklin."

The security guard waves him through and begins to wand me.

"I promise, I'm not going to steal the bell," I say.

"Oh, she will. The pockets in her coat are huge," Hawk says.

The woman leans at us with her wand outstretched. "Don't touch the bell," she says with firmness.

We stand in front of the massive bell and stare at it for a bit. The last time I saw it was on a fifth-grade field trip and I barely remember really understanding how beautiful it is. Now, I can see the fine details, and understand better how incredible the artistry is. The technology used to create this massive broken bit of celebrated history was amazing.

"I want to tap the bell," Hawk whispers. He places a warm hand on top of mine and tries to move me forward.

"Oh god. Stop. I'm not touching this thing." Fear seizes my insides and I yank my arm down.

"It belongs to the people, it wants to be touched," he says.

"Sir, please refrain from touching the bell." The security guard waves her wand at him.

He nods at her and flashes a grin. My nerves are saved by a magic wand and a fairy-God-security-guard in a black suit.

"I don't think it'd be possible." I stare at the bell again and he leans into my arm. "The metal would be super cold on exposed flesh."

My mind switches to an unexpected vision. I'm in a half-off low-necked gown over a petticoat, moaning as Hawk leans me against one of the metal bars that holds up the bell with his breeches undone and his waistcoat providing a shade of privacy as he fucks me. My legs throb and I'm aware of the heat between our bodies right now.

"Come with me," Hawk says.

"Excuse me?" My chest rises and falls with a hitch of my breath. I blink away the vision and am unable to instantly rid myself of the idea of him inside me. I need to apologize to the entire city for the thoughts that crossed my mind for those fleeting seconds. I know he'd have rung the bell after we were done, probably before he even finished redressing himself, but not before he knew I was covered again. This vision must be from my dry-spell. We're friends, and friends don't picture each other fucking one another at a historical site—in historical garb.

"The line is growing, and we still need to get you Italian ice." He wags his eyebrows like he knows where my mind went. But he couldn't know.

We meander in circles for hours, or stand in place for long periods of time to people-watch. Museum after museum have lines out the door, and there are people queued up already for lunch. We aren't the only ones taking advantage of the nice weather. The walk warms us and we slow down once we hit a series of murals painted on the side of buildings. There are glass mosaics and gorgeous murals representing the city and the people.

Hawk's hand is firm against my lower back. He's keeping me close, and it's nice. But, overall, this is more touching today than is typical for us. I don't know how to react to these types of gestures from him. I'm assuming most of it is benign worry for me after the breakup. Him wanting to make sure I'm okay, and to let me know I can lean on him if I need to.

We cross the street, and he tugs me to a bench.

"Oh! I saw this place reviewed online" he says. "Do you want to wait here? The inside looks small."

I opt to stay outside. The bench is nice. Crispness in the air doesn't seem to bother anyone who passes on the street. The bright sun makes the city glow. Passersby are focused on whatever shop or hidden part of the city they're going to next. Hawk disappears down a small set of steps and returns five minutes later with two Italian ices in paper cups. He hands me the chocolate one and keeps the red for himself.

Hawk sits with me on the bench and pulls two pretzels out from under his coat. "The man said we're supposed to dip the pretzel in the ice."

"Sounds gross." I pretend like it's my first time doing this. "I'm in."

Hawk's face contorts and he grimaces mid-bite. I dip my pretzel and take a big bite of the icy concoction. He shifts his jaw and covers his face with his arm.

I swallow down the big hunk of pretzel in my mouth and lean to check on him.

"Are you okay?" I ask.

He shakes his head. A horrified look is plastered across his features. In his hand is an object that looks like a bit of pink and white. Like a piece of a cheap denture or fake teeth.

"That's not yours," I say. "Was that in your mouth?"

"Tell me it's a piece of machinery that fell in." He squeaks.

It looks like teeth. Is not the answer he wants.

"Uh. Yeah. Plastic from a machine." I gag.

He runs his hand down the front of his throat and straightens. I take a napkin from my pocket and put the *plastic* from his hand inside. I then grab both our flavored ices and promptly head to the garbage can to throw them out. When I get back to the bench he still looks pale.

I hold out my pretzel for him.

"No. No food right now," he screeches.

"Okay. We need to reset your brain and your mouth." I stand and hold out my hand for him to grab.

He shakes his head and points at the pretzel. I take his pretzel and mine and throw them out. When I come back to the bench, he's on his phone.

"What are you doing?" I tap on his screen.

"I'm searching what diseases you can get from making out with a stranger's dentures." He flashes the phone at me, and surprisingly, there are results to the inquiry.

"This one suggests alcohol."

He nods. "I don't want today to be remembered as the time I ate teeth."

"They're fake teeth at least." I take his phone and slide it into his coat pocket.

His complexion goes pale again. "What if they weren't fake?"

"They're fake," I say. "It was a piece of machinery, not teeth."

"This is why I need you." He keeps shoulder to shoulder with me for the next few blocks.

We window-shop straight through lunch, as neither of us has an actual appetite right now. The distance from where we started in Old City to where we land on South Street is less than a mile, but there's so much packed between the two places. Besides, Hawk and I have never really taken a direct route together in our entire friendship.

Street performers and bands take up each corner on our walk. We pass by graffiti artists creating masterpieces on the spot. There are dancers and singers pouring their hearts out. Musicians call to us for attention in their quest to draw crowds and make some cash.

Hawk gestures to an outdoor cafe and we take a table. "This looks like a good spot to people-watch."

The spot is central to a line of art galleries and music shops.

"Do you want an espresso?"

"Sure. No dentures with mine please." I flash a smile showing off all my teeth.

"Don't make me vomit." He groans, then disappears inside.

I watch as a cello player sets up and begins to rip blues and melodious scat not even six feet from the table. The muscle in her arms and neck move, emphasizing each emotionally-driven note. I'm mesmerized by her.

Hawk leans down in front of me and gestures to the espresso cups he's placed on the table.

"Dance with me." He takes my hand before I can think of an excuse beyond the idea of being embarrassed as a no. His arm slips around my waist and I fall into him, laughing. My heart races, and butterflies form in my stomach. We dance circles with one another, and as much as I'd normally despise the type of attention where people stare, with him I don't care. Our gazes remain fixed, and for me, the rest of the city fades away. We clap and dance for the entire song.

The musician hits a high note and we stop. We stare at one another and I study Hawk's face, his breathing is shallow, but quickens as he glances at my mouth. I bite my lip.

Claps break our moment, and he turns to take a bow. I bury myself in his shoulder. He guides me to my chair, to my now-cold espresso, and we sit like nothing happened. The cellist nods at us, and her cheeks press up when Hawk smiles. The crowd drops money in her case, and she plays her next song.

"Where to next, Wildflower?" Hawk asks.

"Depends. Do you want to be home before dark? Or, do you want to chill here?"

He doesn't break my gaze. "Mmm ... we can get you food."

"I'm not so hungry." I'm too confused to be hungry. This *is* more touching than we've done in a long time. And, I like it, but I don't understand why it keeps happening. I don't want to get used to the idea of it either.

"Same." He takes off his gloves and rubs the back of his hand. "Are you cold?"

I shake my head. I might be, but my head is spinning from the day already. Thankfully, I'm no longer imagining the bell. Crap. I'm imagining the bell again, only this time it's not the bell. This time, it's in a dusty beatnik bar, where he's a patron and I'm playing piano for a set. Rather than him inside of me, we're busy ogling each other, both of us too cool to make an immediate move. We're in black pants and shirts. The cello player is playing in the background. Hawk walks over and we make out in the open bar without even a hello. This is a very different vibe. One oozing a slow sexy lust, rather than the raw animal-like desire of the bell. Neither, however, belongs in my headspace. My mind is messing with all the emotions I've suppressed for years with this simultaneous singlehood.

"Let's go back to the car, but I'm not ready to leave Philly yet."

"What about the river?" My suggestion sounds stupid and cold.

We get up, tip the cellist, and go back to the car.

The drive to the Schuylkill River is fairly quick thanks to blasting Boys II Men with the windows open. Strangers give us thumbs up as we pass. We park, and he pulls out two beach chairs from his trunk. After a short walk we sit at the riverfront and stare out. There's no green on the trees, and the river is frozen.

"We should come back when the cherry blossoms are in bloom and the rowers are out. The pink over the river is gorgeous." A wind whips and I pull my jacket up.

"I'd like that." He taps his fingers on the arm of the chair over and over, but doesn't look at me.

"I'll give you every cent in my wallet if you tell me what's distracting you." I tug on the lower part of his coat sleeve.

"I've fallen for that once already. You handed me three pennies." He takes off his hat and resets it. "I don't want pennies, but I'll tell you anyway. My jacket smells like cucumbers from dancing."

"I'm sorry? I can get it cleaned if you hate the smell cucumber soap."

He tugs at the base of his gloves. "I never said I hated the smell. Elin—"

"There's a pirate ship we can have dinner on one night." I don't know why I cut him off. Fear, maybe? That he's going to say it's time to go home, that today is over. Or that I'll say something I can't take back and damage our friendship, making the three-hour drive incredibly awkward. I place my hand on top of his, and we sit in silence while the sun shifts behind a large cloud.

He clears his throat. "Let's go check out the artist over there."

I hadn't noticed a tiny woman with a card table and a sketch pad under one of the large bare trees. She must be in her early eighties at the youngest. When we walk over, she nods to acknowledge our existence and keeps sketching. Her supplies are in little containers held down by rocks, so they don't get blown away.

"Anything you want, thirty bucks." She wags her eyebrows up at Hawk. "Except me, I'm taken."

There's a rasp to her voice, and I want to swaddle her in blankets.

Hawk eyes an image on the table. "How much for this one?"

"Thirty, like I said, everything is thirty. I just need money for supplies. If a buyer likes my art, then great. If not, they can sod off and let me sketch."

I need to adopt this philosophy. The piece he is pointing at depicts the river in spring with cherry blossoms in full bloom. It's an illustration with hints of pop art. The work is better than anything we'd seen in the shops on South Street.

"We'll take it," I say.

Hawk pulls cash from his wallet and hands her two twenties.

"I said thirty. I've got no change." She shakes her head at him. "That makes it forty, or you can pick another print and take two for forty."

I pull a twenty from my wallet and add it to Hawk's bills. "How about two for sixty to keep the price fair?"

She nods at me and I point to the image she's working on. "I'm going to give you our, *my* address. When you're done, send it to me please."

I want the reminder from today, and the other one Hawk picked out. While we may never come and sit at the river together to watch the rowers and the blooming cherry blossoms, I like the idea of a day like that with him. The knowledge our friendship allows us to plan for the future, months out, is comforting.

We head back to his car, and he arranges the print carefully in the back seat.

"I'll send this one to my aunt to get framed." I pull my seatbelt across and look at him. "Thanks for everything today."

The three-hour trip home flies. We chat the entire way about music, art, and history. Neither of us brings up Ben Franklin or the dentures. When he pulls up to the condo he gets out of the car and opens the door for me. I stand, and we're eye to eye, the cold air fogging a screen of privacy just for us. He lifts his hand and I swear he's about to touch my face, but instead he pulls off his hat.

"Elin, today was perfect." He grabs the art from the backseat and hands it to me. "These are going to look perfect in the condo," he says. "You should pick out more art and make yourself comfortable since you're staying."

There's an oddness sitting between us. Any other day I'd invite him up to hang out. But I'm still confused about the weird daydreams today. I'm also pretty sure it's my imagination running wild after years of a lack of physical intimacy, or from how close we came to kissing on New Year's Eve. Given that he is not following me up, I'm guessing he feels a little off after today too.

"Elin," he shouts from the base of the stairs before I open the door to go inside. "I'm holding you to seeing the cherry blossoms at the end of March."

"Deal. Have a safe ride home." I open the door. I'm not totally ready for the day to be over, but I know it needs to be. Tomorrow is all about kicking my ass outside the comfort zone. Not that today didn't already shove me into a zone that felt off-limits. I need a distraction that isn't Hawk. Maybe the Bees are right about a transition date after my last relationship.

CHAPTER FOURTEEN

*D*AMN, *THAT'S A LOT of balls.* A heap of soccer balls stacked into a pyramid taller than me sits in the center of the room. *This was a bad idea.* It's too late to reverse time from Sunday back to Wednesday when I emailed to set the new date for this Boudoir shoot appointment after a ton of vodka like it was a good idea. Never make decisions after shots with the Bees.

"Hello!" A gentle voice comes out from behind a black velvet curtain. "Throw your bag in the corner. I'll be out in a sec."

The sound of a zipper sends my attention to the wall of skimpy costumes in the far corner. My thighs would rip through at least half of the bottom row. A black curtain, unseen zipper, and a photo studio tucked far into a warehouse set my nerves on fire. I should have told—who? Who would I tell? Maybe Liv or Rose? No, because they'd want to see the pictures before I burn them.

A tiny woman with big thick round glasses opens the curtain, a stack of wrinkled costumes dangling from her arms. "You're gorgeous." She looks me up and down, tilting her head.

My hand wraps across my stomach, and I nod to the far corner. "Are those for me?"

"Yes! I have to say it was an unusual request, but then, why not?" The clothes from her arms fall into a pile in the far corner.

A scan of the costumes makes me uncomfortably swallow. I should go. I'm not a bustier, naughty nurse, or red-hot devil type. The gorgeous teddies on the top row will strangle my boobs to my throat. None of these are me. This whole thing isn't me.

"It surprised me to get your text so fast to reschedule for to-day." The woman surveys my gym bag and points to a garment bag. "I'm Hattie. We spoke on the phone. I appreciate you understanding about the no refund policy. Small business and all, we do the best we can. Plus, I borrowed a lot of equipment."

My stomach twists and I eye the exit. Please tell me I'm not about to get shoved into some kind of dungeon or have to run outside half-naked. I should've done more research.

Hattie circles me with her measuring tape.

"Tsk," she says. "You're in my safe hands now."

She claps her hands twice, and two minions appear from a back room with brushes and makeup palettes in hand. The taller minion, a sweet woman dressed all in black with a black bob, pale skin, and dark liner, sweeps her thumb across my cheeks. Brushes larger than my head sweep back and forth across my face and tickle below my eyes. Clad all in yellow, the shorter assistant sizes me up. The sunshine tones are a bold choice, but he wears them well. His three-quarter pants are much too short for this time of year, but it's hot in the studio.

The man in yellow swipes a thick brush through my hair and tugs back and forth. "Relax sweetie, you're in wonderful hands. Mine."

There's an awful lot of hands-on effort going into making me look decent enough for a photo.

The woman in black shoves her hand up sideways between our faces, creating a bridge between our noses. She'll probably stab me with the eyeliner if I try to laugh.

"Your eyes are—" She paws at the air. "Rawr."

Can I blink yet? Is it over? Frick. He pulls my hair down and to the front. Put it back, it belongs in a high pony.

"Don't worry. I've got a few looks for you." The man in yellow drops an outfit in my lap.

A pair of black, tiny fit soccer shorts shoots nervous fear through my core. Where's the rest of it? There's got to be more.

He gestures to the fitting room. "Change out here, or in there, really doesn't matter. I've seen tits for days and yours are no different."

That's charming. With a circular gesture, I wave over my chest and look up at him.

He drops a pair of white knee socks in my lap.

I pull my head back in surprise.

The form asked for hobbies. I wrote soccer and music. We couldn't follow the music route?

"I'm confused. What is all this? I thought it was going to be a bed and things like that? Maybe more coverage?" My legs really don't want to follow the directions to the fitting room.

Hattie taps her foot and leans forward. "Trust me. This is better."

I shrug and will my feet to trudge across the floor and out of my comfort zone. I was comfortable for five years—no one's going to see these pictures, so who cares.

A glance in the mirror of the changing room, and I note that my thighs look like muscular tree trunks.

"Maybe we should try something different?" My voice squeaks at seeing myself in the full-length mirror.

A heavy object scrapes across the floor. I take a deep breath, and swallow hard before sliding the curtain open.

"Oh! You look amazing." Hattie clasps her hands together with an enormous smile. "Now take off your shirt."

Excuse me? "I've only got a sports bra under this."

"You don't need that either." She spins on her heels and walks to the box to get high enough to angle the camera down. "Do you need vodka? Beer? Wine? Champagne?"

I shake my head and glance at my feet. My indoor shoes are okay, but not my sports bra?

There has got to be another way. "Maybe—"

Hattie raises her finger. The man in yellow lets out a yip and covers his mouth.

The woman in black helps Hattie down from the box and walks with her over to the goal to stand next to me. "What's wrong, dear?" Hattie asks, maternally. She's probably sweet-talked a lot of clothes from people.

"It's not me." Tears want to burst forward and pour down my cheeks.

She stands up straight and grabs two shots from the side table. After downing the first one, her lips part as she adjusts her glasses.

"Shot?" she asks.

I shake my head.

She shrugs and takes the second shot. "You postponed because you and your boyfriend split up?"

I nod. And without a refund, it'd be a waste of money to not do *something*.

"You're fit. Tall. Beautiful. Strong." She waves her hand across the empty shot glasses. "You want to wallow forever?"

Her fingers wrap around my bicep and give a tiny squeeze.

I shake my head.

"Then let's show *you* what your ex is missing, kick him good." She lifts her hand out. "Trust Auntie Hattie."

I can do this.

I toss my shirt to the ground. She gives a nod and heads back to the camera.

The man in yellow clears his throat and locks a side glance with me. I gesture to the vodka and put out my hand.

"Yes!" He floods the shot glass twice.

I can do this. I rip the sports bra off and put both palms face up. The helpers drop a ball in each hand and position me. My stomach quivers and the tension in my arms shakes my biceps.

The flashes go off several times and all I want is to try something else. It's colder in here than I thought.

"In my bag." I nod to the woman in black. "Grab what's in the red plastic bag."

The assistant looks in the bag and back at me. "These aren't sexy."

"Please." I drop the balls to the ground and reach my hands out.

She shrugs and removes my sparkling new white and deep purple gloves from the bag. They smell fresh from the package and offer a security blanket combined with another shot of confidence. Sliding my fingers deep in the gloves punches jolts of confidence across my body. I pull the straps tight with my teeth and bang my hands together. I'm ready.

Frick and Frack drop the balls in my palms. They stick in place as I turn my wrists to press the balls tight against my chest. I get into a wide stance and offer Hattie a nod.

I'm an athlete. Sculpted, thick muscle—beautiful.

Where did a wind machine come from? The woman in black gives two thumbs-up and a toothy smile, shifting her upper lip past the black studs on her angel bites.

I drop to the floor with one ball and reach out to the net. It's amazing what a pair of gloves can do for confidence.

"These are gorgeous!" Hattie yells. "I told you. I can picture a million boners with a quick glance at these. Popping everywhere."

My cheeks turn sizzling hot, and I wrap my arms across my chest. Sexy woman who gets men to pop like cereal isn't my category.

"What?" She hops off the makeshift platform and scurries over with her camera out. "I'm merely stating the obvious. You've got prime merchandise to work with. Be proud of it, not ashamed and hiding behind those baggy jerseys." She raises an eyebrow and her hand shoots high in the air.

I look sexy. How is that possible?

The man in yellow claps his hands together. "Okay, next look."

"Oh, yay!" The woman in black runs over to the stack of balls and taps a series of white, red, and black balls into the goal, one after the other.

I flick my eyebrows up as the spotlight shifts low. She'd fit in well with the team.

With a shrug, I bite down on my lower lip to hold back the smile ripping forward. Diving into the ball pit she's set up looks too fun to pass up.

"Bring it."

Chapter Fifteen

T HE FIRE DANCES NEXT to the television, and my gaze bounces between the flames and the screen. An entire week and a half has passed since our outing in Philly, and we haven't talked about how awkwardly we parted that night. Tonight is Hawk's turn to pick the movie. His solution is to close his eyes, flick his thumb across the remote and click when the timing feels right. Now, Frankenstein's monster is tap-dancing in front of a curtain. I'm only ninety percent sure he cheated and picked a movie he knew I'd want. I shift to fold into my firmly-planted body imprint on the left side of this beaten couch that's cradled me through years of movie nights.

"I'm setting up a profile for you." Hawk lifts his legs to rest them on the ottoman, and clicks on the laptop keys. "Now, which site?"

I crinkle my nose, staring ahead at the TV, and lean away from him on the arm of the couch.

The sliding glass doors can't hush the thunder outside, nor the pelt of the rain on glass. The trees nestle us safely in the living room, separating the lawn from where the deer wander.

"Ooh, this one is so you can have a hookup. How are you feeling about hookups right now?" He chuckles and nudges me with his elbow. "Think about it. All the hooking up, none of the emotion."

I side-eye him and look back to the screen.

"Yeah. You're right. Too sketchy for you—*you* have a lot of rules." He clicks away on the keys. "This one is your speed. Just show up and get married."

I twist my tongue into a taco and stick it out. Let that be my profile picture. Swipe for me.

There'd be some creep who'd swipe.

I stretch my legs out to claim room for my feet on the ottoman, and tilt my head to my shoulder, avoiding further eye contact with him.

"Pick a site." He whines like a teenager, and bounces his legs.

"All sites are the same." Crap. "Everyone scatters their profiles hoping to meet people, but it's all the same people on each site. There should be a way to condense the sites, see length of sentence on said site, and get reviews from people who had bad experiences."

He leans his head on my shoulder and nudges my arm.

I shrug, and his body dips as his eyeballs burrow warm lasers into my cheeks. He's done online dating before.

"I have a profile," I whisper. This is going to become a thing.

He lifts his legs, plants his feet on the floor, and shoves the laptop onto my lap. "How dare you, ma'am. How dare you do so and not show me."

My lips part, and I take a cleansing breath in through my nose, and out through my mouth.

"It's not a big deal." I turn to face him. His eyes are full of sparkle, and there's a deluge of questions coming.

He shifts closer on the couch, and the side of his arm and leg press against mine. Personal space is gone. He's on a mission.

"Have you gone out on any dates?" he asks.

"Yes, and before you judge me, dating is ridiculously different from five years ago. Example, did you know people do internet searches before they meet in person?"

Hawk looks at me in horror.

"Great, everyone knew but me." I press my thumb into my palm. "I tried. I really did. You'd be so proud. I threw out my normal vetoes like height or weird freckles. I took the time to carefully do my bio data, Height: *5'8*, Eyes: *Moss Green*, Hair Color: *Good question*, College: *Music and Marketing Degree from Private University*. He either liked something in my bio data or that picture you took of me in a blazer at work with my hair pulled back. He was tall—"

"Height isn't everything." Hawk shakes his head.

"Do you want me to finish the story?" I ask.

He nods and I catch the tight twitch in the corner of his mouth.

"I like your height. Anyway, the guy is clean cut, fit, and recently home from living in Sweden where he claims he was a pro golfer."

I blame the high I was on from the photoshoot for sending me on this date. I felt sexy and confident.

"We're in the driving range area with white panels on either side to give us some privacy. There's groans and grunts as people whack balls and I giggled of course because it sounds ridiculous. It dawned on me immediately that I don't want to dive straight into another relationship and I don't want to hook up with ick like him. The whole thing was awful."

Hawk covers his mouth with his hand and raises his eyebrows. "Go on."

"The guy is hitting every ball perfectly. I, of course, suck, because those balls are too damn small and hard. I have a difficult enough time with soccer balls. He puts on his pristine white baseball cap and offers to show me how to swing. The guy gets right behind me, feet either side of mine. He wraps his tiny hands over mine and I can feel the bulge in his pants against my lower back. I had to go all out to control the urge to whack his shin with the club."

His hand drops to his lap and he looks less amused. "Did you leave?"

"No." I give an exaggerated sigh. "I had a handy metal weapon in my hand if I needed it. I shrugged him off and took a step forward."

"I'm never taking you golfing."

I nod. "The whole thing felt gross. Like I'd walked into his standard internet dating play. The best it did was rebreak my dating cherry I guess."

He sucks in his lips and glances down.

"I know there's no cherry!" Why am I telling him this? "I had my cousins' voices in my head, you know. That I'm too old to meet the perfect person."

"That's stupid. They married straight out of college. If you'd done that, you'd have married the gymnast." Hawk rubs his hands together. He's super fidgety.

"There wasn't anything intellectually challenging in my college relationship."

"You need a scientist," he jokes. "Is the fancy golf man gone?"

"The *creepy* golf man is gone. Every time he looked at me it felt like I was covered in slime. Maybe it was the way he was trying to coach me, but that's literally his job when he's not out on tour. He seemed offended I didn't know who he was." I tuck hair behind my ear and tap rapidly on Hawk's leg. "Oh! Here's one to add to your don't do it playbook. He asked if I wanted a revenge hookup. I was invited into the locker room so we could go bang it out."

He shifts his jaw. I look down and catch him clench and unclench his fist.

"I didn't do anything with him." I smile at Hawk and watch the creases in the corner of his eyes soften as his body relaxes. "He started to brag about golf groupies and I laughed in his face which was a bad response. I couldn't stop picturing beautiful khaki-clad women in pearls and perfect hair beating on his car for attention."

A laugh bursts from both of us. The comfort of this place, and the ease of hanging out with Hawk, is what was missing from the garbage date I went on with a former pro golfer yesterday.

"The short version. The dude seemed like a sex starved wanna-be-Cassanova who is a squirt and done. And, I'm not trading a soccer obsession for a golf obsession. I want my equal in life." At least I can play soccer. The idea of following the creepy guy hole-to-hole dries up *my* hole. "I'm doomed to be single if this is the new dating world."

"You're far from doomed. Show me your profile." Hawk clears his throat and taps on the top of the computer screen with impatience.

"Why? I did it about a week ago and I'm not so popular." I close the screen of the laptop. A week ago was after Philly. After I was confused by the mixed messages from Hawk, and tiny pulses of, *what ifs.* What if we tried to date and succeeded? What if we kissed? What if the one thing that binds us together is how our relationship is currently designed? The profile let me shove all those down and half-distract my brain. All I'm getting from the site are blitz communications from guys who scatter the same message across all fresh blood, and prey on whoever takes the bite.

Hey, I like your profile. Translation: *I didn't bother to read anything about you.*

Your pretty. Translation: *My grammar is as fantastic as my sense of boundaries.*

Let's chat sometime. Translation: *I'm too busy to see if we actually fit.*

Or, all of them could be translated as: *I've received so many rejections already, I'm going to hit buckshot and see what happens.*

I'm not accepting garbage and buckshot. Standards shouldn't change when a meet-cute is virtual.

Hawk checks me out, then the laptop, and back to me. His fingers slowly move to the laptop lid and he raises it back up. He reaches in front of me and punches in a website address.

"I'll show you mine, if you show me yours."

The opportunity to see how he works his magic online draws my full attention. *Wait.* "You're on this site too?" I snap out the question as my ears grow hot.

He nods and continues to punch keys.

"Show me yours." I slide the laptop back onto his lap for easier access.

"I thought you'd never ask." He stretches his hands out in front of him and cracks his knuckles.

Gross.

A profile comes up. The image in the upper right grabs at my cheeks and pulls up a smile as warmth spreads across my arms and legs. I took the picture a few months ago during a match, after he'd passed the ball to a teammate when he could've taken the shot. They were up by enough as it was and—well, he's Hawk.

He'd spread his arms wide and done a circle after the pass. His teammate scored his first goal in the "thirty and older" league.

Something small, stupid, but day after day in a stressful job, that moment crowned the week.

"I like this one." I point to the screen. "But, not as a profile picture."

"Boo." He gives me a thumbs down and a raspberry. "I'm happy here. Don't women want a happy athlete?"

I shake my head.

"I'd never click on it if I didn't know you." I stare at the screen and slide my tongue across the back of my teeth.

"Shallow," he says, his fingers pressing over his heart.

I shrug.

"Fine." He clicks on the rest of his images.

Picture after picture are images I've taken and sent. The sushi restaurant, soccer, him and his mom at Sunday dinner. They're so sweet together. He's such a momma's boy.

He scrolls down, and new pictures flash across the screen. Images from when HR came through wanting to capture young scientists busy at work for a recruiting campaign. He wouldn't shut up for weeks about his "perfectly symmetrical face." Their selection of him probably also had something to do with a master's degree from Princeton on his resume, but he preferred to point to his high cheekbones and the dimple in the right spot on his chin.

"None of these are you." I point past each image. "They're you, but not you hanging out." I grab his phone and open the screen. My heart pauses for a second, hoping to not see texts from his boss, or whoever his latest hookup is. Instead, there's a missed text from me: *I'm in the driveway.* My chest relaxes and I smile while looking into his big eyes. "Smile like you're handsome."

"Wait!" He holds up his hand and pulls Curie close for a hug. "You get one of us, you get both of us." He lowers his hand and nods in approval.

I lean back, click the image, and the flash forces both he and Curie to squint. Too close. Way too close. Oops.

He raises a hand to reach for the phone. "Much better?" His squint turns into a rapid blink. "Next time, no flash this close." He rubs his eye and pats Curie's head before looking at the photo. "If *you* say to use this one, I will."

I nod. "Also, send it to me. I don't have any new pics of cute Curie."

"Gorgeous Curie." He pulls his arm and fist in tight for celebration. "Yes! The new picture works!" His laugh is warm, inviting, a flirt that's impossible to not join. He's an intoxicating mix of happiness and energy.

I need to stop staring at his mouth. "You're ridiculous."

He uploads the image from his phone and it pops up on the computer screen. Much better. And who doesn't love a dog? He rubs his hands together and checks the phone.

"You think it happens that—" There's the red light flashing on his phone. "—fast?" On the screen is a red envelope in the upper left corner. Really? It's that easy for him?

He returns his attention to the profile on his laptop. "Look. Would you click this if you didn't know me?"

A scroll past his punny jokes and self-deprecating humor takes me to the meat of his profile.

Likes: *Women who read and take care of themselves. Women who like me.*

"Your requirement is women who read, and like you?" I laugh. "You've done well with this?"

"I *don't* want a woman who doesn't like me. That's stupid." He gestures at the screen. "These things are dumb. No one reads the descriptions. They look at the pictures."

Rude. "*I* read the descriptions. Am I doing it wrong?"

"Of course you do. You probably also have a comparison chart somewhere too." He points at the red envelope, now with the number "four" printed on it. "Guaranteed. They read nothing."

"You sound like a tool." I shake my head. "I'd never click this profile."

"But Curie's photo!"

"I'd have no opening line." She is adorable, but I'm completely biased having helped him pick her out as a puppy. He wanted to go with Pavlov. I suggested Pavlova, and he called me out for going from scientist to ballerina. Marie Curie flew from our lips at the same time, but too many of his aunts are Marie or Maria. Curie was cute and fit her tiny inquisitive self when she was only ten-weeks old. At nine, all she wants is snuggles, treats, and to snore loudly on the couch. "*Nice dog*, what kind of opening is that?"

"Best compliment ever. I'd respond." He raises an eyebrow, leans in, and drops to a whisper. "'Cause it's no different from meeting someone at the park."

"Bullshit. You're pickier than me. You dumped a girl because she liked Nickelback." I knuckle his arm to get him to move back to his place on the couch. "I'm going on record—there's nothing wrong with Nickelback. You sing their music and full-out dance. It was a bullshit excuse to dump that poor girl."

His mouth gapes open, and he presses the back of his hand to his forehead. "There are no photographs. No proof of this slander." He drops his hand to his laptop. "Maybe there's one video, but we promised not to discuss my youthful missteps in music."

"I promised no such thing." I stare at the envelope in the corner. How can he not click it? I want to see what's behind each one. Do I sound desperate when I message people? Do these women respond to men better than I do? "Scroll down."

Dislikes: *Princesses. HA. I'm fairly open.*

"I hate princesses." He looks straight at me, rolls his eyes, and playfully sighs. "I'll delete it."

I gesture to the laptop and shake my head. "Scroll." These women really aren't reading.

Hobbies: *Comics, reading, stuff. Ask me, I hate these things.*

He's not taking this seriously at all. Based on the number six now showing next to the envelope, maybe guys don't have to try hard.

"This profile is ridiculous and says nothing about you." I run a hand over my thigh.

He points to the picture of Curie and pouts.

"Not good enough. You're going to get garbage responses."

"Oh, you're the expert now? Single for a hot minute, freshly dipping your toe into the cataclysmic world of virtual dating, and suddenly an expert." He hands me the laptop. "Here, fix it. Who am I? What are my hobbies?"

"You're serious?" My jaw drops. Tiny jolts of excitement cross from shoulder to shoulder. *Bring it on.* I crack my knuckles and stretch my fingers over the keyboard.

"Charming. You should do that on all dates." His nose crinkles high with disapproval.

I concentrate on the screen and retype his profile.

Likes: *I need an intelligent woman to banter with or I grow bored. My dog. She's amazing and supreme in my life. I'm not a full sports nut, but there's something exhilarating about running up and down a soccer field in small bursts.*

I can talk about movies all day, and make obscure references to films I'm certain only I've ever watched. But, please laugh at my jokes, and I'll laugh at yours even if I'm lost.

Dislikes: *Nickelback. (Change my mind.) Leeches. No other reason than they are creepy AF but super important to medicinal history. They can exist, just not near me. I'm not into dating vampires, werewolves, or princesses. Unless you come with a full castle, then we can talk. You'll also need a guest castle for my family.*

Other Details: *My closest friend says I'm a big loyal softie who puts my friends and family first. I'm the guy you can not only count on, but who will make you laugh and pick you up when needed. Whoever I end up with needs to be warm and caring.*

"You ready to read it?" I turn the monitor to him and work to look anywhere but the screen.

He puts a finger on my hand while he reads. "This is me? This is how you describe me to people?" His tone is tender. He slides his hand on top of mine and gives a small squeeze.

I frown when he moves his hand. The clacking of keys drives my attention back to the screen.

"What are you doing?" I thought it was good.

"Relax. I'm keeping it but making it sound more like me."

He makes a good point. I write more flowery than he does.

Hawk puffs his chest up and spins the laptop in my direction. Okay, if I didn't know him forever, I'd respond to this one. Hell, I'd respond now if he kept rubbing his forefinger against the back of my hand. At least I'd have an opening line or two.

I lift an eyebrow and give a nod. "Super better."

"Super-awesome-now-show-me-yours."

He bounces up and down in the seat, rocking our cushions.

"Oh my god, stop bouncing so I can type." I click slowly on the keys, dragging out the inevitable.

"Faster!" He stops bouncing and sits, nodding his head with each keystroke. "It's the same site!" he shrieks with excitement.

Relax, sir. Relax.

He spins the laptop in his direction, and his eyes dart across the screen while his lips move. At least I can tell where he is on the page. He shakes his head back and forth. "No. This is not good. This is bad."

He's honest. Honesty is good? "Creating profiles is stupid. I spent hours on this ridiculous thing and the best I could come up with was *college educated, reads, loves her friends fiercely, plays soccer, likes sports, and has an athletic build.* And, some creepy jackass informed me "athletic" didn't mean "athlete." Which was made further gross when he messaged to tell me I identified my body wrong." I bite my pinky nail. "Next time I'll do duck face and quote from Isaiah Berlin's definitions of ethics and human relations. Because, according to you, no one reads."

He snorts and pulls up my profile picture. "This picture is awful."

"The picture is fine. I don't need to have my boobs out, or wear short clothes to get messages." That's not the attention, or the guy, I'd want. My phone buzzes in my hand.

I click open the text and there is an image from a game we lost a few months ago. I'm suited up in my burn your retinas out neon yellow goalie jersey, smiling from inside the goal with my hands wide. This was before the game even started. My hair is in a tight ponytail, and the sweat hasn't taken over yet. Hawk motions with his thumb to the left. I swipe to the left and the next image is me in full extension reach, my body parallel to the ground with wild hair, missing the ball as it goes into the net.

"Open your app and post those two." He punches the keys on this phone, and places it on his leg.

"I look like garbage in the second one."

"Powerful. Not garbage. You don't want some dude to think your sole purpose is to be *his* cheerleader."

Fair. Blunt, but fair. My feet fidget on the ottoman as I slink into the couch.

"Disappearing will not get you out of this." He hands me a water. "Put your password in."

I raise an eyebrow and cross my arms.

"Come on," he groans, playfully. "You can delete it when we're done. Fair is fair."

"Don't make me sound dumb."

He raises two fingers in the air while I punch in my password. "Scout's honor, but I'm not adding Berlin. I like it, but maybe save some of your nerd for after you have a few dates." He flashes a grin, showing his super straight teeth. "Yes! Success." His hand shoos my attention to the television.

He wants privacy. In my account. Go ahead and answer the trash emails I've gotten.

"I'm opening your messages."

I grit my teeth and my chest tightens.

"You liar! There are so many messages in here!"

"Most of them are trash." I sigh in frustration. "I'm not good at dating."

"You're fine at dating. You're not good at selecting people." His eyes move left to right on the screen as he reads down.

"Wow. Now I knew men could be—wow. Some of these are awful. I'm answering them."

"Uh, no. Bad idea. What if I run into them in the future?" Oh, hello, I sent you a nastygram response online. Please don't punch me in public.

"They need education on how not to talk to women." He slams on a key and lifts his hand from the keyboard. "That one says 'hi beautiful.' Two words isn't trying."

Whatever he responds can't be good. Funny, maybe, as long as you aren't on the receiving end.

"You answered two of them." He tilts his head and nods.

Approval? Confusion? Did I pick wrong?

Hawk shakes his head, before resuming his initial task.

"Likes," he says. "Bread. The more artisan, the better. Soccer, to burn off the bread and make friends."

"You make me sound like a bread eating robot." Curie wanders to my side of the couch, huffs, and snuggles in for attention. Hawk's hands are too busy for her right now.

"Traitor," he says to her in a frank tone. He grabs his dark blue, thick-rimmed glasses, and squints at the screen.

He's sleepy.

The clock flashes eleven. A work night is not the right time to do this. I'll be dragging tomorrow. Then again, there's no difference between staying up watching TV alone 'til midnight, or being here past eleven. At least here I have company.

"She loves me." I snuggle her and wait for Hawk to stop decimating my profile.

"Done." He declares, and shoves the computer onto my lap.

"Hobbies: Peek-A-Boo Champion. What does that even mean?" Dumbfounded is a state of existence. Well, it's not worse than it was before. Punchier, more sarcasm, and more cutthroat. "Likes: Playing sports. Dislikes: Watching sports 24-7." Fair.

"I tightened it up. Again, no one's really going to read. They're going to check out your picture. Once in a while you'll find a guy who reads the description. Only respond to them. Personally, I'd date the hell out of a person with this profile."

Out of a person, or me? No one but him is going to respond to "peek-a-boo champion." This is ridiculous. I might as well say I'm a thumb model.

"This gets one week. If I get weirdos responding to me, I change it back. Deal?" I extend my hand.

He takes my hand in both of his and gives a definitive shake. "Deal." He releases me and looks at the television. "You won't need the profile. The woodwork men will come out soon enough."

"Woodwork men? Do they bring whittlings as offerings? Do I get an assortment of carved accessories?"

"Nah. Thad's already asked about you, same with some other guys on the team. You'll see. Give it time."

"Time? I've been single for the longest I've ever been. I don't remember how to flirt, or how to date, and I'm failing this online thing as you've pointed out."

"Stop. Everything takes time." He yawns.

"Fine. I'm going. Check in with me tomorrow and let me know if the quality of messages from women goes up with the improved profile." I lean in to give him a hug and linger a second to inhale the scent of clean cotton on his shirt. Clean white shirts are a weakness. Simple, relaxed, and they highlight any grooves of muscle on a man.

His fingers thread through my hair and a welcome tickle runs down my arms. "Or, you could take a break from dating. We can hang every day and have the best time."

I stand and reach to pull him up off the couch. "That sounds an awful lot like I'd be a cramp in your dating life."

Curie grumbles and wanders to Hawk's bedroom. She's done for the night. The springs on his bed creak as she thumps down on the mattress.

He nods and the light from the TV flickers on his face. My gaze drops to the fullness of his lips and the natural, extra tint of red they carry. What is wrong with me? I've got to go.

I shove my hands in my pockets, and pull out my keys before giving him one more quick hug, soaking in the citrus from his hair.

He follows and leans against the open doorway, his shirt rising high enough to show a peek of waxed stomach. "Text me when you're home safe." His hand drops to my hip and his thumb traces a circle on my side, sending a too-welcome shiver up my spine.

A warm ache spreads throughout my body and I want to return the sensation. Instead, I pull back to fight the urge to lean into him further. This is Hawk. We're friends and we don't touch each other with this type of intimacy. No one else can pull me in with the softest touch like him.

I cut across the frosty lawn to my car, refusing to look back at his sculpted silhouette, no doubt still hovering in the doorway. He always waits for me to get in my car.

Mixed messages. Crossed-signals. Over-analysis of what's not there. Get in the car and go home. He wants me to date, or he wouldn't have helped set up a better profile.

CHAPTER SIXTEEN

H AWK CROUCHES AND THROWS sticks atop the blaz-
ing fire pit in his mom's backyard. "You *can* sit closer—come block the wind for me." His fogged breath sits still
in the air until the wind picks up and brushes it away. He had
a hankering for smores, and now, here we are. The crackling
fire doesn't replace the awkwardness we created two days
ago rewriting each other's profiles, and yet tonight's like any
other for the two of us. The flames illuminate his solid frame
and the angles of his face, as his big green-brown eyes stare
deep into the fire. He stands, and his biceps twitch, pushing
out against a cream-colored, waffle-knit shirt. A gust of wind
rustles the turning leaves around us, and unsnaps a button
on his tear-away pants.

Hawk closes his legs tight as the breeze finishes whipping through. "Brr." He wraps his arms around his stomach
mid-shiver. "Seriously, it's warmer over here."

I shake my head. Why am I staring at his bicep? "I can see
you better from across the fire." I pull my knees up and wrap
my coat over my legs.

"Want a blanket?" His gaze cuts across the fire as he nods to the house. "Or do you prefer to freeze while eating marshmallows?"

I reach out and grab at the air for a stick. "Marshmallow and stick please."

He hands them over.

I scoot my chair closer to the fire, letting its warmth kiss my skin. *This is better.* I watch as the flames catch the marshmallow, igniting it to a glorious, flaming charcoal of goodness at the end of the skewer. I draw the marshmallow in and give a swift puff to blow out the fire. Marshmallow oozes from the top. "Perfect." Is it too hot to bite? I should bite it. Patience—or nothing will taste right. I glance up.

Hawk's shaking his head and staring back at me, laughing between shivers. "You scorched the poor thing."

"And now he shall die." I pull the marshmallow off the stick and eat it with over- exaggerated chews. "Murdered."

He brushes his hand over his hair and leans forward. He sets his skewer on the edge of the fire and waits patiently for the marshmallow to cook.

Who has time to wait like this? Burn it. Blow it. Eat it.

"Music?" He presses on his phone, and low music fills the gaps between the pops of the fire and the whistle of the wind.

I load on another marshmallow and mimic his cooking technique. This will take forever.

"Any updates?" He inspects his marshmallow. "Any new prospects?"

"Ha. No." Screw patience. I shake my head and move the marshmallow closer to the fire.

He picks up his chair and shifts closer to me, leaving a chair-width gap between. "You look like you're on fire from there. Super distracting."

"How's your onslaught of prospects going?" One of us should have a decent dating life. "Is Curie winning you dates?"

He sneers and inspects his marshmallow.

A smile draws across my face while my marshmallow burns like a torch.

"Things aren't—" He takes a bite of the marshmallow. "Graham crackers are stupid. They get in the way."

"That's a weird segue, but agreed. You really only want the chocolate and the marshmallow. Graham crackers *are* the inferior ingredient."

"When's your next date?" His voice is soft, and the flames hold his focus.

"Five days." Please don't ask who. "I'm not good at it, you know. I should cancel and save them me."

"What's stopping you? You're the girl always in a relationship. What's different now?"

"Recovering, unsure, haven't had sex in almost three years. Out of practice in dating—" Crap, I over-shared. The lump in my throat isn't going away, and I can't take the words back. Stupid gorgeous night sky and music. Stupid full moon.

"Back up. Back up. You haven't had sex in almost three years?" His dropped jaw and blank gaze aren't helpful.

I shift in my chair and look down for the bag of marshmallows. Shit. Let it go, ignore it, move on.

"You and Nate—you dated for almost five years."

I nod and shift my gaze to my feet.

"How is this something I don't know? Why wouldn't you say, oh, hey, Nate is an idiot and—"

"Because we don't talk about that stuff. That's the line." The clear line *we* established over a decade ago.

"But, three years?" He smacks his forehead. "How does that even happen?"

My heart sinks, and my feet want to run to my car and drop this busted marshmallow to the ground. I bite my lip.

"What's the excuse?" His tone carries concern and astonishment. "I know it wasn't you, 'cause I know you. You're—you." He leans toward me and taps my elbow. "Come, on. Kidding aside. What was the deal?"

I pull my hair to the side, blocking part of my face. "He played so much soccer. Or worked. And when I tried, he didn't find me attractive anymore, I guess."

"Uh, no. That's ridiculous."

Easy for him to say.

"Remember the golfer I went on that awful date with? He texted this morning to say I'm not up to his standards." I peek over at Hawk's blank stare and bite my bottom lip.

"He did *what*?" Hawk runs a hand over his five-o'clock shadow. "Do you believe these idiots?"

I shrug. "Can we focus on eating marshmallows?"

"I'm sorry, no. This is ridiculous. *They* are ridiculous." He puts his hands on the arms of his chair and taps his fingers. "You're freaking beautiful. Stop going out with jackasses."

I switch my gaze to the fire and shrug again. Tears form and my chest tightens. "I'm not—"

"Don't you say it." His shadow shifts with the dancing flames.

Two tears trace down my cheeks and I glance down, letting them fall to the dirt.

"I'm sorry, I have to—" He stands, timidly walks to my chair, and crouches in front of me, the fire behind him. His thumb brushes away a stray tear, and my chin lifts with the assist of his soft fingertip. Hawk and I search each other's faces, holding for much longer than a friendship allows. When his lips part, a pull in my arms and chest urges me to him, but instead I push back in my seat. My body's angry for not allowing me to potentially misread a situation and destroy a friendship, not this one.

"Why can't you see how great—" His voice cracks and his shaking hand moves away to brush his cheek while our gazes never waver. "This breaks the rules, but the rules are old." He nods his head and leans forward.

Is he? I nod. We don't kiss or date. We don't venture down paths that may or may not be of interest to us in order to protect the best friendship either of us has ever had. We agreed on this years ago. At least a decade ago, when we saw two friends of ours explode their own friendship, and the aftermath of their breakup still looms any time we hang out as a group. Hooking up. Sex. Dating. All of it ruins friendships, but right now I want to throw away the bullshit rules of maintaining a friendship and get kissed and held by my best friend. To feel someone who cares about me wrap their arms around my ribs and want to kiss me—to *be* with me. But I don't want to lose him, or want him to do this because he thinks it'll make me feel better. My heart pounds in my temples and ears, tears sitting at the ready.

My gaze traces down his face. "Don't you dare kiss me out of pity," I whisper.

"Never." His eyelashes tickle my face and his full, pillow-like lips press against mine.

Outside of my quickening pulse, my entire body feels weightless while his hands move to my hips, lifting us to stand. He tilts his head, and his soft lips press against mine. He's kissing me? I'm kissing him. A pity kiss, but a kiss.

His hands slide back to pull my hips forward—sending a flash of tingles through my core—pushing our bodies flush together. My arms wrap around the thick biceps I eyed earlier and up around his shoulders. Being eye-to-eye has advantages, no awkward lean or strain to reach the other. Stop brain. Relax—HA. His arms squeeze around my waist ... what am I doing?

This is Hawk. *Hawk.*

He pulls away. "Stop thinking."

Yeah, okay. Like *that's* going to happen. Stop thinking. His lips part with mine and my tongue grazes the inside of his lower teeth. Leaning forward, our foreheads pillowed together, he lifts a thumb to stroke my cheek. Our lips separate, and he pulls back.

"Beautiful," he says, catching a breath.

I open my eyes and catch his glance. As if glass, the moment between us shatters—we broke the no kissing rule. He softly stares back at me, and my heart beats faster and faster. We can't undo it twice. Can we? Do I kiss him again? What even just happened?

"Ow!" He releases his grip and his hands shoot behind him. "Ow, fuck that hurt." He laughs and jumps away from the fire.

"Are you okay?"

"An ember bit my ass." He keeps trying to glance at his butt in the dark.

Thank you fire. I stifle a laugh behind my hand and kneel to grab my phone from the ground. "Turn around, let me see it."

"I'm not letting you look at my ass right now." He shifts his weight. "Don't turn on the—"

I hit the flashlight button, and it glows brightly in front of me. I look up, and then back down and flip my phone to the ground, catching the shadow from the bulge in his pants.

"I'm sorry. I don't know what to say right now." He's flustered.

Well, that's, yep. I don't know where to look.

He holds his butt, limps to the chair, and grabs his skewer.

"I should—" I point toward the driveway.

Hawk shakes his head and shoves his hands in his pockets. "Please stay."

He's just staring at the damned fire.

"Night Hawk." I wave and leave. Don't look back. We'll be fine. We're always fine.

Shit.

CHAPTER SEVENTEEN

DEEP BREATH IN—NOPE. THAT one didn't clear my lungs. It got stuck on the block, resting right ahead of my conscience. The fire pit incident happened five long days ago and neither of us have broached the *what was that and why* topic.

As much as I'd like to, I can't quite convince myself it was a completely misread, hormone-filled moment likely caused by the ambiance of the clear night sky and the cool breeze. That we were just inspired to share one another's heat by the crackling blaze. My head has gone through every scenario possible including one in which we were an actual couple. That us kissing one another was well overdue, and some precursor to a different version of us. But the couple thought quickly disappears since his actions in general don't seem to align with this idea. After all, he revamped my dating profile.

I trust that my idiotic best friend kissing me out of nowhere meant I didn't fall for some page from his playbook. He wouldn't do that to me. My best friend, whose broad shoulders were bathed in moonlight before wrapping his warm arms around my waist to pull me in. What is happening? I blink back the moment and look down.

The goals tonight are simple. The first is to continue to pretend like nothing happened at the fire pit. We're adults who can push lusty feelings aside to protect our friendship. And the second is not to have a repeat of the fire pit. Except maybe toasted marshmallows, because they sound delicious right now.

I crash down onto the couch next to him and he winces as I land. His hands grab for his knees, and he winces in pain.

I give him a once-over to see if I've inadvertently stabbed him with something from the back of the couch. "Your legs!" I point to the bandages soaked through with unknown fluids on his thighs.

"What the hell happened?" I lean closer for a better look. "I probably shouldn't do that again."

Hawk's grin greets my face as I look up.

"There was an incident last night."

"That's an understatement. You've got bandages!" Calm down. He doesn't need me freaking out and taking care of him. "Are you okay?" I sit up and wave in a circle around his lower body. *Yikes.*

How could he not tell me he's injured?

"I told you I'm fine. Stop looking so worried." He strokes my arm.

"Petting me like a puppy will not get you out of spilling—" I grimace and my stomach churns. "Bad choice of words." The air punches at my inability to not stare down at the thick glossy ointment coating his thigh. "How high up does it go?" My eyebrows push up as my hand reaches to pull up his shorts to see the extent of the damage.

He shakes his head and pulls his legs together, closing off the gap of his basketball shorts. "You do not want to do that." His hands fold and hover above his lap. "There's no unseeing once exposed."

"I'd have taken you to the hospital, you stubborn prat." Sitting up stretches at the twisting in my stomach. "Did your mom take you?"

Hawk shifts his gaze high, sighs, and looks back down. "Stop asking questions, please." His tone softens to a whisper.

A tug of tension pulls at my throat. "Must've been some date."

"Don't." He raises his hand.

"Your date must've been shook!" I cut him off again. I should hug him, or comfort him, or I don't even know what. But touching him, given my lack of coordination, will surely fail and I'll injure him more. I heave a shallow sigh of empathy instead. Much safer, though not as effective.

His thumb spreads the exposed combination of liquid from his burns, and ointment, across his skin.

"I take it the date didn't go well then?"

He shriek-laughs. "She glommed on like a stage-three-thousand clinger! Do you know what I had to do to banish that woman?"

A warm smile spreads through each cheek. "Stage-three-thousand sounds super high. I thought ten was bad, but three thousand? You must've been laying on the thick charm."

"I work my magic well." He rolls his fingers through his unkempt hair. "Too well in this case. I wanted to eat, and she attacked with an open mouth as I was getting ready to drain the pasta. The boiling water was going to go everywhere, and came dangerously close to poor Curie." Crinkles of pain rise on his forehead. "I tipped back and pulled the pot in my direction, causing a tsunami, and shrieking, when the water cooked my legs."

Curie offers a low whine.

A stranger? A stranger took care of him after he poured boiling water on himself? Why didn't he call me?

"You know what isn't a sexy sound?" Hawk raises an eyebrow. "Me, shrieking. Luckily, it missed my important bits and they remain in solid working order, surrounded on either side by puss-filled blisters. I'm damn sexy right now." He crosses his arms over his stomach.

Snort laughing is the wrong response, but when his voice cracks, I can't help myself. "Sounds like an awful situation." My fingers reach across Curie's fur, and I scratch at the sweet spot behind her ear.

"You mock me in my hour of need?" He grins as his phone glows on the table.

"How many times has she messaged you today?" If she was on the prowl, there's a good chance he threw her an okay sign.

"Thirty," he says flatly.

"Thirty? She feels guilty then."

"You'd think, but no. She offered to come and—" He covers Curie's ears. "—suck my noodle."

My heels dig into the slick driftwood coffee table. "I can leave if you want your noodle sucked. I'm the last person to block you from enjoying searing pain and pleasure at the same time."

He raises his eyebrows and his lips part.

My lips part to draw a heavy breath. "No? This is a bad idea?" The couch dips as I lean back and twist to get into a comfortable position. "Wipe that look off your face."

"I think she likes scars. She finds me freaky and attractive now." He lets out a heavy sigh. "I'm not that freaky, and I'm worried if a first date earns me second-degree burns, I'll be in a body bag by our third date."

Without a chase, this date stood no chance. One of the key aspects of Hawk's dating life always includes his brand of courting rituals. If he can't make someone laugh, genuinely laugh, he loses interest fast. Though, I've never known him to turn down sex.

"You'll be well laid by your third date."

He waves off the comment. "I don't need a woman who comes at me like a piranha. I'm lucky to have legs, Mr. Longfellow, and a tongue at this point."

He's fine. Complaining, analyzing, and fine.

I drape an arm over my forehead to shield the light and absorb the calm of the room. If I look down at his legs, my stomach will retch again. Puke on top of burn might be too much for even Hawk to handle.

Sitting here is nice. Talking is great. I close my eyes and see giant piranha teeth gnashing at his face and giggle.

"Sorry."

"It's not funny!" His hands smack against his stomach. "I blame you."

"Me?" I sit up.

"It was your profile that led her into my life! Your advice gave me excruciating burns." He nudges me. "Put the ointment on me."

Two can play this game. "I think I'll text her back from your phone and profess your desire to get lathered in ointment and strapped into a swing."

He snatches his phone from the table with a loud grunt. "No. She'll show up with ointment and a hook in hand."

I grit my teeth and my stomach trembles, keeping the bubbles of giggles down.

"I'm not opposed to it—but not with her." He pinches at my arm. "Not your fault, you know that."

I know, and at the same time I can't shake the sinking feeling he may end up scarred from following up on the profile I made him.

An irregular lump throbs in my throat.

His fingers lace through mine, and our palms press together.

He whispers, "Comfort me?"

"I'm not rubbing ointment on you." Keep the ooze over there, thank you.

"No, just sit with me and watch a movie." He pouts, and rubs his back against the couch until he finds a sweet spot.

The screen clicks on, and he thumbs through a mess of colors, quickly settling on an old Ginger Rogers and Fred Astaire movie we've watched at least twenty times. He'll be asleep in no time, but at least I'll have Fred and Ginger. I glance at his face, and note tiny winces with each shift of his legs. Those burns will have him off the field for a few weeks at minimum. If nothing else, I'm glad to be here tonight to make sure he's all right, even if it just means getting ice for his swelling.

CHAPTER EIGHTEEN

"H APPY WEDNESDAY!" HAWK HOLDS the door open.

I gesture at his swollen legs. "You shouldn't even be here." Based on what he said last weekend, he still has at least two weeks before he can take the field again. The bandages on his legs are clean, and he's not wincing as he shifts his weight.

He smirks. "And miss the new season drama?"

Sweat, minty muscle relaxer, and stale air billow across the airy space. The lobby echoes, and whistles blow on the fields off to the left. A teenager in a blue referee jersey sits with his feet up, engrossed in his phone. Hawk slides his team's check across the counter and balances a ball low on his foot.

"What are you going to do if I steal that?" My stomach twists as I gaze over at the spot on the wall below the scuff marks, where I sat over a month ago, crying like an idiot. "Why are you here so early?"

My toes slide the ball off his foot and pull it to the worn carpet. Not even a tiny effort to keep the ball? He *must* be in pain.

"Gimmie yours." Hawk reaches behind him. "Dear sir, hello. I have checks."

I shrug and pull the folded check and form from my pocket for Hawk to finish the registration.

The man puts his phone down, and the screen is streaming a match. The three flatscreens above him are playing matches and soccer news.

"Why are *you* so early?" Hawk asks, shoving a long receipt into my hands. "Our players need to sign updated safety waivers. Apparently, *someone* got injured bad in the championship match."

I stop walking and eye him. "Fight, or dirty slide-tackle taking out a leg?"

He nods. "Fight."

Damn it, Nate. Useless brick wall, this isn't the pros.

"Same team even." Hawk hums and opens the door to the empty fields. "Can you imagine going to the championship match and getting into a fight with your own team?"

I look down at my shoes and stumble through the heavy metal doors, doing my best to pretend I didn't lose five years dating an idiot. Part of those five years had to be wonderful. Why else would I stay so long?

"Is he okay?" I drop my bag on the corner of the bench, and pull my cold rubbery gloves from their bag. "Did Nate hurt him?"

Nate's temper on the field—and his mouth—are notorious. He'd never even dare raise his voice around me. Fight? Yes, absolutely. Ignore or pretend the world is fine every day, yup.

Hawk opens the gap in the net. "You don't know, do you?" He taps a few balls over the white lines on the field.

I look at him, and his grin is a little too large, and way too happy.

"Thad laid him out." Hawk extends both arms to the side and rushes for the center, pulling his forearms together, and dropping a shoulder. "Nate went down. With a capital D." He flops his body out wide across the ground, staring up at the metal cantilever.

I look over at my goal with furrowed brows. My fingers grip my hips tight, and the open space in the goal stares back in invitation. *Don't engage Hawk in this.*

"Are you here to play, or do you like rolling in spit and blood?" My arms swing wide, stretching at my shoulders. "You should put that in your profile. Enjoys rolling about in spit and sweat." I turn and flash him a smile while tapping the goal post.

He rolls to his side, and strikes a pose with an arm propping up his head while his other hand rests on his hip. "Don't pretend like you don't know."

I take a deep inhale and stretch my arms high above my head. Hawk doesn't even play on their team. This place is so gossipy.

Hawk jumps up, with both knees lifting high in the air, and lands solid. "I'll admit, I didn't hate seeing the blood come from

Nate's nose." His hand touches his face and he taps the balls to me.

"I don't know what you're talking about." Line up the balls in a perfect row and don't make eye contact.

"I told Thad you'd be here early," he says, chuckling.

"You did *what*?" I punt a ball across the field and point at it.

"He likes you." He shrugs, and jogs to the ball with his head held high. "Dolph was running his mouth and all of a sudden Thad lost it. Took him right out. Thad's a good dude."

I punt another ball to the far corner and point.

"Uh!" He grimaces, jogs off, and taps the second ball high in the air to juggle with it on the way back. "We set up your profile, and you didn't give me updates or stats, which is simply rude. Thad's a great guy. Much better than Dolph."

His smirk could use another jog. And, Nate's back to Dolph. He's always Dolph when Hawk's pissed at him.

"Why'd he get laid out?" I ask. Thad lets his feet do the talking, not his fists or his shoulders and never his mouth. He's calm and talented. I grab water from the side and take a long swallow.

"I don't know the details. Somehow it involved your name and one of Thad's sister's names. I can guarantee you I'll *never* hit on one of his sisters." Hawk makes a weird face and points to the bottle. "Did you bring that?"

I shake my head.

"Me either." He shrugs and taps a ball into place on the line.

I spit the water from my mouth in a giant spray across the field.

"Sexy. Damn sexy. You should record that and put it on your profile." Hawk points at a ball. "Practice throwing?"

I step and exaggerate a hip swish back and forth, laughing at my unsexy self. "What's the punishment? I'm assuming a red card and out of the game?" I pick up the first ball from the far side of the line and let the weight find a steady place between my gloves. My arms heave back, and I throw the ball forward, sending with it the frustration of Nate's existence.

Hawk shakes his head. He snaps his finger and points to the next ball.

"You want me to go on a date with Thad?" I force myself to sound positive.

Hawk puts a ball on his hip and fidgets with his ear. "Thad's dreamy. I mean, I adore women, but he's spectacular. Why wouldn't you go on a date with him?" He snaps at the next ball.

I yank my arms back over my head, then throw the ball. It lands right in front of his big toe. I give a nod, and pull up the next ball, ready to go again.

"Nice!" He looks down at the grass and taps the ball back to me. "Do you still like Nate?"

My palms squeeze the ball, trying to pop it like a balloon. "No." In fact, I'd like, at a minimum, the last three years of my life back. "Why is dating so awful?"

"You've been on one date! One!" His chin lifts and we stare at each other. "I've been out here dating how much while you're in steady relationship after steady relationship?"

"You like dating though." I hook the ball into my arm and swing it over my head like a shot put. The ball bounces less than ten feet in front of me and trickles to the side.

"No one *enjoys* dating. You're constantly on your A-game, trying to win the person over and hoping they don't hate the real you as it plays out. I want the person that likes the real me from the start. I want the one person for me."

"That requires you letting them in from the start."

"I let you in," he says.

I ignore the comment and walk to the center circle to stretch. "You never said what happened to Thad."

The doors in the back open and slam shut as a few new players enter.

Hawk juggle passes the ball to me and we trade back and forth for a few hits. He knocks the ball high enough to hit a beam, and shoots his arms over his head to duck the ball's return.

"What happened to Thad?" I rub a gloved hand over my lips and raise my eyebrows. A cold rush settles on the field from the overhead fans kicking on to circulate the already frosty air.

"Suspended for four games." Hawk says in a frank tone. "Both of 'em. Once Dolph came-to, he was running his mouth at Thad and saying awful things." His voice cracks, and his eyes travel high as he taps another ball into the air.

Awful things about me. "So they're both out."

Hawk shakes his head. "Whole team. Thad turned to tackle Dumb-Dumb for his stupid mouth and the team backed up their captain."

Nate's not a small man, but after he takes a hit, he's a giant baby. He'll cry to everyone 'til he gets a call, then strut like a chicken back to the goal. Four games are enough to not allow them in the championship match, which will bother Nate more than Thad.

"Why didn't you tell me this sooner?" I punt a ball at him with extra oomph. My hardest, most direct kicks with pinpoint accuracy always come through my instep.

He playfully shrieks and jumps to the side.

"Were you here? What were you doing when all this was happening?" Yelling is pointless. He's not at fault for their actions. But simmering the frustration of my recent decisions would be easier if it weren't all so public.

He gestures his palms to the ground. That's calming no one.

Hawk kicks a ball back and forth between his insteps with straight legs, faster and faster. "I was on that field. The game was on this field."

Oh good. I'm standing at the scene of the stupidity.

"Everything stopped as things picked up. Our field stopped playing and then mayhem. They almost called the cops." He rests his hands on his hips and smiles at me, still tapping the ball from left to right and back. "I got them to *not* call the cops—so in theory, I helped. But I also talked to Thad after."

A hot flash of energy pulls up through my arms and across my neck.

"Thad likes you." Hawk stops his awkward jig and his hands fall to the side. "I get that you aren't up for anything serious and I don't know what he wants. But I do know that no one wants to be a rebound. I know I couldn't handle being one. He's a great guy who will treat you good."

I'm glad Hawk gets it, because why would I be hunting for a rebound? I *was* the rebound. The five-year rebound after Nate's fiancée left him.

Dating should be easy. Find someone, have common interests, and get those wonderful butterfly feelings.

I miss those short bursts of flutters when something funny or happy happens, and then glancing at one another in understanding without needing to speak. I want the sparks. The funny. A person who isn't afraid to kiss me and doesn't ignore me.

Hawk points to the goal. "My turn to take shots?"

"Sit your ass back on the bench before you rip open the blisters."

He sticks his tongue out at me and clears a space on the bench.

I bend my arms up and twist my torso left, then right. With a wide step to the side, I separate my feet to ready for the next shot. Did Hawk come to watch my match and not play? Crap. The orange hue of the ball rushes at me, zinging my chest just before it knocks me to the ground.

Chapter Nineteen

T HE NUMBER OF HIGHLY embarrassing moments I've had on the field can be counted on one hand. Two nights ago was number three—when the ball leveled me on the field. Opening my eyes to Hawk crouched on one side, and Liv on the other, with a circle of yellow and black jerseys around me was more embarrassing than the ball knocking me out. I broke the most basic rule of always pay attention to where the ball is, and now I'm paying for it with a frosty ice pack sticking to the ball imprint on my chest.

I have an entire tortuous week before I can play again because they're concerned about a possible head injury. Which leaves Hawk and I our next option: to hang out and take care of each other like a rapidly aging couple-that's-not-a-couple. He's refused to leave my side since I came-to on the field; which hasn't helped dissuade me from wanting his lips on mine again. He called out of work both days in case I need anything, even a water, while I heal from the game. I woke up in his arms on the couch this morning, and I swear I felt him kiss my forehead last night. I may have—absolutely *did*—pretend to be asleep when he woke, just to keep his warmth on me a little longer. For those brief snuggled moments, it felt like we were a couple which was nice. Then my brain reminded me he said Thad would be a good person for me to date, a clear signal he's not interested in me right now. I wiggled from the bliss bubble in his arms and woke him up.

I can't get the kiss out of my head, nor the weird ass image from our trip to the Liberty Bell. There's a lot I don't think I want to forget either. But that means I'm not really watching the television and am, instead, well aware of the tingle in my lips when I look at his.

"What?" I wipe my cheek and take a peek at Hawk's dry bandages. "Do I have something on my face?"

Hawk glances at me and back to the television no less than five times. When I turn to face him, we lock onto each other, the way we did at the fire pit—alight with hope and desire. Are we really going to do this? Again? Please.

The touch of someone is enticing. But Hawk? The man who thinks a seven for seven is an amazing week. Seven different dates, with seven different fucks in one week. A mental trophy of sorts. I'm fine with seven different fucks. Hell, multiply it. But, I'm keener on it being one person. This is where we differ. A lot. And, I couldn't handle being his dusty trophy.

And even still, whenever I need him, he's right there.

We left the fire pit unfinished, undiscussed, and here we are again, staring at each other. Making out with someone doesn't have to mean dating. We've kissed already. Physical intimacy is one of the few details of our lives we've kept separate, and tonight, sitting next to him, I keep shifting in my seat, wanting him to try and kiss me again, completely unsure of why.

Our gazes split as I pretend to stretch my neck, crinkling the melting bag of ice, and severing a replay of the moment at the fire pit we both refuse to acknowledge.

He leans in, and a tiny giggle flutters up my chest and out through my lips.

"What?" He asks, pulling his torso back, his voice squeaking high. "Does my breath smell?" Furrowing his brow, he huffs into his palm. With a deep sniff, he shakes his head.

I swallow down a larger chuckle. He looks over my shoulder as he bites his lower lip. Do what happened the other night. It's simple.

I cough to cover another laugh and clear my throat. "Let's try again."

Hawk crosses his arms and tilts his head like a confused puppy. "Are you going to laugh at me again?"

I shake my head. "No?" Maybe.

"Well, that's so convincing." His voice hits a puberty high crack. "It's only me."

I nod and take in a deep breath. It's only me? Does he realize what that even means? There is no one I trust more than him. Despite that, this is still new territory. There's this tiny nag in me throwing up blocks, worried about being tossed aside when he's bored of me.

My lips part and hover close enough to feel the gentle exhale of air from his mouth. I peek open an eye to find he's staring back at me. Another obnoxiously loud laugh erupts from my mouth, and a pang of worry seizes my heart.

I suck in my lips and bite down as I open my eyes. Well, crap. He looks so ... confused?

"You're not okay with this, are you?" He scratches at his cheek and glances down.

The bag of ice drips on my shirt and ceases the trembling tickle in my chest. "It's not that. It's every time I see your face I laugh."

"I'm that horrible looking to you?" His tone suggests a joke, but one drenched in a heavy ouch.

"Shut up. You know you aren't ugly." I shake my head.

"True. I'm in the realm of hideous." He flashes a wide grin and runs his tongue over his lips. "Would a bag over my head with lip holes help?"

"You. Are. Ridiculous."

He covers his face with wide fingers. "Better?"

"Stop making fun."

All I want to do is see if the fire pit was a fluke, and forget all the other nonsense. Instead, I can't stop giggling like I've never been with someone before. I lean in, kiss the back of his hand, and lean back.

"Oh, baby." He rolls his eyes back, pulls his hands down his cheeks, and lets out a groan.

"This. This is why it's weird." A full belly laugh pulls through, filling the air. "You're, you." Knowing it's *him* kissing me is different from *seeing* him kiss me. When the structured lines of his face get close, my nerves flare a warning and a protective shyness takes over.

"Wildflower, I *only* want to kiss *you*. I need to kiss you." His hands land at his sides with an exaggerated smack and his tone shifts to serious. "Do you actually want to do this?"

The way he says "Wildflower" melts me. I nod repeatedly and pout my bottom lip. My chest holds the tingles, the desire, the pull to him. "I don't know what's happening. It's like each time we get near, one of our magnets flips over, shooting us far apart."

"Oh. Talk dirty to me with science. Two poles of a magnet repelling." He leans back and gives an approving nod.

The issue isn't the repelling, it's the pull. The thing I'm stuck on from the night we kissed is, *he kissed me*. He scrambled the natural balance of our friendship, messing with the normally clear division line. We crossed into the unknown and he was burned. Literally. I don't want to get burned or set our friendship ablaze in a grand bonfire. And yet, I want to be kissed—by him. None of this is logical.

He pulls me into his bedroom and points to the gamer chair. "New idea."

My lip quivers up. "Do I need a blacklight on this thing?"

"Masturbation is perfectly natural, thank you very much." He tosses my bag of ice onto a pile of tissues in the trash can.

A sour taste floods my mouth, and I purse my lips. "Gross." I jump up and push the chair away. Every inch of this room is probably drenched in semen, and now all I can see is imaginary semen dripping down the walls and coating all surfaces.

"Let me explain something." Hawk roots through his closet, tossing items to the side. "Any guy's house you go in, there's a good chance you're sitting in a spot he released."

Well, that's just gross.

"I also clean. Constantly. And I disinfect, because I'm not a disgusting monster." He lifts a crocheted black tie from his closet, walks over and holds it across my eyes. "Too skinny."

I pull my head back and blink away the soft tie. "What are you doing?"

"Experimenting." He tosses the tie on the oak desk and heads to the nightstand.

"Care to share your hypothesis?" I ask.

He nods, spins to face me, and triumphantly lifts a sequined purple sleep mask from the drawer.

"That's different." What in the world? "You aren't putting some kink you used on one of your exes on me." I shift in my seat.

"I'll have you know this is mine." He snuggles the silky part against his cheek and smiles. "Gift from the most beautiful five-year-old ever, to keep the night time monsters away. In this case, to help us *see* differently."

I let out a short, frustrated sigh.

He offers a wink and lifts the mask to cover his own face. "Sit and relax. Trust me. If I'm wrong, worst case you laugh again."

I sit in the molded black leather gamer chair. My fingers rest gently on each arm, and the muscles in my stomach dance from the flex I'm holding down to pretend I've got my nerves in check.

He kneels in front of me and lifts the mask up. The fabric caresses my eyes shut, coaxing the remaining muscles in my face to relax. A mild scent of lavender doesn't work to calm the flutters in my stomach. "Did you spray something?"

"It's the mask." His tone is tender. Soft. Close.

Butterflies scatter up my arms and chest. "It feels weird, but I'm also looking super fierce." I toss my hair back over my shoulder a little too enthusiastically and it smacks against the headrest.

"Heh. You look good with sparkles." Hawk's voice feels further from my face.

The room feels calmer and blackness surrounds me. I pull in my lips to wet them and they just barely part.

"What's the hypothesis?"

He slides his trembling palms under mine, and gently lifts me to stand. The anxious giggles fall quiet. The pulse in his wrist beats against mine.

"That you'd—"

I tilt my head just slightly and lean forward before he can finish his sentence. His soft lips press back on mine, and his mouth opens just barely. I can feel his smile against my cheeks. My hands slide up his chest to his temples, while his arms slide around my waist with a touch so light, it feels safe.

I take a step forward, and his heartbeat vibrates against my chest. Some things aren't possible to hide when the body can't control a tell. My fingers glide over the shadow of stubble, and back down to rest over his heart.

His hand slides up my neck and pulls the tie of the face mask. I take a step back, stumble into the rolling chair, and slide across the room. I blink into focus, and Hawk's ass is doubled over as he silently laughs, dangling the mask in his hand.

"I may have destroyed your hypothesis." I laugh, and tears stream down my face. "Super star."

"I hadn't added in—" He wheezes from laughing too long. "—the Elin variable." His face is a deep red across his cheeks and beneath his raised eyebrows. "Are you okay?"

"Always." I untangle myself from the chair and the bed. "Bruised ego, and maybe thigh." No matter how many times I tug at the base of my shirt it doesn't want to lay straight. "What was the hypothesis?"

"That I'm a hideous monster." He winks. "Or, that you want to. But then you see my face—your bestie of all besties—and get nervous. I get it."

Every ounce of air in my lungs whispers out. Well, damn. "You're not hideous," I mumble.

The Hawk train of women still sits at the forefront of where I don't want to end up. He's all the right and wrong components in a partner for me, and at some point, he'll be the one to call off whatever this thing is between us where we kiss and hang out but don't talk about what's happening. But the little jolts of happy nervousness I get around him make me foolishly want to try anyway.

CHAPTER TWENTY

CANCELING A FIRST DATE is never a nice thing to do, especially not on a Saturday night. Mr. No-Name-Needed surprised me with an excellent opportunity to stand in a hotel lobby and go to a signing event for retired professional basketball players I care nothing about. I was gentle with canceling on him and offered an, *I'm so sorry, a work project came up last minute. Have a great time.*

What really came up is me choosing *me* tonight. My head's still spinning from whatever is happening with Hawk. I don't completely know what any of it means, and I don't want to change anything by asking the wrong question. Kissing him is nicer than I want to admit, and yet still a dash terrifying.

No regrets.

Now I'm busy blowing steam into the abyss of the coffee shop and staring at the bulletin board of things I *could* do, instead of sitting here solo. Poetry reading at the bar? *Not tonight, I'll giggle if it's too out there.* Join a rock band? *I'll pass, not my style of music.* Bread baking lesson? *Interesting, but I'd need a partner.* Attend a burlesque show? *Probably more fun to go with my team than solo.* Nothing on this board is quite slamming a "get off my ass and claim an adventure for the night" feel. I glance down at my phone. I could call Hawk, but that'll risk him reading too much into our odd make-out session from yesterday, and me canceling the date I had for today.

The golden keys on the piano near the window distract my gaze. Eons ago, I played here regularly with established musicians who wandered through. The owners like to book up-and-comers like I once was, and well-established musicians who sneak through when they're headed to a performance at the arts center. I stopped practicing, or really playing, when my life was almost entirely at the pitch. Now, I'm not sure how out of practice I am to try to play for myself.

"I can pull her out for ya if you'd like." The barista points an elbow at the tucked away piano.

"I'm good. Thanks for the offer though."

He gives a half-frown and nods.

The shine of blood red ink and white letters on a black post-card stapled to the lower left of the board draw my attention. The card offers an invitation for a "transformative evening." With a long slow blow straight ahead, the steam rising from my mug parts like curtains to let the rest of the letters dance while I read. Experimental art isn't typically my cup of tea. But a night out surrounded by free beverages, and snacks on floating trays, captures my interest. To sit here all dolled up for a date that's not happening because I need a night to think, and to distract myself from the memory of Hawk's tongue sliding across mine, is a waste of tights and eyeliner.

I chose myself, and now I have to follow through.

My fingers smack against the ledge of the table. Tonight, I'm choosing art and free cheese. This is a calculated risk. If it's terrible, I can come right back here and sit in a silver soda chair listening to music while watching couples flood in from their happy dates.

I drop a five on the table, and offer a half-smile with a nod to the couple that's been hawking me—to the point of obnoxious—for my seat. The cup clacks when I put it in the bin, and the glittery piano keys shimmer "goodbye" as I exit through the back door and head toward the gallery.

Floodlights shine on colorful murals encouraging love, peace, tolerance, and hope on the side of the old factory-turned-gallery.

With my head held high, I brush through the open gallery doors. Inside, a rapid heartbeat and ... squishing ... echoes through speakers to fill the otherwise almost-empty room.

Am I early? There's no-one here. No, everyone else is out for dinner and chats while I listen to ... someone experimenting with lotion, maybe? Jelly? Please let it be a separate exhibit, and not what I'm going to.

A hostess sporting a corset, red tutu, top-hat, and fishnets rides over on a milky hoverboard with a set of silver noise-canceling headphones.

"Welcome! Please take this, and put these on. If you swipe in different directions, you can enjoy the space without sound." She winks. "Or, each space has its own accompanying soundtrack." She bats her peacock feather eyelashes, revealing emerald eyeshadow. "If you aren't comfortable on the hoverboard, you can skip it and walk through the exhibit."

I offer a smile, and let her place the headset over each ear before I stand on a hoverboard for the first time in my life. When I step on the board, relief takes over my body and I stand tall. I'm incredibly thankful for the stomach muscles I've gained playing goal. A tiny tilt of my feet, and I turn straight into a wall.

The hostess giggles, cocks her head, and puts her hands out. She points to the path on the floor, and grabs my fingertips to guide me along the first arced line.

My stomach twitches, and I shift my weight to keep balance. What drunk painted this line? How am I going to view the display and not crash?

She releases her fingers and gives me a thumbs-up. My training-wheels are off, and I'm free to follow the line. I successfully steady the board and grab a pamphlet.

The inside page directions read: *Use the board to follow the path, like a sperm through the exhibit.*

I look up, and blink at my reflection in the frosted mirror. The mirror is part of the exhibit and a painted white tail pokes out from where my ear should be. I bite down on my lip to pull myself together.

I am a sperm. I haven't been one in a long time, but tonight, I'm a sperm.

The bonus benefit tonight is an ab workout with each flex on the hoverboard to maintain balance. A tall, elegant man rolls forward on a red hoverboard, clad in a maroon speed suit with a magenta hula-hoop surrounding his body. If I'm the sperm—is he the egg?

"Drink?" he offers.

I pluck a glass of champagne, with raspberries bobbing against the bubbles, from his tray. "Cheers."

"Cheers." He gives a nod, and without spilling a drop, does a double circle, bows, and heads back to the far room.

Champagne will go everywhere if I try the double circle.

This isn't so bad. I'm out alone, enjoying something new, and nothing smells like sweat, mint, or tiny rubber balls.

Too soon for the tiny rubber balls. A collage of mixed balls is piled strategically inside a shadow box frame, giving modesty to a painting of a man sitting spread eagle while staring upward. With a sip of bubbly goodness, my mind prepares for whatever the painting is staring at. I glance up, and two painted bowling balls hang above the picture.

The semen trail leads me to the next space, framed in deep wood tones. Music. I forgot about the music. A quick slide of my finger across the headset, and the sound of pouring rain with light jazz eases my nerves. Three egg-men in roller-skates come out with trays of cheese, truffles, and strawberries. A cursory glance around and I'm still *it* in terms of guests. I sneak a truffle and a strawberry from the tray before promptly shoving them into my mouth. They smile and do a lap, lining up on either side of me while I take in the series of oversize black, white, and red photos. Each with an image of a beautifully sculpted body, red highlights exaggerate natural muscular curvatures in poses of moderate modesty. One frame is blank inside, except for a black post-it with red writing reading: *sold*.

Good for the artist.

The man with chocolate truffles offers his tray and uses a free hand to point out the usage of white in the most unusual of spots in the photos to make the subjects pop.

Hawk's never going to believe this. I chuckle and grab another chocolate to fight my urge to text him. I can do this solo.

The men skate off as the trail winds around to a latex-covered door, complete with what will forever be the largest clitoris I've ever seen. The woman with the tutu is back, and motions for me to tap my headset off. Whatever's beyond those labia holds both my intrigue, and my horror. I may never be the same once I go through those walls.

"Use your shoulder to go through." She pulls back a curtain, and reveals a small slit in the latex. "There's two layers."

I glance down at the hoverboard, then squint back at her.

"I can break the hymen if it's easier for you."

With rapid blinks, and the last swallow of champagne, I stare down at the beast in front of me. "Do I stay on the board?"

She nods and taps the music on my headset. The noise in the room is gone, and the void is disorienting. My mission is simple—break through the latex, and don't fall from the board. In short, infiltrate like the good sperm I'm meant to be.

The hostess motions the air to offer a push, but I shake my head.

I dip my shoulder and head low, flicking my ankles down fast on the board to gain speed. My body works to barrel through the latex, and the sheets stick to my face until I'm free from the curtains. The silence is peaceful. Fans blow hot air at a steady pace on either side of my face, and heat flushes my cheeks. The room is filled with artistic sculptures of toys I've got many questions about. Along the back wall are historical dildos with placards of their owners' names, offset by an assortment of toys used by famous people. I stare at them, dazed, waiting as if they'll spring to life. Yep, that's the name of my favorite women's team goalie on the one that shouldn't be humanly possible to use. Well then. Good for her.

My fingers tap against the phone tucked neatly in my small bag. One little picture? I could send it to Hawk.

Then he'll ask why I'm texting him on a date.

The trail loops me back to the door I initially came through. What happens if I go full force and smack into someone trying to come through?

A red button to the side of the exit reads *"push me."* I smack the button with an open hand, and the audio in my headset shifts to the sound of crashing waves. I shake my head. If my vagina sounds like waves when an ear presses to it, I'll be doing Kegels every moment of every day forever.

The path out is easier than the path to get inside. White confetti and silly string blanket me as I exit. The artist throws confetti up over her head. I squint through the raining sperm confetti and the woman's tiny frame and black hair in a tight bob come into focus. She's the photographer from the boudoir shoot.

"Elin!" Hattie pushes her glasses up. "You've been reborn. Go be adventurous!"

With who? Myself? The only other person possible right now is Hawk. Between the fire pit and last night, he and I are innocent compared to what Hattie probably means. Last night was adventurous for me. Finding the guts to initiate anything with him spins the flutters in my stomach into twists, fearing he'll realize it's me and change his mind.

I laugh and glide over to her on the board. "You remember my name?" All the jobs she has, the countless costumes, and she remembers my name.

She rises to her tiptoes and gives me a hug. "Who could forget your name, or that figure!" She waves over one of the eggs and takes a glass of champagne. "Did you get the proofs I sent?"

I wrap my arm across my stomach and nod. "Wait, is this your show?" The quality of the proofs she sent are gorgeous—it's the subject matter I'm still working on having confidence in.

"Did you enjoy it? I'm experimenting with something new." Her intoxicating smile and hopeful eyes are that of a sweet kitten, a fierce, ready to bite calico with sharp pointy teeth, always willing to play.

"Marvelous. You should be super proud." I brush confetti off her shoulder and step down from the board.

The remaining members of her squad of tutus and eggs return with cheese.

"We haven't had many people come tonight," she says, with a tinge of disappointment. "Is it too much?"

"I'm sure they'll all come soon enough." For her sake, I hope this place gets packed, and she sells everything off the walls.

"Aunt Hattie can teach people a thing or two about seeing their beauty." She shimmies and takes a sip of the champagne.

She gives me a hug, and a small wave, before jumping on the hoverboard and disappearing through the giant vagina with a smile plastered on her face. Her entourage follows her through, and the clitoris lights up like a bright pink disco ball. My cue to exit, and end this date.

I'm ready to be adventurous—within limits.

Don't think, just walk through the doors, and shut off the thoughts. This overanalysis my mind goes through each time I make a decision is too much. At some point, I need to turn my head off. I rub at my neck where Hawk's lips dipped to my skin a few nights ago, and goosebumps trickle down my arms. The front door opens with a creak, and I walk down the brown carpeted stairs I've run down hundreds of times before.

"In here!" Hawk's voice yells from the hallway.

Jitters flutter in my stomach

"Shouldn't you be on a date meeting used-up basketball players?" Hawk mumbles around something in his mouth.

Where is he? My insides are vibrating. I glance around the room second-guessing the determination that brought me to stand in the middle of this room, with a low fire going, and alternative music blaring. Was he expecting me?

"Was the guy a winner at least?" He pops his head out from behind the arcade machine and slips the screwdriver from his mouth, letting it roll across the hearth to the floor.

"Do you really want to know, or are you just making conversation?" I eye him up and down, scrunching my toes in my shoes.

Hawk doesn't *need* to know I canceled my date due to an overloaded brain. Not seeing Hawk as, well, *Hawk*, isn't easy. His cocky smile, and mussed hair from studying whatever needs upgrading on the machine, pull at my nerves.

Just pretend it's like the other night—without the blindfold or tripping over air. He's a man with hands, a sculpted body, a tongue that can flex well, and a warm sensual touch. A massive upgrade from anything that requires batteries. And one who can melt me with a single stroke of his finger down my arm.

Hawk throws a smirk back at me, comes around to the front of the machine, and folds his arms across his gray tank top. "Tell me how it went." He scratches the side of his head and leans confidently on the machine. "You went all out tonight, huh?" His unabashed ogle begins at my feet and finishes on my face.

"Who knew you owned a dress so ..." His eyebrows arch, and he rubs his palm down the side of his jeans.

All black. The best I could find in my closet to put some effort into not wearing jeans and a t-shirt, or my training gear, was to piece together anything black. Black knee-high boots over black tights that give the illusion of rose tattoos down the sides of my legs, with a short black dress sporting an off-shoulder cutout is the fiercest I've felt in forever. My fingers grasp the end of the long, silver waterfall chain that dips almost to the edge of my skirt.

He squints and leans forward. "Is that shimmer?"

I take two steps closer, slow blink to let the light of the machine reflect off the bronze sparkle on my eyelids, and drop my keys on the couch.

My palms rest on either side of the machine around him, and I bat my eyelids. I can compartmentalize this. There are two Hawks. The first is my best friend, and the other is the good looking and funny Hawk with a magnetic personality and a body chiseled by the soccer field. Right now, I need the second one with a dash of the first. I want momentary impulsivity with the second one, with the flirt. Adjusting for the calculation, my best friend, the first Hawk, will still be here after this. He won't run, or make fun of my awkwardness. This is our rule.

"You're wearing makeup." His fingers reach back, pulling the joystick forward and setting off the music on the machine. "Eyeliner, burgundy lip-gloss, your hair's down and straight. Who are you pretending to be tonight?"

"Don't sound so disappointed." Damn. What was I thinking? Sexy isn't my thing.

His hands wrap around my waist, erasing my thoughts, and he pulls me forward for a long deep kiss, igniting the blood coursing through my chest, and drawing a powerful throb between my thighs. I grab the joysticks and press against him, leaning on the machine. His fingertips sweep up my shoulders and tickle down the sides of my arms. His fingers fall from my skin, and I press my chest closer against his.

Hawk pulls back and drops his lips to the side of my neck, flicking his tongue deep into the dimple above my collarbone. His palm slides down the side of my hip, adding a surge of inhibition to my hands as I glide the tips of my fingers across the flex of his stomach.

"You're killing me," he whispers into my mouth.

He tips his head back and stares up at the ceiling. My fingers dip lower, grazing the trail just below his belt line.

"Time out," he utters a low note and his knuckles turn white, gripping the edge of the console. "You didn't answer my question."

Is he serious? My hand is right here, my legs are turning to jelly, and I'm ready and willing to push the lines from our last visit, and he calls a time out?

I pull my hand back and stare at him with hope, taking my time to tame the tingles.

"What's the question?" I pull my hand off him.

He leans back on his elbows, and raises his eyebrows. "What happened on the date?"

"I went to a gallery opening instead." I bite my lower lip.

"Uh, huh." He pulls air in and pushes it out slow. "Did you two—*have* you two ...?"

Ah. I shake my head. "Nope."

His hand releases from the edge of the console, and his finger traces the edge of my nipple.

Pull me back in and kiss me. Pretend I'm a person he wants to touch as much as I want to run my hands across his body.

"Is that what you're worried about? That I hooked up with someone then came here?" I brush my cheek against his and then lean away. "Do we need ground rules?"

He nods. "I don't want to be second-hand kissing someone who just kissed you, or more."

"Same." I press my hips against his and pull his hands to the edge of my skirt. What's his hesitation? My clothes? Is my makeup that bad? Is he having second thoughts?

His pupils grow large as he cups my butt. He lets out a soft exhale and slides his fingers across my back. A gasp releases from my lips and he masterfully unlatches the bra through my dress. He cracks a smile, and in a very un-Hawk fashion, laughs nervously.

Hawk grazes his knuckles against the thin fabric covering my nipples, squeezes them gently, then pulls my mouth to his. Hungry, I slide my tongue past his lips, and his hips grind against mine.

He moans and pulls away. "I need to know what the rules are here." He gives a tight gasp, and lowers his hands to the outside of my thighs. Waves of heat course through me and make my thoughts go fuzzy.

The idea of this moment has crossed my mind more times than I'll allow myself to truly acknowledge, and I'm super nervous. Nervous I'm doing something wrong, that I'll ruin everything, or randomly jerk and accidentally hurt him. Nervous in a way I've never been around him before, nor in a way I've ever been with anyone else. I slide my hand down to where his ribs and abs meet, and with shaking hesitation, I rub my thumb up and down. *I'm touching Hawk.* Maybe the fifteen years of build-up was too long. He's going to laugh or pull away.

He takes a deep breath in with closed eyes, then opens them, and stares at the ceiling as my thumb flicks up. "Elin, I can't do this with you without knowing what it means to you. I take us, in whatever definition you want to make that word, seriously."

I let go of him and take a step back to adjust my dress and try several times without luck to refasten my bra as I walk over to sit on the couch. "Yeah, let's set some guardrails."

"I prefer to view them as bumpers." He folds his hands across his chest.

Bumpers! We can get whatever this is out and be okay because we have bumpers. I can do bumpers.

"I really feel like these rules should have come a lot earlier. Like maybe I could have used them at the fire pit ..." He's far from wrong there, like maybe we should have revisited our rules multiple times over the past fifteen years. "Rule one, no second-hand kisses."

Second-hand confirms this thing we've been doing isn't leading to dating. I lift my chin to try to keep back the tinge of unexpected hurt pricking at my throat.

"So we're dating other people and making out?" I ask, playing it as cool as I can, and failing miserably.

He rubs at his jaw. "We've talked about this. No one wants to be a rebound, but I don't want you diving into dating another moron."

I rub my hands on my thighs. "Are you volunteering to be my warmup coach? My bumper? Or are we rewinding to where we were before the firepit?" Rewinding is impossible.

"Bumper. I trust you to help me not date the wrong people, and I'll do the same for you. This is one bestie helping another with no strings attached except that we remain best friends. That last part is key."

He has to know how stupid this sounds. Yet, it's a green-light to keep kissing him and touching him which is what I want right now.

I rub my thumb into my palm. "If we do this, I agree to rule one of no second-hand kisses."

"Agreed," a nervous shriek comes out of him.

I stick my tongue out at him with a faux gag. "Imagine if it was a secondhand blow job!" I cringe at the nervous non-sense that just barreled from my head and out my mouth.

He blinks at me blankly and takes his open seat on the couch. "Rule two, no second-hand blow jobs. And, there's nothing in dating stating you have to kiss someone on the first date. It's sexier when the person doesn't kiss on the first date, makes the chase more fun."

I laugh and curl into his side. "If it has hit the level of rule two, rule one got thrown far out the window."

"Fair." He rubs at his face and puts his arm over my shoulder, pulling me closer. "This is a disaster waiting to happen. Agreements like this fail because someone always develops feelings."

My stomach twists. He's not wrong. "Rule three, if one of us starts to experience feelings for the other—outside of the love of friendship—we can bail with no questions asked, and no friendship lost." I swallow down. *Don't let that be me.*

"You love me?"

He pokes my arm and scrunches his face like a duck. "You know what I mean."

His face softens as he glances at me, sending a flutter strong enough to make me worry about rule three. Younger me broke this rule several times before. I panicked and ran straight into the arms of my college boyfriend and then Nate. Right now, I want to kiss him and not think.

"We could sit here all night listing rules. My boundaries are rules one through three, and you're in charge. We go as far, or as backward, as you're comfortable with." His tone softens, and he kisses my forehead. "I trust you to be honest when you finally admit how much you love me, Wildflower."

I can't look at his face, but feel my cheeks flush. "Let's hit reset and start out basic and slow. We wave a yellow flag to stop if either of us is uncomfortable, or has a dating prospect that may turn serious." These rules are manageable. "We need to be careful to not get caught in public."

He raises his eyebrow with a spicy little grin.

"Not what I meant." And, his rule, the one about pacing, has been in existence for the majority of our friendship. Which is why I trust him here. At least now we have our feelings out and open—kind of. "Oral sex to be negotiated at a later date."

He blinks hard at me with flushed cheeks.

"Too much?" *Too far?* My heart thuds against my chest.

Talk of a blowjob sucked the air from the room, and now we're trying not to look at each other while I parse the rules of our agreement. I hope we can do this and still be friends.

Chapter Twenty-One

Determination and courage. Two nights in a row of hanging out is nothing new. There's just an added level of "different." Last night left my head reeling when we slammed the brakes to lay out ground rules, and now all I want to do is to get to the part we didn't yesterday. All day my head kept reverting to the heat between us last night, and right now the tingles still rage deep in my belly. Three plus years of no sex, and now all I want to do is stay in bed and feed the desire 'til I pass out.

I push my shoulders back and march through the door. Hawk's nod over to the couch is inviting, but the couch isn't why I'm here. I don't want to sit and watch movies. Hawk's eyebrows furrow as I draw closer, and he reaches his hand out. I grab his hand and pull him in closer.

"Well, hello." He brushes my hair back and pulls me in. "You had a date today?"

I shake my head. "Please don't ask questions."

His lips part and press against mine as his arms wrap around my waist to pull me tight. His firm hold matches the tightness in my own arms. I loosen my grip and lean back.

My hungry mouth isn't ready to part. I slide my hands down his biceps and squeeze them, pulling back my head. With a racing heartbeat, I lean back in, but my lips graze his cheek instead of his mouth. I open my eyes, and his stare deep into mine. *Move, talk, do anything.*

Hawk releases my hips and takes a step back, running his fingers over his agape mouth. *Say something. Laugh, crack a joke, ask a question. Don't stare at me like that.* I can't read him. This isn't something I can read.

He shakes his head and sits on the couch, rubbing a hand over his face.

"I'm sorry." My lungs grip as I try to talk.

He shakes his head. "No, I want to." His fingers pull his cheeks down, then fall to his bouncing knees. "Argh!"

Tears well as the air in my lungs pushes out. I turn to the door and take a step.

His hand grabs mine and I turn back to face him. Door or couch. Door or couch. If I leave, I'll be playing this in an endless loop until I see him again. I'll text him, I'll cry. This isn't how this should go.

Hawk tugs at the back of my shirt to pull me forward, guiding me to his room, and spins me toward the desk by the far wall. I glide my hand up his smooth back and his torso puffs up.

Three years is too long to stay pent up. Being turned down over and over by Nate grew to be expected, but Hawk ... to be crushed by Hawk would be beyond awful.

His lips part, and he presses his body against mine, hiking me onto the desk.

"Bumpers?" he whispers.

I tug at his hair and press my hungry lips against his. Flutters shoot across my chest and down to my throbbing thighs. He lifts my leg with a tight grip as his jeans press against my pelvis.

Slow down brain. Tonight's not the night to throw him down. We have rules. Set rules.

"Are you okay?" he asks.

I moan a yes into him. Hawk kisses the hollow of my neck and pulls at my hips, he lifts me from the desk to roll onto the bed.

Rules are for a reason. Yet I want to rip off his pants.

Rules are for a reason.

To maintain our friendship.

The gentle kiss behind my ear, and the press of his palms against my sides, rips my stream of thought, chucking it to the side, replacing it with a hot bolt of desire.

My chest rises and falls with each press of his hips against mine. He keeps his gaze on my face and slides a warm palm up my stomach, causing it to flex as I arch my back. His hot breath hits my ribs while he tugs my tank top high. Why didn't we even try for fifteen years? There has to be a reason ... my mind goes blank. His teeth gently glide up to my chest and his tongue flicks before moving up the column of my neck, caressing in intricate circles at the base of my neck, sending my legs to press into the mattress.

"I have to stop," he whispers in my ear. "We set a bumper ... and my body ... I want to make you feel so good all over. I want to explore every part of you, and we can't right now. We agreed to slow."

Argh. "Above the waist? We can do above the waist?" The words pour quickly from my mouth.

"I can do that." He groans and slides off his shirt. A ripple travels down his arms and he tightens his muscles. He stares at my face, his eyes studying me as if reading the deepness of my inhales amid his pause. He bites his lower lip as his gaze shifts to lock with mine. I want to feel the dance of our bare skin pressing together.

Why is he staring?

"Everything above the waist," he repeats.

The palms of his hands press the sides of my ribs, and he pulls me closer to him.

I sit straight and toss my top to the ground. Why didn't I plan or prepare? Heat fills my cheeks. I'm sporting an object akin to a mermaid's wardrobe. He runs his thumb across my back and unhooks my aquamarine silk bra with ease.

Hawk leans forward and peels down the straps on each side, adding a kiss to each shoulder.

He tugs at the side of the straps and stares at my chest.

I brace, waiting for judgment to come.

How many? Imagine the variety of nipples he's seen. Saucers, quarters, thimbles, different sizes, dark, light, where do mine fit in? Mine are the worst, and that's why he's staring. I swallow, staring at the sweet angles of his jawline. I shift on him, gliding my fingers to trace the definition of his bicep and up to his cheek. Now it's too late to undo anything, to turn the dial back and just accidentally make-out with one another.

"Damn," he whispers.

His hands slide up my back and pull my torso down to him, pressing my nipples to his muscular, smooth chest. He looks deep into my eyes while his fingers glide across my lower spine, sending a bolt of electricity between my thighs. I suddenly want to throw the "no full-blown sex let's take baby steps" rules out the window.

I want more of him. All of him. He opens my arms wide. I arch up and away, and his lips pepper my collarbone. When I give a quiet gasp he stops abruptly, and we split apart from one another.

He moans.

I want to pull him on top of me. Instead, he brushes his fingers softly down my sides and blows out a slow breath.

He's staring at me and not moving.

"I'm sorry," I say, rolling my head into his shoulder.

"Why would you be sorry?" Hawk turns his full torso to face me, and places his hand on my hip, sending more electricity through my body. "You have nothing to be sorry about."

"But you stopped." I hit pause on myself to keep from remounting him and tossing all cares out the door. "I did *something* wrong. Or, it's too weird."

He leans over and locks his mouth on mine, dragging his tongue across my lip to seal them shut. "I need a second."

No, he's right. My arm flops to the side, and our gazes linger.

He brushes his thumb across my lips, and cups my cheek with his palm.

"I'm that bad?" I pull the blanket up to cover my stomach, and look at the stack of books on the far wall.

I glance over at the perfect imperfections of his face, and a softness invades my body, washing away the hormones.

His eyes linger on my face, and his chest relaxes to a more natural rise and fall.

"Can you look away?" He gestures to the wall. "Gimmie a sec?"

I can feel the top of the bed bounce as he bangs the back of his head against the mattress. I bite down on my lower lip.

Now what? Now I'm half naked in Hawk's bed and he's fully charged for a night of multiple rounds. Yet he called it off to respect the rules. I slide my straps back up, cupping my breasts back into place.

"You didn't have to cover those," he whispers, kissing the back of my neck before running a hand across the side of my breast, then down my ribs toward my waistband.

I pull my stomach in as his fingers glide, tugging at the gap in my pants.

"You aren't making this easy," he says, burrowing his head into the curve of my shoulder.

Navigating this new zone is leaving us both reeling, but destroying our friendship over one night of sex isn't worth the risk. Instead, I'm working on dipping a toe into the world of the physical after years of rust.

I roll to face him, and graze my fingers across his scruffy cheeks.

His palm smacks over his forehead, covering his face. "Do you even know—"

"How out of practice I am?" I cover my face with my arm. "I'm sorry. I'm so awful and if you want to stop now, I get it."

His fingers sift through my hair and rest behind my head. "You are far from awful. If this is rusty, I can't imagine where we'll be in three months."

His fingers stroke the back of my head, and his gaze settles on my face.

I take a deep breath, and hold it until my lungs want to burst. He said three months. I let the air slowly escape my nose and watch the rise and fall of his chest. Will we still be doing this in three months?

Hawk clears his throat and pulls his hand to his stomach as he rolls to his back. His hand drifts to conceal the rise still pulsing against the sheet.

If I were another person, odds are he'd throw me out the same way he's thrown out so many of the women I've shaken hands with, smiled at, and pretended to learn their names. *Please don't throw me out.*

But this is an agreement. This is part of it. I glance over, and Hawk is sitting up, pulling his shirt back on. Nothing makes me feels less sexy than when the man I'm with quickly gets dressed. Granted, I grabbed for the sheet first, and am contemplating every tiny decision we've made since our bodies slammed on that desk.

His fingers slide between mine, and our palms press together.

"Promise me we're okay," he says.

I sigh as he tugs at the sheet.

"We're okay," I say. What other option is there? What the hell are we doing? "Nice tent." I grimace. Wrong thing to say, why do I always pick the wrong thing to say?

"There are many places I can think of to put him right now, and most are not on the menu at the moment." He flicks his eyebrows up and rubs his hands together.

I shake my head. "Yeah, I don't think I want to watch you do a clean out."

"A clean out? Really? You're gross." He rests his hands behind his head and shifts his hips, adjusting the blanket higher.

This always ends in disaster in the movies. Two friends hook up and that's it, the end of their friendship. Jealousy or feelings come into play. Yet, when I glance over, it's still Hawk. The guy who doesn't give up on me on the field, who is loud in public, and who doesn't care what people think about him. Who pushes me to try new things he thinks I'll like, like joining the Bees. I'd said to him a million times before we joined how fun it might be to be on the field instead of kicking a ball in his backyard. He's known me long enough to hear all the times I've thought aloud, *wouldn't it be cool if.* Ultimately, it usually comes down to, *wouldn't it be cool if we found a way to do some random fun thing together.*

We can manage this new world. I can handle a little more grinding and kissing. But tonight is done. All that's left is to figure out "what now."

I let go of Hawk's fingers and he stares blankly while I pull my shirt on.

"You don't have to go." Hawk pats the space on the bed that still holds the shape of my body.

"I have to get something done for tomorrow." I close my eyes. The reminder of his fingers grazing my collarbone crosses my mind, and a shiver runs down my spine. "Besides, if I stay, it's different."

"True." He nods his head and clears his throat. "It's late though. You hate driving at night."

I raise an eyebrow. I've got to go. Before one of us makes more decisions in a sideways direction. Maybe he doesn't even really want to keep going, and it's in my head. I need to think, to navigate this and to figure out how I, the person who only does anything sexual in a defined and committed relationship, willingly pressed my chest up against my best friend.

The man I find dates for, and play wing girl for. The man who's seen me fall on my ass drunk, and helps me find my feet when boyfriends didn't enjoy my silliness, but saw it as stupidity. Hawk never sees me as stupid. He's Mr. Positive when it comes to compliments and encouragement. The person I call when I'm excited and happy, or about to fall apart. Only, right now, I can't call him while my head swirls through the desire to keep touching and exploring him, while also wanting to fall asleep holding his hand with his breath against my face.

I snatch my keys off the table. Hawk sits up with a sheet over his bent knees, watching me pace.

"You good there?" He asks. "You look ... flustered."

"Ha." Yes. Yes, yes, I am. "You good?"

He nods, and lifts a hand to my hip, drawing me forward for another kiss. Instantly, my legs fail and turn to jelly. Don't fall into him, keep moving. To drive to his condo and sleep in his extra bed.

"I can't—" He gestures down. "I don't really want to knock over a lamp or a couch with what's going on under this sheet right now. Especially not when my mom could suddenly appear."

My ears grow hot and I raise my hand. I get it. Stay there. I need to go home. To figure out if I'm an idiot for diving into him, and pretending like neither of us will get hurt if we keep repeating this pattern. I don't want to be hurt.

CHAPTER TWENTY-TWO

IF NOTHING ELSE, I'LL get a decent cup of Chai out of this date, and a chance to clear my head from once again falling mouth-first into my best friend. I'd rather be with Hawk in his bed right now, but I'm following the agreement. If, and more likely, when, Hawk asks how dating is going I'll be able to give some kind of answer thanks to this guy who looks nothing like his picture. First off, his hair is salt and pepper, but in the photos it was deep brown. And, I'm not completely certain, but he doesn't seem like 5'10. At best, he's 5'7, an inch shorter than me. I don't care about height when dating, except when someone lies. Following my gut to get a tea on a Thursday after work was dead-on. At worst, we have fifteen minutes together. If those fifteen minutes go well, we have an unlimited supply of coffee, and open mic night in an hour. I fake brushing crumbs off the sleeve of my teal satin shirt and glance at my watch.

Seriously? It's been seven minutes. My tea is still hot, and he's droning about some field in Nevada where he does computer work. Yes, sir, I can see why dating and meeting women is difficult. Maybe don't lead with the fact you work in a bunker several times a year and talk about—what is he even talking about?

I flick my fingers through my ponytail, and a waft of Hawk's fresh linen detergent cuts through the monotone of the man across from me. My concentration is shot, and I can nearly feel Hawk's fingers press against my sides. I nod, pretending to find something interesting. The fresh linen isn't restricted to my hair, but my shirt, my pants. It's everywhere in the condo, from intertwining with each other again last night. The corners of my mouth twitch to hold back my distracted smile.

The man across from me straightens as if someone coached him on how to sit for a date and his glances settle everywhere but my face. "Yeah, I've been lucky to have this new job. Government contracts are great because—"

Stop the self-sabotage. Okay, look past the jeans swallowing his legs, and the ill buttoned top—those are superficial. Good job in software with the government is a plus. No mention of sports what-so-ever. He seems calm and snorts at his own jokes. Ugh.

If only I could remember his name. Does he really need one? Nah. I dub thee, Nevada.

I take a sip of my warm cinnamon Chai and glance across the airy café. The floor is covered in lacquer over old sheet music, and there are tablets placed atop carved music stands next to each table so you don't have to interact with anyone when ordering. The baristas, dressed to the nines, stare off into the distance, seemingly ready to grab the stage—utilized for open mic events—and the microphones, on their breaks.

The streamlined burgundy velvet couch on the far wall looks inviting and comfortable, but there's no way I'm sitting too close to him without a table barrier. If he makes a move like the golf guy tried on our first date, I'm likely to dunk tea straight in his lap. I'm not ready for that, and now there's the simple comfort—complication—of Hawk. If there weren't an agreement, at this point, I'd swear we were dating. But, we're not. If we are though, what does that mean? Do we need to talk about things again?

I take another sip, and bask in the milky warm cinnamon. At this point, I should be a partial owner of the café.

Banjos and mandolins hang below a row of ukuleles. In the corner, a man sets up a barstool below a single spotlight from the ceiling. A handwoven rug beneath the stool, worn from years of metal chair legs rubbing below each artist up there, hoping for that moment of discovery. Waiting for some bigwig to swing through this tiny town on the way to the Poconos and lift them out of monotony.

"My cat misses me a lot when I travel for work." Nevada swishes his shoulders back and forth, rocking the legs of the table atop the sheets to Brahms Lullaby.

His cat misses him? Is this sweet or creepy? A smile forces its way to the forefront, and I place my clay-colored mug on the stack of old guitar cases turned into a table.

"What's your cat's name?"

His cheeks turn up and his soft brown eyes twinkle against the beams of light working their way across our table.

Nevada straightens his brown bowtie and nods his head forward with an eyebrow wag. "Tardis."

Why is that—oh! Finally, something I can respond to. "Shouldn't he make a good time traveling cat then?" I throw a half-hearted giggle his way.

Come on. Anything? No laugh at all? The strong desire to say thank you and goodbye sits on my tongue.

"Oh no, he'd hate traveling." Nevada furrows his thick brows and shakes his head. "He can barely stand when we go on car rides. Tardis throws up everywhere."

Well, my vagina has officially left the building. He's staring at me as if I'm the one who said something odd. Well, who knew all it would take was a joke to get him to check his own watch and the door.

A beeping sound draws my attention to his phone, and an alarm bell is going off.

Feed Tardis scrolls across the screen.

Bastard had an exit plan? Feeding the cat is his exit plan. My phone rings and Liv's name scrolls across the screen.

"Do you need to get that?" he asks, picking up his phone and clicking to get rid of his date alarm.

I shake my head and smile. "Nope, I'm here with you. That'd be so rude of me." Take that Mr. Nevada who has to go feed his cat.

The end is near, and the tea tastes a little sweeter not having to be the mean one.

"I'm sorry, my cat's on a strict schedule." He clears his throat. "We can do this some other time?"

"Well, you know what they say, never get between a man and his pussy." I grin, tilting my head to the side. And then it dawns on me—that was a Hawk joke. His confidence infiltrated the date through me.

The man stares at me blankly, his lips parted.

"Thanks for understanding." Nevada pulls on his long trench coat, and plucks a pair of fingerless gloves from his pocket. "I'll call you."

No, he won't. I wait 'til the bells on the door jingle behind him, and he's disappeared up the street, before claiming the far side of the couch for myself, and watch the performer tune his twelve-string. Sour notes vibrate against the soft music playing overhead.

I flop my phone back and forth on my leg and stare at the blank screen. With a shake of hesitation, I flick the screen on and punch out a message to Hawk. The night's young enough, maybe he's around. Unless he's on a date of his own.

Elin: *I'm being skipped for pussy vomit.*

Before I can put the phone down, a response vibrates against my palm.

Hawk: *I need clarification. I've got a lot of images in my head right now and none can be right.*

Elin: *Watching too much porn again?*

Elin: *Join me at the coffee shop?*

Hawk: *Yeah. I'm at the record store. Be there in a bit.*

The record store is five stores down. He could be here in either three minutes, or he'll get lost scanning the stacks for the next few hours.

I glance at the coffee counter and wave over a barista to get a fresh cup. It's a guy with black, slicked-back hedgehog hair. He's always here, and his name is Mark.

"Okay, before you take my order, I need tips on how to do that." I gesture to his immaculate guy-liner, and trace a finger under my eye.

A faint blush crosses against his snow-white skin, and he points to the woman wiping down table tops. "She's in cosmetology school and amazing. Designed this whole look."

I need her number, and to figure out how to look less like I'm fresh off the field.

"Any interest in being on the list tonight?" He nods to the gold piano tucked into the far corner.

"Tempting, but not tonight." I lift my lip and offer a half-pout of apology. "I'll take another one of these—"

"And a black coffee." Hawk's voice pushes through the foul notes coming from the corner, and he flops down on the other side of the couch.

"Finally!" My body relaxes, and I look over at him with a small grin.

"So, pussy vomit, huh?" He smiles, and his fingers walk to my side of the couch.

I shrug, and watch him walk his freshly manicured silver nails back to his side of the cushion line. "You little liar."

"Can't a man have nice nails and not get judged?" His voice squeaks high as it booms with confidence across the café. "Now tell me about pussy vomit. Because let me tell you, nothing turns me on more than that wonderful phrase."

I give an annoyed grunt. "Mid conversation he decided he had to go take care of his cat. Which is fine, because we clearly weren't right for each other."

Hawk rubs on his chin stubble. "Now, hear me out. Maybe he really has a sick cat."

Fine. Be the voice of reason.

Mark, the barista returns with our drinks and leans down. "This one's much better." He whispers at me and throws a wink at Hawk. I bite back a laugh.

"Are you singing today?" I ask Mark.

Mark stands up straight, nods, and gestures to the corner. "Soon as he's done."

Please, someone bail this poor little rich boy out of the corner with his badly executed experimental jazz. I should be nice, he's the one up there trying and having a blast, not me. The woman at the table next to him is locked in, and claps every chance she gets. She clearly either knows him, or *wants* to know him better.

"This place looks great." Hawk glances around the café.

"Did you see behind the bar?" I gesture to the record players lined up on the back wall. "Friday night is now record night.

You get a discount if you bring in a record from the store you *clearly* weren't at before."

He places his fingers on his chest. "I was, but then the nice lady I was chatting with wanted to get her nails done. Who was I to refuse a free manicure and a human to talk to?"

"Only you." I shift against the sadness that floods my body and inspect my nails. Asking for details will only get me answers I don't want right now.

He takes a long sip of his coffee and sighs. "Alas, it wasn't meant to be."

Hawk slides down the velvet and shoos me further to the arm, making a wide gap of space on the far side. He leans his back against me, shifts his attention to Mark and gives a wave. The warmth of Hawk's back spreads comfortably into my arms, and I lift my fingers to tangle through the flop of his soft hair.

The gentleman with the twelve-string sinks into the end of our couch and pulls up a glass bottle of water.

"You did great," I say.

I glance over, and the woman at the far table is making googly eyes at him. I feel you girlfriend. That's what I want, googly eyes with reciprocation. Mark stands in front of the microphone, tips his forehead down, and releases a long sweet note before belting out all of his grunge pain. Hawk snuggles his back down further and I can feel his soft heartbeat against the side of my chest. Everything feels right, natural, while the music plays and he leans against me. I can happily stay here for hours.

Bounding up the steps to the condo two at a time is a direct reflection of why too much caffeine late at night is not a good idea. Between the music, rich cinnamon goodness, and Hawk, the time flew, and suddenly the open mic night was on the last song. I'm wide awake to poke at, and annoy, my partner in most crimes—the one with fancier nails and no cares as to what the world thinks. I need to be more like him in that way, the embracing who I am as much as possible and ignoring the voice in my head telling me to pull back.

Hawkism of the night: *People will clap and cheer for those who are open to being vulnerable.*

"You don't have to walk me inside." I glance down the steps at him, half-hoping he'll ignore my statement and pull me tight against him inside the condo.

His thumb drums against the wood railing and a flop of his hair flicks back as he gazes up at me. "I ... er ..."

"You want to come in?"

The corners of his mouth lift as he rubs the back of his neck. "It's not what you think."

"Sure." I gently bite down on my lower lip when I open the door, and stare down at his mouth. Impatient butterflies dance in my belly, anticipating that he'll make a move.

Instead, he passes me, runs a hand through his hair, and gestures at the fireplace.

Oh my god. I blink several times, and clap a hand over my mouth. My breaths come in rapid bursts before I sit on the floor and stare at the monstrosity over the fireplace.

That's me, it's not, but it is. The image above the fireplace hangs in a charred barn wood frame, and splashes of red highlight the gentle lines on my abdomen but fail to cover the birthmark near my bellybutton. There's no face or legs, but the image is from my boudoir photoshoot. An artistic version. The original proofs from the shoot are tucked away safely in my phone. White thick brush strokes blur the edges of my goalie gloves as they hold up two soccer balls. My jaw drops. How did this even happen? My throat turns dry. Was there fine print in the photo contract?

I clear my throat again and again, but nothing allows the words to pour forward.

"Well, what do you think?" Hawk taps his foot next to my thigh, and scratches his chin. "I will say, it's a conversation piece." He crouches down and sits next to me on the floor. "My eyes almost shot out of my head when I saw it, but in a good way."

I elbow him gently in the rib. "Well, fuck."

"I went to this weird little art exhibit on their opening night. I saw two people struggling to load in last minute pieces and ran to hold the door. I was then shoved inside and told to enjoy the exhibit as thanks." He nods and snort laughs. "I'm sipping champagne and munching on a strawberry, and then nearly died when I looked up." His elbow blocks a second jab. "My initial thought was, no, my best friend would tell me if she posed for something like this." He slides his warm hand over mine. "Then I met the artist. Eccentric, rather horny, but a nice lady. Apparently, your boudoir photo shoot encouraged the entire series of these black, white, and red images. She kept saying that your shy confidence screamed to be drawn out." He gestures up at the painting. "This is the result of you being her muse. As your friend, it's artistically beautiful and really well done. The piece is also hot as hell."

Did he call me or the image hot? "You bought it?" I turn and gaze at the side of his face. The artwork didn't have prices on it, but I can't imagine the piece didn't set him back a good bit.

"Damn straight." He turns and joins my gaze. "The little horny lady seemed great, but I know you, and knew you'd be mortified if people saw it. Not that you should be, because you're dripping strength and sex in this. Plus, so few people will know it's you since there's no face." He runs his thumb across my cheek and a wave of warmth scatters down my arms and chest. "But your ball boobs, great touch."

I laugh and lean back on my hands. "You lost me wanting to jump you at 'Ball Boobs.'"

He looks back at the image. "Well, it's essentially glued to the wall, so now you have to see your ball boobs, and the strength of the woman in that picture each day."

My jaw drops. Any moisture that was once in the gape of my mouth is now gone, and I'm in desperate need of water … or his mouth on mine.

"Kidding," he says. "I made panels for it, or we can find somewhere else to hide it. I didn't know what else to do once the framing was done."

I lean my head against his shoulder. "We can keep it here for now." Weird, but I'd rather know who is seeing it than it being at his mom's. "Thanks for doing this." If I'd seen the image at the exhibition, I'd have focused on the flaws and wanted to destroy it. Worse, if anyone in the league saw it or recognized me, I'd be hiding under the benches at games in utter fear of judgment.

"You'd do the same for me." His soft fingertips tickle the inside of my palm, sending shivers up my arms and neck.

I laugh. "You'd be standing naked, feet apart, with your thighs holding a ball in full glory."

"Maybe I should call the artist and see if she wants a series of these." He stands to pose in front of the image, holding a fake ball between his muscular thighs.

After another glance at the image behind him, I stand up and press my lips against his. His strong hands glide to my lower back and he kisses me back with gentle tugs at my hips to guide us to the couch. My body is hungry for him, for the kindness of purchasing the artwork, for how much he knows me and how confident we can be with one another. I tug his shirt off and toss it to the floor, biting my lip as my eyes trace down his smooth chest, and the sculpted soccer abs he gets shy about. He stares down at me, his gaze dancing across my face as I pull off my shirt and bra. Our bare chests draw together, letting the heat of our bodies meld us. The nervous shakes from days past are gone, and all I want is to be under him, feeling our hips pressing against one another while our mouths and hands work at each tiny nerve. My body flushes with anticipation while his fingers play at the edge of my pants, and his thickness stiffens against my inner thigh.

CHAPTER TWENTY-THREE

WHOEVER IS KNOCKING ON my door on a Sunday morning at eight a.m. is officially the worst person in the universe. I want sleep. Not visitors who think it's cool to bang louder than bigfoot himself. I run my hand through the tangles in my hair. They'll have to deal with unbrushed teeth.

I open the door and the sun drives straight into my skull. Squinting isn't helping me feel fierce, or like I can gather the energy to yell. The figure in front of me shifts to block the sun and my eyes settle on Hawk. This is the opposite of the worst person in the universe. He's in the good jeans that highlight his ass, and a paint-smeared dark gray hoodie with a leather toolbelt hooked around his waist. Next to him is a pile of supplies, more tools, and what I hope is breakfast.

"Good morning, Wildflower." He leans forward. "May I come in?"

I stare at him, my eyebrows nearly touching. "This is *your* place, and you have a key."

"Not today. You have a lease and as a proper landlord I reviewed your application. In order to make you feel comfortable, it is my responsibility to make sure this place is good to go. As your best friend, I'll point out that your night time shorts are on inside out and backwards."

"Were you watching porn last night?" I push the sleeves up on my gray sweatshirt and yawn. "Did it involve a handyman?"

He gasps and nods fervently. "I most certainly did watch porn on Friday night. Yesterday, I was too busy to watch anything. And one of them did involve a handyman, which then led me to think about you."

I stare at him blankly.

"Not like that," he shrieks. "I thought about what would make you more comfortable so I drafted plans and thought, *what would make Elin happy.*"

What would make me happy? If he knows, it'd be nice if he'd share because I'm still lost navigating parts of that same question. Right-side out shorts and a coffee would be a start. I glance down and lean forward to pick up the package next to his feet.

"Sorry. That is one of the other things I did yesterday. All the mail for the condo was forwarding to my mom's house. The package came a few days ago but was buried under a pile of pots on the table." He grabs his gear and tips his chin up. "Is it all right to come in?"

The brown packaging reads Philadelphia and an instant warmth crosses my body. "Always."

Hawk brings in large bag after large bag and situates them in the living room. We didn't hang out Friday night or yesterday. Which meant quietly hanging out on my own and taking the entire time to read as a distraction. I was heavily distracted reading certain scenes and he managed to slide into my head replacing the author's main character. I place the package on the side counter and turn on the kettle. He rushes in front of me and grabs matching mugs from the cabinet.

"Is this my landlord or my friend making coffee?" I grab the package and pull the top off, watching as he grinds fresh beans for the French press. "This is the picture from the woman in Philly!"

There is a softness to seemingly cold image. The river, frozen like on our day out, and off to the side are two people sitting close. One in a beanie with a bright scarf around a leather jacket, and one with gray sunglasses on their head. She managed to nail us both down to our accessories and hair color. I let out a happy sigh. The picture is as wonderful as that moment was.

"I like it. We look like an old married couple," he says.

I go still and keep my focus on the image. We do. My heart races and I can't stop focusing on the couple in the picture—on us.

"Best friend in desperate need of caffeine." He walks over to me. He places a thin, green package between his teeth, leans one arm against the counter, and wags his brows. He then rips the package open the same way they tell you to *never* open a condom for fear of ripping it, and I can't move. I'm planted to the ground and can't break looking at his mouth and the wrapper as it falls to the floor.

"More porn?" I ask.

"Internet. It looked hot." He pulls up the cheap breakfast tea bag, raising and lowering it in unison with his brows.

I shake my head and refuse to admit it's confusingly hot. The kettle goes off and he repositions himself at my side. He pours the water into the glass French press first, then into his own cup.

"Oh wow. That is worth a lot more than thirty bucks." There's a twitch in the corner of his mouth like it can't smile wide enough. "Where do you want it?"

A burst of excitement hits and I nervously chuckle. He's asking to put a picture up of the two of us, even though no one will truly be able to know it's us from the back. The whole thing is like a little secret makes my pulse race. I rub on the side of my neck and point an elbow to the wall above the couch.

"I'll need to get it framed first." I push down on the press and pour the coffee. "The other one is against the wall in the bedroom."

Hawk puts his cup on the counter, and then dashes to the bedroom returning with the framed image from our trip like a trophy. He places it next to the couch. There's just enough space to put the two pictures side by side with an inch-wide gap between them so they don't feel crowded.

"I love it. You should pick out more things to put up." He walks to get his tea and nods for me to follow him to the couch.

The moment I take a step to follow him it dawns on me I'm not wearing a bra and look like I wrestled squirrels last night. I sit next to him, my posture straight, hoping if I preen myself enough, he won't know how badly I want to run and take a shower. Or that he won't know I suddenly care to *not* look like garbage in front of him, and I'm still trying to wrap my mind fully around why.

He blows on his cup of tea. "Do you want to take a shower while I get set up?"

Thank. God. "Yes!" I stand slowly so as not to tip the coffee on him, or the couch, and tiptoe to the bathroom. "Knock if you need me."

He scans my face and traces my body straight down to my bare legs. "Just getting a mental picture. You're a cute mess."

I stick my tongue out at him and disappear into the bathroom. Once I turn on the water, I can hear him banging around in the living room and hear heavy objects being slid around. A loud crash makes me jump.

"Are you okay?" I shout over the fan in the bathroom.

"Uh. Yeah." He grunts, and what sounds like not one but two bodies sliding across the floor, is concerning.

I wrap myself in a towel and come out of the shower. When I peek out of the bathroom, he's busy unrolling a rug pad near the far wall. With drips of water hitting the floor, I shuffle into the bedroom. I pull on an old, black Bees jersey with a yellow side stripe I seldom wear, since it's for the field and not the goal, in haste. With the shirt barely on, I snatch a pair of athletic pants off the floor and nearly topple into the dresser trying to pull them up.

When I come back out to the living room, he's biting a pencil and measuring the area on the far side of the couch. His concentration face is cute and scrunched. The rug pad on the floor is centered between the fireplace and the opposite end of the wall. He keeps moving with his eyebrows pinched, and rubs the back of his neck while his mouth moves. I can't hear him, and assume I'm not meant to.

"There're bagels in the bag if you'd like." He crinkles his nose as he spreads the measuring tape up the wall. "There's a lox bagel for you, and a cinnamon toast one for me."

I pull two plates from the cabinet and set the bagels on them. "I didn't know landlords built things while their tenants were in."

He waves me off and presses a flat board against a pencil line on the wall. "According to the application, my tenant likes to play music. Since they also mentioned the desire to turn this into the sex capital of the condo association, I'm going to soundproof a bit so we don't get complaints from the neighbors."

My ears are hot. "While watching porn, you decided we needed to soundproof?"

"No, but I can see where you went with that." He stares at the drill, then over at me as I'm mid-bite into the delicious lox and cream cheese bagel, with extra cucumbers and capers. "Can you come hold this board?"

I leave my breakfast on the plate and walk to him, swapping my hands with his on the board. He grabs for the drill and follows holes he pre-drilled.

"Perfect. See, if soccer doesn't work out, you can always go into holding wood." His cheeks flush.

"I'll keep that in mind." I snort and sit next to him. "Is there a reason I have a floating board on the wall above a random rug?"

"Can you be patient?" He points to my plate. "Go eat break-fast and face the opposite way. I want to surprise you, but also want to hang out with you."

My stomach grumbles while my chest feels like there's a hummingbird going full speed inside me. I take a seat at the table and stare off at the door and cabinets. "You want to hang out with me?" I tease. "You've never been so direct before. I like it."

Objects clink and clunk, and he lets out a whimper or two, but I don't look behind me because I want to hang out with him too. Even if that means staring at the front door while I finish my coffee. The satisfying sound of peeling plastic comes from his direction. The sound repeats at least twenty more times.

My cup is empty. Even those last bits of bitter on the bottom. The press is on the other side of the room and I promised to not look.

"Let me know if I'm going to trip." I get up from my chair and walk backwards toward the counter to fill my cup.

"Three more small steps back," he says.

On the third step, my body presses against Hawk's warm softness. He wraps himself around me in a hug and kisses my cheek. I melt into him like a lazy sloth and take a big whiff of fresh cut wood from his sweatshirt. This is nice.

"Sorry, I couldn't resist." He squeezes me tighter and a wash of calm takes the room. "I'd have gotten the coffee for you."

Coffee. I was headed to get coffee.

In a daze, I head back to my seat and swing my legs. He brings the press over and refills my cup. Indie acoustic guitar music streams throughout the room and there's a positivity to each song that plays while I sip coffee and listen to him hum.

"What's this station?" I sway while the singer lulls me into their world.

He mumbles.

"What?" I ask.

"Wildflower." He shuffles and there's a big whack on the wall. "It's a playlist I made. I figured, if I had calm music I might not get as stressed out if you hate my surprise."

Being taken care of is nice. I bounce my leg under the table.

He grunts and takes a few heavy steps. "You don't chill well at all."

I don't. I'd rather help. "I like this mix of songs."

A rush of impatience hits my bladder. I drank an entire press by myself and didn't use the bathroom when I woke up or took a shower. A whimper comes out of my mouth and I cross my legs. He's humming happily to the music and now and then words are threading into the air. Select words like *sweet*, *wild*, *beautiful*, and I'm fairly certain he even sang the word *love* under his breath. But not having direct sight, and being distracted by the water balloon hoping to burst from my bladder, I squirm more.

"Hawk," I whimper. "How much longer?"

Objects are sliding around behind me, and there's a bang of a hammer. "I have like an hour left."

An hour? I'll pee the entire floor. "Um, how close of friends are we?"

"That's a ridiculous question." There's a grinding–sander, maybe? "Bestie of all besties."

Bathroom now. I stand from my seat and take tiny backward steps. "Beep. Beep. Beep." I continue to beep, walking backwards with crossed legs, holding myself and doing my best not to laugh.

Hawk, on the other hand, laughs so loud the neighbors downstairs bang on their ceiling. He rushes to stand in front of me, and places a hand on each of my shoulders. Please don't let me leak. I'm not willing to cross the wet my pants line with Hawk. He may not care, but I will.

"Beep. Beep. Beep." he says, guiding me to the bathroom and shutting the door between us once I'm inside.

"Stay in there for the next hour." He raps on the door. "Need anything? Hot towel? Cookies?"

"Go away so I can use the toilet!" Stage fright hits. I can't go. I sit and wait. Nothing comes out.

"How do you pee so quietly?" His footsteps pass the door into the bedroom and then cross back in front of the bathroom.

"Seriously, I thought you said you had to go. Need me to sing for you?"

Make him stop. I've never had this issue before. What do I care if he hears me go? It's a natural body function. Though, I don't think I've ever farted in front of him either. Left the room to go do it, absolutely, but never with him in the same room. What is wrong with my brain? Where are these thoughts even coming from? He's not even in here and I can't seem to let myself pee.

The front door opens and shuts. Pee flows from me like a waterfall for what feels like an eternity offering sweet relief. The front door opens and shuts again and I pull myself together. A quick flush of the toilet and an elongated handwash buy extra time. But, what does one do in the bathroom for an hour?

"Hawk, as fun as it is to be trapped in my—your—bathroom ... can I at least open the door?" I turn the handle and open the door a crack, hoping to not destroy or take an early peek at anything he's been working on.

He's waiting outside the bathroom having shed his sweatshirt and exposing one of my extra, black Bees shirts. It looks nice on him. When he turns around to show it off, the back reads Axelsson and I giggle.

"Can I get a tryout?" He leans against the doorway of the bathroom blocking the view of the main door of the condo.

Damn it. He's gorgeous in this light. I stroke back his hair and leave my fingers on the side of his face, drawing him into me. He leans in and we kiss softly.

He closes his eyes and blows out a breath. "That was sexy as hell."

I kiss him again, wrapping my arms across his upper back and we stand quietly, pressing our lips together, feeling out the heat of the moment without rushing anything. He leans back and I study his face. His chest rises are slow and heavy, his lips are flush, and he's gently rubbing his thumb on my lower back.

"This is nice," I say.

He nods and takes a stagger step back. He seems as dazed as I am by today.

But, I'm in a bathroom. His bathroom. My bathroom. Our bathroom?

I slide down the doorway and sit on the ground to give him time to complete his project. I'm happy here, even on this tile. He rushes into the living room and returns with a large pillow.

"I thought this might help if the floor is cold." He shakes his head and blinks several times. "Give me like ten minutes. You can help me from there."

With a straight back and legs crossed, I sit quietly on the pillow for the next ten minutes. I no longer care what he's doing or building. I no longer care about much else other than wanting to feel his soft lips against mine. The way his thumb grazes my skin does me in every time. How is it he knows my body so well, so fast? That kiss wasn't about wanting to jump one another and reach a climax. Perhaps I'm misreading or searching for a feeling that isn't there. I've done that in relationships before.

His voice shakes. "Okay, come out and take a look."

"Do I need to close my eyes?" I take a second before stepping out of the bathroom.

He flicks his ear back and forth and I follow his concerned gaze to the far wall. On the wall is a floating desk with a small piano bench beneath it. The color is whitewashed, like my old bookshelf. Above the floating desk is a smaller bookshelf he's placed a series of old music books onto, and a picture of Curie in a glowing party hat.

Hawk reaches his hand out to take mine and walks me closer to the wall. On the floor is a thick green rug with deep gray swirls throughout. The walls surrounding the desk and up on the ceiling have designer octagonal acoustic tiles in different shades of gray. Now that we're closer I can see and hear the tick-tick of a white and rose gold metronome on top of the shelf.

"This is stunning." I stare at the craftsmanship and run my finger across the rounded edge of the desk.

He takes my hand and guides it to the center where there's a divot. "I hope you don't mind, but I got something with some assistance from your teammates."

I pull up the divot and this isn't simply a floating desk. When I lift the top, my piano keyboard, the one I'd left behind when I came to the condo because I wasn't sure about anything in that moment other than getting out, is inside the desk. The entire piece he built is a floating keyboard stand that converts into a desk. The books on top of the shelf are mine, from my old bookshelf at Nate's, and sadness wars with happiness inside my chest.

"You hate it don't you?" He presses on the bridge of his nose. "I knew I should have asked. Thursday night you looked so sad at the piano. Like you wanted to play, but didn't. I miss seeing you play. Not that you *have* to play for me. But, I'm sorry. I'm an idiot—"

I grab him and kiss him. It's not only the piano. The entirety of our friendship, he's always been different from other people I've known or even dated. He's a weird standard no one else can stack up to in the long run. But, if I admit this, everything ends, so I need to keep playing along and waiting on edge for the world to break apart when the arrangement is over.

We sit on the bench, kissing instead of talking. I kiss him to say, *I like you* in ways I'm still not one hundred percent sure I'm allowed to say for fear it'll ruin everything.

Hawk yawns and leans on me. I rest my head on his and play a lullaby until he falls asleep. Once he's out, I turn off the sound on the machine and continue to play well into the evening. I can do this with the sounds in my head, the rest is muscle memory. Like Philly was a few weeks ago, today was amazing. Above the couch, safely on the wall, is the artwork of the Schuylkill River in the spring. I'll take the other to be framed so the matched set can be set up properly. Hawk is snoring on my shoulder and I don't want to move. If I move, he may fall, and after he took care of me all day, it's my turn to take care of him.

CHAPTER TWENTY-FOUR

I SLIDE MY PHONE out, and my fingers shake against the cold as I punch out a message to Hawk.

You free?

The hour drive home, at night, from a date at the Jersey shore on a Thursday after work, spins my head. Tonight was stupid, and I knew it would be as soon as I agreed to go. The guy wasn't my type, and the only reason I said "yes" is this senseless fear I need to keep moving ahead with first dates to honor the agreement with Hawk.

Sunday scared me. Monday and Tuesday at work I kept re-playing Sunday with Hawk in my head trying to figure out what everything means.

There's been a weird shift between Hawk and I, but I've felt this way before, and then tackled by the blunt truth that how I read people isn't always accurate. Any time I think we're coming close, Hawk and I get shot apart again. Even if I line up every little moment, I'm likely overreading that he likes me as more than friends. I can't let the shift in our relationship due to potentially simple lust, and long-suppressed curiosity, be the end of us.

The date on the boardwalk was simple enough. We met up on the freezing boardwalk for arcade games, skee-ball, and a little healthy competition with the pinging of tiny metal pinballs. A very "New Jersey" date.

In the short time there, a couple had a proposal orgasm, the kind where there is loud groaning intertwined with shrieks of pleasure. They were practically dry humping from joy on the machine next to me. I cringed, but also wished Hawk had been here to see it with me. He'd have congratulated the couple and joined in celebrating. When I looked at my date, who was conventionally handsome, but incredibly full of himself, I knew he wasn't for me. To add a cherry on top of my gut feeling, he took off his scarf in the sweltering arcade, revealing hickey upon hickey. The kinds where it appears a person was experimenting with vacuum attachments. Like the person at home—his wife as it turned out—knew to not trust him, and laid her claim all over him. It's one thing to hook up with someone. Dating is dating. But to have the previous person's mark staring at you in the face is like inviting another person to bed. I'm not interested in married men or ruining relationships.

I excused myself quickly after he stated he had a wife.

I pull up to the condo and gingerly walk up the front steps to find Hawk sitting in the cold with his back against the door. He stands and his hat beard falls into place.

"Shitty night?" He holds out a bag of popcorn, and a box of gummy candies, with a sweet smile. "Thought you might like—"

I step into his warmth with a strong impulse, and press my full body against his, anxious to forget the night. To forget the unavailable moron who got me to drive an hour from home when I could have been here with Hawk, watching a movie and eating popcorn.

There's no hesitation from Hawk as the candy and popcorn drop to the wooden deck. His hands draw me in close, gripping my hips. Wet lips claim the hollow of my throat while he takes my keys and forces the door open with his back, sending us tumbling to the floor.

He yanks up my shirt and tosses it to the side, allowing the breeze to tickle at my neck. I lean up and pull his shirt off, tossing it behind me to land on the couch we almost made it to.

A long-drawn exhale slips out as Hawk's fingers intertwine with mine, and his soft lips trace between my breasts, then down, hovering a whisper above my waistband. Unintentionally, I shift my stomach, trying uselessly to hide from the exposure of laying out on the gray rug in his—*my*—condo. Tufts of thick fabric tickle against my back as my shoulders press deep against the floor, forming a tiny trembling arch mid-spine.

Turning off my head isn't as difficult this time. He's seen—*touched*—this half of me enough times that there's no doubt I'll still be reeling when he leaves. Pushing it further couldn't harm—whatever *this* is.

I push up my upper body. His teeth scrape gently across the side of my hip, sending a jolt of desire through my jeans. He works his way up to my cheek and gives a soft kiss. We pause to exist in this space together. Everything in my brain right now is Hawk. Our lives are tangled together so tightly and I want more of him. I press my hands flat against his chest to roll him onto his back, and study him as I straddle his throbbing bulge.

His eyebrows flick up.

I take a long breath. *Be confident.* A swallow at the hesitation building in my mouth and mind leaves only one option. To trust him to not laugh or call me out for being completely not confident when it comes to my body—or knowing if *anything* I'm doing is right.

I lean over him to close the space between our bodies, my purple bra grazes across his chest and sends a twitch down his stomach. With a moan, I move down his body, kissing a line down the middle of his chest and stop at the top of his pants. I move my hand up, and curl my fingers below the elastic on his tearaway pants and his stomach drops low.

He lets out a shaky groan. With a gentle stroke, I press my lips on the outside of the fabric and glance up.

"This isn't—" His head tilts back and his Adam's apple flashes high as he gasps for air.

My fingers work at the sides of his pants to release the snaps for easier access, and he clamps around my ribs as he pulls himself into a sitting position.

I've done something wrong. He's hesitating.

Hawk draws me forward and wraps his arms around my lower back. He shakes his head.

"Are you sure you want to go a little further?" He hooks his thumbs into the sides of my jeans and kisses my lips.

My heart pounds, and the throbbing between my legs is only increasing. I nod, and that's all he needs before he grips my hips and pulls me in tighter. His lips trace from behind my ear to my collarbone, and my head tilts back, sending my hair into a waterfall. I deepen my straddle and he shifts to push me up into a high kneel over him. His fingers gently tickle my inner thighs to open more space. He slips down the top of my jeans, and I nearly topple over as we try to inelegantly slide them off. I wrestle with the pants and almost knee him trying to get my underwear off. I wince, bracing for him to change his mind thanks to my lack of coordination.

Hawk gives a soft chuckle and runs his fingers down the sides of my thighs. "I've got you, Wildflower."

In so many ways he does. He gently pulls my hips up over his face, and his warm mouth encircles my wetness. My entire spine shoots straight up, and he moves my hands to his head as he leans back.

I can't think. His stubble sweeps against my inner thighs as I grip his hair while he trails his tongue along my flesh. He hovers over the wetness, adding depth and waves of heat to my core.

He slides a finger inside me and then another finding a tempo that makes it near impossible to not collapse down over him.

My eyes flick open before rolling back and closing. I can barely catch my breath, and I don't want to.

Trust him.

My stomach clenches, and I bite down on my tongue to keep from letting my moans echo through the condo with each slide and flick of his well-practiced touch.

After, I grab my shirt and lay it across my chest.

"You know, I've seen those." Hawk points back and forth between my breasts and lets out a laugh.

His pants are no further down than when we'd started, so I roll to my side, press my palm against his chest, and rest my hand on his collar.

Hawk lifts his thumb and traces it across my lips. "These are dangerous." His pupils dilate as he stares back at me.

I pull the shirt higher to cover my face. "Did I do something wrong?" I sputter out.

He tugs down on the shirt to look at me, his head propped up with his hand. "What on earth are you talking about?"

I flick my tongue against the side of my cheek, and shift my legs. His palm slides down my stomach and rests atop the dampness we caused.

"Not at all. I'm savoring learning new things about you." His fingers trace down my center. He slides across the slit, sending a twitch of desire and invitation for reconnection through me. He lifts his eyebrow.

Hawk barely touched me, and all I want is for him to slide his fingers back inside. This is what a long dry-spell gets you. A soaked rug, and the desire to slam my body against his for the rest of the night.

I sit up, and his hand slides off my lap to the floor. I tug my shirt on, skipping the bra, and lay back on the rug.

"You didn't want me to—" I slide my hand over his hardened shaft.

"Oh. No. Don't get the wrong impression. I'm just—we don't need to jump from A to Z. You said kissing, and that led to more than kissing." He winks at me. "I'm following the rules in front of me."

His fingers slip through mine as he pulls away the shield I've created for myself.

"I was more worried I'd—" He looks back up to the ceiling.

Break the tension. Tease him. "Think I was really a hideous monster? Be ruined for all women forever with my sweet ability to go deep on your banana?"

"You're gross." He wraps his arm around my side. "You know, there's a perfectly wonderful couch behind us. Possibly some popcorn on the stairs. You feel like watching a movie, or going another round?" He pokes at the soft spot on my side.

I nod and brush my fingers across his still visible erection.

His body shoots straight up. "That was cruel." He laughs and stands, a tad hunched.

I throw back a devious smile. "I'll grab the popcorn and movie. You know where the bathroom is if you—"

His voice cracks high. "I'm not about to crank it in the bathroom!"

I lift both hands and offer a wink. "Never said that. I figured you had to pee."

His cheeks turn red, and he limps over to the bathroom. "I'm only peeing, I swear."

These baby steps we're taking are hot, but confusing in the moment. Now all I want to do is everything again, but based on history, we're done for tonight outside of light teasing. Tonight's disaster only reinforces my desire to skip dates to get to the part where I hang out with Hawk.

CHAPTER TWENTY-FIVE

FEELING THE SLAM OF the ball is exactly what I need to clear my head right now. Wednesday took forever to arrive. Too bad I'm certainly not stopping any goals tonight unless I can figure out how to ignore my desire for Hawk's fingertips running between my legs, as his lips press into mine.

It's possible I dove into dating too fast. I'm not ready. The arrangement with Hawk is still a little weird and distracting. Who am I to have a hook-up buddy—with Hawk of all people? The more we hang out, the less it feels like we're only hooking up. I'm fooling no one, not even myself. He's more than a hookup buddy.

The theory that it takes almost half the time you were in the relationship to heal from it is mortifying. When do I count from? The moment Nate and I stopped truly being in a relationship, or when I broke up with him? If we go from when the relationship died, I should be fine, and not hesitant to try new things.

If we count from the date when I broke up with him, it'll be another two-and-a-half years until I'll feel like myself again. That can't be right.

I'm breaking a habit, not some deep eternal love.

I trace the ball with the outer edge of my foot before punting it up the field.

Eek. A sharp left trajectory grazes the shoulder of a player on the other team. She whips around, throws a thumbs-up, and blasts the ball back to me with her foot. I'll need to pay attention to her. She's more than accurate. She's got to be their goal poacher. I'll be watching for flashes of blue tie-dyed socks when she ramps up the field.

Snap out of it and focus for forty-five minutes.

I glance in the direction of a banging door, and my stomach drops. Nate and Hawk enter from opposite sides and offer nods. I stare up at the ceiling, which gives me a second to gather myself. Nate's been MIA since New Year's Eve. Charming, there's no one draped over his shoulder. His black peacoat's collar is popped high, and a white polo peeks out from underneath. His worn jeans are clean at the ends—he's been shopping.

"Heads, Keep!" Margaret yells.

A ball whizzes past my nose, and the vibration of the air knocks me back, smacking a clamp over my throat.

She tugs on her collar and jogs over. "Caught you sleeping."

I glare at her with my hands hovering over my nose. I'm a fan of my nose. Small enough, even shape, and sits well on my face without major bangs or bruises from defending the goal.

"Pay attention before someone parks their bus in your box." Liv punches my arm. "Forget him. He's an ass looking for attention. Focus on manning the goal."

Liv and Margaret line up on the goal line and point.

"Check your angles," Liv calls.

I glance over to the bench and Nate's taken a seat next to Hawk, near my bag. With spots blurring my vision and a twist of my gut, I cut an open angle at Margaret. They can have my back.

What if they talk? Nate's not dressed for a game. Did he come to see me play? Is he still angling to "coach" Margaret? She's well out of his league, and waiting for an opportunity to embarrass him on the field for his behavior toward me and her. As fun as it would be to see Mr. I-Coulda-Been-Pro-In-my-Prime get defeated by a former D-1 athlete, leaving the drama off the field is always my preference. She holds the title of friend, ultimate defender, protector, and all around the type of person everyone should have in their life. I'm a jerk for the fire pit, for not encouraging Hawk to go for someone like her.

"Wake up!" Liv yells.

I glance back, and the ball's tucked into the lower net.

"When in the hell?" I mutter under my breath, diving low to pull the ball.

The black beads stick to my face, refusing to fall without a heavy rub. I rub my forehead and squint to hone-in on Liv's next shot.

This is fine. Everything is fine. The person I used to sleep with is now sitting with the person he hates. The person whose mouth makes my legs weak.

I glance at Hawk, and note that he's grinning. He doesn't need to see inside my head to know his finger is hovering over my internal panic button. I shift my attention to the ball, and a wild arc shot wraps around my body while I hurl myself without hesitation to the right.

"Whoop!" The unmistakable boom of Hawk's clapping, loud enough to get all the attention, echoes over the field.

Ignore him.

"Come on, Elin!" Hawk yells.

"Whoop!" Nate's tone is encouraging, happy even. "You've got this! Stretch your arms up!"

I shake my arms out at my sides, trying to rid myself of the hot prickles urging me to go hide in the bathroom. Is he finally here to see me?

The ref blows the whistle, and my team scatters into position for kick-off.

With a quick scan, I size up the other team. Their goalie's busy popping up and down, expending unnecessary energy she'll need against Liv.

"Margaret! Watch her," I call, pointing at the woman with the blue socks.

Margaret nods. "Welcome back to the game, Keep!"

My team barrels up the field, and a loud pop, followed by a fizzle, bursts overhead before the field house goes black as night. Small red squiggles above quickly dissipate, but the emergency lights don't even flicker on. I'm stuck in the goal, with no view of anything, frozen, with my hands above my head.

"Fuck!" Liv screams across the field.

The referee blows a whistle. Like we were all going to keep playing in the pitch black. That's safe.

"How long do we wait?" an unfamiliar voice cuts up the field.

Someone from the other team, maybe?

I tug the collar of my jersey high to cover my ears, and a shiver runs down my back as the last of the heaters hiss out.

"Don't worry your panties, ladies." The cheeky ref says. "I'll check what's happening."

The minute these lights come on, he'll be clothes-lined real fast. How does the ref plan on escaping the black net of doom without a cellphone or light? The stupid teenager from the front desk should fix this. He's got to see on the cameras that the room is black. Unless the power is out there too.

With a deep sigh, I flop to the floor and spread out like a starfish. No one can see me rubbing my face, or feeling the spinning disorientation of the pure blackness.

I turn my head as the turf crunches nearby. One? Two? Maybe three people are headed my way.

"Elin!" Margaret yells.

"Margaret!" I yell back.

"Keep talking!" She giggles.

I'm imagining her bumping into half the team on her way through the vast cavern of the field.

"I can sing for you," I say. "Any preferences?"

"*Big Balls*!" she shouts.

"Ha. I like it."

I stand, reaching my arms out to steady myself, then start humming loudly into the field. Outside of the hook, I flub the rest of the song.

A hand grasps my left hand, and I relax. *Finally.*

A second hand grabs my face.

"My cheek!" Who grabbed my face? "Where do you think my hand is?"

"Oops!" Margaret laughs from her belly and removes her hand.

A hand lands on my shoulder and another takes my open hand.

I stare ahead. There are three hands around me.

Cellphone lights flash on, and Hawk's face glows on the field next to me. He's got the hand on the same side as Margaret, whose nails gently press my shoulder. My heart skips, and I swallow down at the awkward rising in my stomach. It's one thing to date or hook up with people in the league, it happens all the time. But when you're all touching each other at the same time, the comfort level feels off, and a little dirty.

Hawk nods and lets his fingers slip from my hand. I turn left and find Nate. His hand is wrapped around mine as he glares at Hawk.

Something punches my chest from the inside. "Let go, Nate."

The doors leading to the field open wide. I release Nate's hand and follow Margaret out the door.

The hallway fills with chattering teeth, illuminated by a hoard of cellphone flashlights. The teenager is on the phone, unable to control the high pitch of his voice. Emergencies are clearly not his strong suit.

"Good news! We didn't lose!" I shout to Liv.

Liv throws a thumbs-up and cuts through the crowd to join Margaret and I.

"How come no one came to help *me* through the net?" Liv raises an eyebrow.

"Because your butt was already up field." Margaret resets her ponytail and pulls on a jacket.

A tap on my shoulder pulls my attention from Liv and Margaret.

I turn on my heels, offering a full grin only to come face-to-face with Nate. My smile drops.

"Can I get a few minutes with her, ladies?" Nate asks.

I shake my head.

"Of course." Liv's voice drips disgust.

"Where could be more private than in the middle of her team with all these other strangers." Margaret clears her throat. "We'll be right over there."

Rose's hand passes the side of my face, her middle finger at full salute.

"You've got a solid fan club." I cross my arms and drop my gaze to his shiny black shoes. "Those look impossible to play in."

"They keep sliding on this grass." He sighs. "Can we not make a scene?"

I lock into his emotionless gaze. At least it's public. He won't be able to wiggle out of bullshit.

"Speak." I shrug and fold my arms. "They're going to close back in if you aren't fast."

A quick glance over my shoulder reassures me that the entire team is there, staring at us, complete with Hawk crossing his eyes at Nate. Stifling the rising snicker relaxes my stomach.

"I thought we could talk, or maybe get a few minutes to figure out next steps." His tone is tender and sweet.

I shift my weight back to add a little distance between us and run my tongue over my teeth.

"Do you want to go sit in my car?" He rubs the sides of his arms.

"I'm good. I have to see what's happening here first." We've argued in the car enough times, I'm not doing it again.

"You have to watch the other player's hips when they're shooting and react immediately," he says. "You'll stop so many more shots."

I stare at him. His face is tight, serious.

He stands up straight, and scans the far wall.

"I know you too well. You aren't here to coach me." I shake my head. "What do you want?"

He stares at me, shifting back and forth without meeting my gaze. "You still have stuff at my house."

"I'll be there next week to get it out," I say flatly.

The twisting anger in my stomach isn't helping.

"Why are you even here?" I ask. "Why mess me up when I'm trying to play?"

He shakes his head with a half-smile, and flicks back his hair. "I didn't know you were playing. I'm meeting my new captain."

"New team?" I ask.

Not a shocker that he landed one, but so soon. Most of the teams here don't want to deal with his mouth, or are pissed about what's already flown out.

"Green." He sucks back his upper lip and bites down, flashing his lower teeth.

I nod. That's Hawk's team, and I guarantee my best friend is not going to be okay with being back on a team with Nate. He's going to flip out when they bench him or he doesn't get to play goal. Green has the only goalie in the league better than him. If it weren't for a new team, I doubt he'd have ever asked me about the last of my stuff at his house. I'm not even surprised he's here to take care of the love of his life—soccer.

A glance past Nate's shoulder and Hawk is clutching a purple jersey. That's the switch. They've swapped teams. What on earth did Hawk do to get purple to agree to the trade? Unless, maybe, Thad as captain initiated the trade.

Claps and cheers cut through the room, and the field lights up as if the sun itself rose to let us back on the grass. But our opponents have already left. Those of us who remain filter from the lobby, back out onto the field and the sidelines.

Nate shoulders his way through the crowd to his new friends and leans against the wall. He can sulk and stare all he wants, this is his own doing.

I glance over at Hawk. He's too busy eyeing up Nate to grab his attention.

The lights might be back on, but the heaters aren't. Wisps of condensation cloud around me as I stride across the field to grab my bag. Rose is changing out of her Bees jersey for a lime green sweater when I reach the bench, and Liv is busy stacking loose balls on the ledge to help clear the narrow walkway between the wall and the net.

Rose bends over, flicks her hair down over head, then swoops it into a slick ponytail. "When do you get the proofs back from your photoshoot? I was thinking of getting some done too." She whips her head back up, and narrowly misses hitting Liv's eye with her hair.

Liv takes a step back and blinks hard.

Ugh. My lips twitch and I dig my heel into the grass. Liv chucks a ball at me and it slides right between my palms with a smack.

"Nice!" Rose winces and sprays the side of her shin with a pain reliever.

Liv looks me up and down, and I glance away to avoid eye contact.

"Oh! She's got the proofs and hasn't shared." Liv clicks her tongue. "Gimmie."

Rose and Liv flank my arms and tap my shoulders like impatient toddlers.

"This body isn't meant to be in front of a camera."

"Oh, shut up." Rose makes grabby hands. "All bodies are meant to be in front of a camera."

"Come on, phone out. Let's go." Liv reaches for my bag.

I grab my phone from my deep brown corduroy jacket and flick over to my email. If I don't, these two will raid my belongings until they get the pictures.

"I'm jiggly, and my face looks funny." I click open the email and scrunch my face, bracing for the laughs.

"Hey now, these are gorgeous." Liv grabs the phone from my hand.

Rose nods and wrestles Liv for the phone until they settle on holding it between them.

"Why don't you like them?" Rose looks at me and uses two fingers to zoom in on a photo. "They highlight all the sexy."

"And the pretty." Liv nods and waves her hand in my general direction.

"My face—"

"Is gorgeous, shut up." Liv turns the screen toward me.

I'm staring back at myself in black and white, with full makeup on and my hair set back from my face. My eyes look enormous, and I'm smiling. Smiling isn't smoldering, it isn't sexy or sassy, it's ... wait, I'm smiling. I swallow back my urge to be defiant, and hold out my hand for the phone.

"Not until you admit you're smokin' in these." Rose pushes the phone to Liv.

I shake my head.

"Team vote?" Liv yells.

I shake my head and lower my jaw. "Give me that before half the field sees."

Liv pouts and shakes her head. Rose puts her hand on the side of the phone, shielding the photo from any prying voyeurs walking past the net.

"I think this should be where we do a team photo." Rose nods at me. "How amazing would it be to have pinup soccer pictures instead of a boring traditional team picture?"

"No. Are you trying to ping boners across the league? There's no way something like that would stay quiet."

Liv flicks a finger across the screen and gives a thumbs-up. I glance over and my stomach twists—it's the original image of the morphed photo from the art show. Only now it's me in the raw, without the artistic flair, and instead of headless like the artwork, I'm staring down the camera.

"Stop being harsh on yourself." Rose nods at my folded arms. "You need a confidence boost. Can I send them to the team to kick you?"

I shake my head. "What if they share them?"

Rose laughs. "We don't have assholes on this team."

"They'd have to deal with me." Liv lets out a short growl and a giggle.

Given the giant image of myself over the fireplace at the condo the pictures will get seen eventually. I relent my initial inclination to say no and offer a thumbs-up to Rose.

"I need a verbal yes so Liv doesn't have permission to murder me."

"Ugh. Bees only." I lower my hand and pull a hoodie over my jersey.

Rose grabs the phone from Liv and hits buttons. "There, all done and sent to Bees-Field."

I drop my bag to the floor with my stomach. "Bees-field?"

Rose nods. "The group email."

I shake my head and want to vomit everywhere as phones ping across the field. Liv squints at me and hands a bottle of water to stop my choking.

"The entire league. You emailed the entire league. The Bumble Bees, is B-Bees." I whisper out and stare at my phone. It's too late for a recall message. Every single member of each league has the proofs from the photo shoot.

I glance up at Rose who has tears welling and a cherry-red face. "I'm no longer a Bee, am I?" Her nervous chuckle cuts at my heart.

"Now you're a legendary Bee, as is Elin." Liv laughs and glances around the field.

A group of referees are grinning. The doorway feels much farther than twenty yards. Rose grabs my hand, and Liv cuts a line up the side of the net to the door.

"You're always a Bee." I squeeze her hand.

Tears pull forward as I fight the urge to collapse to the floor, and cry or laugh at how stupid I was to say okay. When we hit the hallway, we pass Hawk and Nate, both staring at their phones. There are worse things in life than this, but this isn't good.

Nate looks horrified.

Hawk glances up, sees me, and mouths: "*Oh shit.*"

I nod. Oh shit, is right. With sheer focus, I exit the building and pour myself into the car. I'll be "naked goalie" or "ball boobs" for the rest of my time here.

CHAPTER TWENTY-SIX

I'VE RECEIVED NO LESS than eight hundred texts, and emails, covering everything from girl power to date requests after the pictures were sent a week and a half ago. The league officials even emailed, requesting we limit group sends to *actual* announcements—though they appreciated the images, and ruled they were "not porn." AKA, the Bees can stay in the league.

The hallway of the indoor soccer field house now boasts a headless version of me, in poster-size, squeezing a ball between my gloves with definition I didn't know I had in my biceps. Thankfully, the commotion around the images slowed over the past few days, and I can almost laugh about it. Almost.

Rose is buying my beer for the next month, because it's the only way I could convince her to not quit the team from embarrassment. She wanted to make up for what she'd done. Accidents happen. Half-naked, well-intentioned accidents happen, and it's stupid to be mad at someone you care about.

The bright lights of the sports bar, and the clamor of cheers, mix with tense pauses as replays of the Saturday morning European matches play on the big screens. Everyone does their best to avoid score alerts or updates on their phones so they can enjoy the games, as if they're live. Grease and spicy buffalo sauce scent the air, sending a low rumble across my stomach. Pitchers of beer slosh across tables as fists pound on the high tops, challenging the referees who can't hear us.

Fried cheese, pickles, chicken—essentially fried everything—sit in half decimated baskets in the center of our table. Rose raises her arm for the server, and signals for two more pitchers of watery beer.

"I saw the strangest thing after the last match." Ariana shoves a jalapeño popper into her mouth, and looks off to the television. "I could've sworn I saw Elin and Hawk making out in Hawk's car like horny teenagers. Then I thought, that couldn't be right."

My mouth is dry, and the silver napkin holder is suddenly the only thing I can focus on. Don't look anyone in the eye. I grab for my water to fight the desert forming in my throat.

"Funny, I heard a rumor they were cozy on the couch at the café from one of the guys in the men's league." The head of the beer fizzles in Liv's fresh pint. "Drink and talk. Spill it all." She wags her eyebrows at me and fills my beer.

There's no answering this well. "Hawk and I—" Should've been more careful. I shove a mozzarella stick in my mouth and chew slowly.

"Are finally dating?" Rose holds an open palm out to Liv. "Pay up."

Liv shoots a shush finger in front of her lips. "All she said was Hawk and I. Let her finish."

"Let *him* finish." Ariana takes a slurping sip from the top of her beer. "Mmm."

Ariana! She's supposed to be on my side. Quiet, sweet, and not egging on their nonsense. I shoot her a playful glance of death.

"We aren't dating. He's dated half the team, including Margaret." If we were, this conversation wouldn't twist in my throat as I waited for judgment.

"Margaret is fine. I saw her making out with the new British ref." Liv taps on the table.

He's cute, good job Margaret. "We have an arrangement." I twist in my chair to face the screen, and lock my feet around the pole—because it feels like it's the only thing holding me above ground.

"Arrangement? Like, if you two aren't married in the next few years, you get hitched and have beautiful babies?" Rose slides the basket of fries across the metallic tabletop.

"Or arrangement like he bounces her until her eyes roll back?" Liv asks in a matter-of-fact tone, shoving a fry into her mouth. "What?" She scans the table as our mouths gape.

"We aren't—we've mainly—you know." I dunk two fingers deep into my beer and then slide them around the rim. My cheeks grow hot and thinking through what he and I have done which is much more than a quick dunk in both my imagination and in real life. I wish he were at the table with us, tracing circles on the inside of my palm and laughing with everyone.

"What the hell even is that? Cause if that's your vagina there are exercises." Liv tilts her head, leans across the table, and looks down. "You poor, poor dear." She blows a kiss, sits back, and twists the seat back and forth. "She's crying out for help and an orgasm."

Rose leans across my lap with her hand to her ear. "I can hear her."

Tinges of embarrassment spark across my chest, and the door is too far away to be subtle.

"Lube me. Lube me," Rose says through the side of her mouth.

Why do I hang out with these people? I stare down at my distorted reflection on the table.

Ariana taps my chin up. "If you don't tell us, we're going to keep guessing. She needs to be happy. You *need* a happy vagina."

I squint at the far table. A group of men in hockey jerseys are passing a pitcher, engrossed in their own little world. I should switch tables. What are the chances they'll be talking about sliding past the goal line?

These women are my loves, and I know better than to not answer. They'll dig, or bluntly ask Hawk. If I answer, they'll pretend they know nothing and wander around in smug bliss.

I clear my throat and glance at the bubbles rising in the pitcher. "The agreement is we do everything except—well, one specific type of penetration."

"Penetration. That's what the kids are calling it these days." Liv places both hands on the table. She straightens her back, and pulls in a deep breath. "I have a series of questions."

I play with the napkin on the table. "I may or may not have answers."

"Has he eaten your papaya?" she asks.

My eyebrows pull together. "Yes. Also, I'll say, I've never had my papaya eaten so well." Truth be told, the way his tongue flicks from strong to delicate makes me want to not be sitting here right now, and to replay last night with him again. I shift in my seat as the memory of his touch sends electricity between my thighs.

"Ooh. Damn." Rose throws her napkin on the table. "My papaya is equally edible." She pulls her cell from her pocket and clicks away on it.

"Booty call?" I ask.

Rose nods and bites on the tip of her thumb, staring at the black screen.

Liv stretches her fingers out on the table. "I'm the one asking the questions here."

"Yes, ma'am." I sit up straight and lock eyes with her.

Liv focuses on my mouth. "Have you enjoyed his milkshake?"

Really? I'm not answering this. I stare at her.

"You heard me. Have you made him spurt, either in your mouth, or on you in some way?" she asks, shaking the salt shaker for additional emphasis.

Rose's jaw drops. "Elin, you don't have to—"

I nod before she can finish, a flush working its way across my face. I'd never have the balls to ask these questions, and I don't know why I'm answering.

"So you've penetrated." Liv bites into a french fry, grinning. "Is he good at least? We all know he's well-practiced."

There it is. Everyone knows how much practice he's had, and how little variety I've had. In fairness, maybe the variety he's had likely helps him navigate this arrangement better than my brain.

I tap my heel. "It works. Plus, he knows what he's doing." Thick vibrations of desire pass down my sides. "We don't take the irrevocable step. That's the agreement. The final step is irrevocable. I only do that with people I'm in a relationship with."

Rose checks her still-dark phone and frowns. "Friends with benefits are nice."

So I'm learning. "I was, uh, out of practice, after the last relationship. I didn't want to go on a date and then, like sexually explode all over someone who barely knows me."

"Sexually explode?" Liv raises an eyebrow, and waves at a man at the table next to us who's turned to check out our table. "I'd say there are many men who wouldn't mind a sexual explosion."

That's not what I want, or how I date. Prudish of me maybe, but I'm not a prude. I want courting, and *then* sex. I want all the things in combination.

Ariana looks me up and down. "And Hawk wins with the orgasm your date was hoping for."

I shrug and lean back, taking a swig of warm, hoppy beer. "I suppose we both win."

Rose taps on the dark screen of her phone and crinkles her upper lip. "Does he date too?"

I nod. "We both go on dates, but neither of us can hook up on the dates."

"The real question is, why won't you let him shove his thingy in your hooha? You don't *have* to be in a relationship to let him slide it in." Ariana makes a crude circle with her fingers and slides a spoon back and forth through the gap. "None of us are going to judge you for wanting it."

I shake my head and pull the mug of beer to my lips. Two more gulps and I know she's still peering at me.

"Have you at least done *that* for him?" Her voice cackles high with a laugh.

I swallow wrong, and cough as the beer shoots out of my nose. I slam the mug down on the table, and Rose pats my back. Blinking away the tears looking to settle my sinuses only encourages their smirks. They have no cares about the match on the TV.

"If she's not a swallower, she's not a swallower. That's perfectly acceptable."

"Will someone say *penis* already?" Liv dunks the fried pickle deep in the ranch sauce and takes a hard bite. "Damn, that's good." She flicks her jet-black hair back, and checks out the guys at the table next to us—who have ceased their conversation, and are busy staring at us.

I let out a frustrated sigh, and wink. "He doesn't need to use his penis. Trust me."

He agreed to this, and no penis to vagina penetration wasn't a solo decision. There are a million other ways to have sex, or be intimate. Sure we've had a few close calls, but each time we've gotten too close, he's respected the boundary and we've worked it out.

I glance over at the hockey table with a fry half in my mouth and one of the men waves back at me.

Liv elbows my side. "Isn't that—"

"Thad." Nervous flutters in my stomach work to send the "stay there, don't come here" vibes.

Nope. He's getting up, and locking his damn gorgeous focus on me, and heading over here with the wrong type of jersey on. I need a mute button to silence this table, or a delete option so I can remove myself from the room.

"Hello, sir." Liv extends her hand, with her fingers pointed down for a weird handshake that seems more like she wants him to kiss an imaginary ring.

"What's your *position* again?" Her fingers clutch the outside of the pitcher, and she refills *my* glass.

He raises an eyebrow. Liv, please, not right now.

"I float, but mainly I'm a striker." He waves at his table, then tucks his hands in his pockets.

"You're saying you play the field." Liv shakes her head. "Tsk, tsk. Same. I'm good at pushing the balls up, or keeping them away from her."

I bite down on my lip to avoid a burst of nervous laughter. She's enjoying herself a little too much.

Thad rubs the bridge of his nose, and he tilts his head slightly. "Did you just—man." He shakes his head and a tint of pink fills in his cheeks. "I have to go through you to talk to her?"

"Yup," Ariana chimes in, narrowing her gaze on his rosy face.

"Did I interrupt something?" Thad's voice cracks and his Adam's apple bobs on a long swallow.

I gesture to the empty seat at the next table. "You can join, but they are—"

"Wonderful women who will interrogate you." Rose cuts in.

Relentless, and geared up to swallow a man whole was my initial thought, but Rose is right. Wonderful. They are wonderful.

Awkward discomfort kneads at my chest while Thad pulls over a chair, scraping it across the checkered tiles before sliding it between Rose and I.

Please don't say anything about the email and pictures.

He gestures to the server for a beer, and shifts awkwardly in his seat. "I have four sisters. You can't rattle me."

Mistake. Large mistake, sir. Do not challenge the lionesses.

"One condition though." He points to his table. "We get equal footing."

"Your condition is a table of half-decent looking men?" Ariana holds up seven fingers and swishes her shoulders back and forth.

Could have been worse. She could've averaged them out to a five. Maybe she was counting Thad in the group.

Liv and Rose peek back and nod. "Agreed."

What happened to no men? This beautiful, vulgar table is infiltrated.

"Nice to see you off the pitch." One of the men waltzes over to the table and pulls up a chair between Liv and I.

I force a smile and offer a half nod.

Crap. Another member of Nate's old team. I cough to clear the thickening in my throat. He saw me throw the shoes. He saw everything. Then again, so did Thad.

A third and fourth chair from his table fill in on either side of Ariana.

"I need answers." Liv points at each of the men "What is a proper amount of time to see someone before you can glide your puck in their net?"

Thad drops his chin down. "Doesn't it depend on who was in the net first? Or if she wants your puck in her net?"

"Personally, I'd take Thad's puck in my net any day," one of his friends chimes in. "I've heard he's a good puck."

Ariana snorts loudly and covers her nose. Rapid blinks pull down tears from her red face while she fights a laugh. "Agree. Who doesn't like a good puck?"

"Ariana!" I rub my eyebrows as dread weighs on my chest. This group likes to push boundaries pretty far.

"Okay. So now what happens if you've done all the work of lining up the shot, and you're ready to slap it in, but then say some guy—" Liv squeezes the shoulder of the man next to her, and steals his beer. "—Skates through and slots it in the five-hole between your goalie's legs. You're left there with a stick all ready to go, and yet, nothing to do but whiff your wood."

"Who on earth would slide through and steal a shot like that? Besides, Thad's gonna make the shot every time." A higher-than-expected voice squeaks from the giant man on the other side of me.

He's way too big for that mousy voice. Don't laugh. Sip the beer and don't spill.

Rose shakes her head. "Oh sweetie. No. The question is—never mind."

The mousy voiced man's eyebrows contort with confusion, and he glances at Thad.

They were fully warned.

"Pardon the more direct language, but that'd be a dick move." Thad shakes his head. "You don't go for someone else's shot at dating a person. If you've decided then you've been working on it, planning. You've made the determination that you want that person, and don't want to pass it. Someone sliding in at the last second is like a slide tackle plowing through your legs from behind. That's why there are penalties in sports. The penalty in relationships is no one can see the internal wounds left behind. Now imagine though, you think you're the one planning, wooing, falling for someone and then realize they may have their attention on a different person altogether. Someone you respect and like. Then you take a step back because the timing isn't right." A tinge of raw pain escapes his timber. "But what do I know? I can't even keep my sports analogies straight." The pink's gone from his cheeks and he gulps down his beer.

Ariana leans over to Liv and taps the table.

"There are balls and penalties in hockey?" Ariana whispers loudly.

Liv shakes her head. "No balls in hockey."

I wave to the server for three more pitchers of beer.

"If you were interested though, in oh say, borrowing a goalie from another team," Liv presses her focus on Thad. "To be clear, this person is by all known accounts a free agent. They can go wherever they choose. How long do you wait before making a move?"

Thad clears his throat and laughs. "Hypothetically?"

His arm rests across the back of my seat. I straighten and lean in to grab for the frothy amber pitcher. This is a good time to disappear.

"Hypothetically." Liv raises an eyebrow. "Goalies, like her, are in high demand. So how long do you wait? Is it when the rubbers on someone else's cleats are grazing the back of your leg? Or when someone's about to swoop through to take a shot?"

Thad keeps his gaze on Liv and nods. "Fair question. I think it depends on if the goalie is ready for a new team. Maybe she's not ready yet."

"Or maybe she needs a few solid shots in the net," Rose says around the edges of her cup. "Speaking of nailing shots. How many balls have you sunk?"

"Oh, snap." Ariana slams two fingers in her beer, knocking it over.

Thank you, Ariana! Beer spills all over the round table and cascades off the side. Rose and the men grab for napkins and pull the liquid into a tiny beer pool in the middle of the table.

Thad's fingers brush the side of my arm, and I look straight into his eyes. My chest turns to twisted mush.

He clears his throat loudly. "Fun fact. I need a new goalie."

"Weird that you picked up an extra striker instead. Seems like the opposite of what you need." I grab for a new napkin to move my arm away. "I can't imagine Nate went down quietly."

Thad shrugs. "Hawk said he'd step in, but I may give it a shot for a while." He moves his arm from the back of the chair and props his elbows on the table, glancing over at the television.

Is this still about soccer?

Ariana's squeaky laugh cuts across the table. She's engrossed in conversation with Rose, and the two gentlemen on either side of her, while the man to my other side chats up Liv.

Thad takes a sip off the head of his beer. "Relax, I'm not asking ... yet."

I steal a sip of my beer and glance at the dimple in his cheek. He's so clean cut compared to Hawk. Not a hair out of place, and a much gentler way about himself in public. Thad's all the right parts intelligent, sweet, and enough muscle to get lost in. If Hawk was here, he'd work to help tease, or push the men flirting with my friends, to make a move.

Hawk's body fits with mine. We're the right height and form to mold together. With Thad, I'd be making out with his chest, or he'd be doing some kind of weird bending action to make it work.

I take a final fast swallow of beer, check the time on my now fuzzy phone, and send a quick message while the table settles up.

CHAPTER TWENTY-SEVEN

EARLY HEAD-BUTTS FROM CURIE woke Hawk and I up on the couch as the sun rose. I don't remember texting him to come over after the bar last night, but the evidence is in my phone, and I can still feel his morning stubble on my cheek despite the empty cushion next to me. Now, I have to get through Sunday dinner and pretend as though I don't want his arms around my waist while I lean on him.

At the Occhipinti house, we'll start eating by three o'clock—four at the latest—after a ton of appetizers get devoured. Hopefully, he snuck in before his mom started cooking early this morning. If she was strong enough, she started prepping yesterday.

The stack of cars at the base of the driveway is at least five deep. A small hand waves at me from the other side of the glass on the front door, and points down to the garage entrance. One bottle of chilled wine won't make a dent in the amount of recycling in the can later. Showing up empty-handed is rude.

A deep cleansing breath of roasted garlic, and marinating sauce, makes my mouth water.

I step into the den. The fire's going, and a pile of Hawk's cousins stare vacantly at their phones on the couch where we've ... been. My cheeks grow warm.

"Where's Hawk?" I ask.

The eldest points straight above his head and gives a half wave. That's more dialogue than I was expecting from the seventeen-year-old. Poor kid. He'd probably be happier out with his friends, or a girlfriend, than being here for another Sunday dinner.

At the top of the stairs, the long table is set, and lit votive candles cast shadows among the peach-tinted water goblets. A mess of Hawk's aunts and uncles sit with coffee, parked in front of the bay window, keeping tabs on the street.

"We see you, Elin." His Aunt Gloria raises her cup to her lips, pressing another layer of thick red paint to the porcelain. "You look good. You've lost weight."

I shake my head and smile at her. "Nah. No weight lost, but I appreciate the compliment." How is that ever a compliment?

"You're standing taller. Something's different," she says. "Oh, you got a new man, maybe?"

I bite the insides of my cheeks and glance back at the kitchen, searching for an escape route. "Eh. I'm excited to see you." I turn and kiss her deep stripe of rose blush.

"You need a strong fellow." Aunt Gloria's husband chimes in with his grizzly voice.

"You're taken." I gesture to Gloria, her lacquer lipstick catching the glow of the table lamp. "And I'm pretty sure I can't cook half as well as your wife."

"She only keeps me for my body." He huffs, and flashes a single gold tooth through his crooked grin.

Aunt Gloria raises her cup. "I made him round, so I'm keeping him."

"I'm buying you that dress." He turns to his wife. "You'd look damn good in that dress, like Elin."

"Eggplant isn't my color." She whines. "I've got too much olive in my skin. But it looks good against those shades of pink in hers."

Uh, hello. Someone come get me. My chest flutters.

Stop it, nerves. Today's no different from any other Sunday dinner. No one here knows how Hawk's strong hands made me tremble under his chest, or how loudly my tongue made him moan last night. Nor that I'd like to grab his hand and go hide in a closet to make out and feel him against my skin.

"Sorry to break up the party, but I need extra hands in the kitchen." Hawk moves past me and refills their coffee cups. "Besides, I let her around you too long and she'll decide I'm not cool anymore."

My fingers adjust on the neck of the bottle and press it against the flutter of the ribbon across my dress.

Hawk nods and marches me into the kitchen. He sucks in his lower lip while his eyes linger on my cleavage. With a shake of his head, he drapes an apron over me, wrapping his arms around my waist to tie it in the back.

A wooden spoon bangs against the sides of the too-tall metal pot of simmering sauce. Hawk jerks back, and rubs his hands across his stomach.

His mom raises an eyebrow at the two of us. "You two do that in front of all them, and they'll have questions." His mom throws more basil into the pot, and clinks the lid back on.

I walk over and give her a tiny hug.

"You've got sauce duty." She presents the spoon to me, and sits in the gunmetal chair in the corner. "Hawk, don't forget—"

"Taken care of," he says.

He stomps twice on the floor and yells down the staircase. "Come up and help."

No response. The phones have likely dragged his little cousins into their network, so they no longer have to even flick their fingers across the screen.

"Not going to work." Mrs. Occhipinti gestures out the sliding glass doors to the back deck.

His cousins are busy kicking a ball around the backyard and knocking each other down.

"Man, they are brutal." Hawk looks me over. "How are you going to kick with us if you're dressed like that?"

"You leave her alone." Gloria's voice chimes through from the living room, waking his grandmother. "If I had cleavage like that still I'd wear it too!"

"If your boobs still looked like that, my stomach would get more exercise." His uncle chimes back.

Great. Never, ever, ever wearing this dress again.

Hawk's grandmother clears her throat and gestures for me to keep stirring. She'll be back asleep at the table in no time, and still claim she's made the best sauce. Mrs. Occhipinti comes over, pulls my hair off my neck, and swoops it into a low bun. In one motion she loosens the yellow silk scarf from her neck and wraps it across the front of my hair, beneath the bun.

Hawk's jaw drops, and he pokes at the lemons on the apron. "You look like one of them," he gestures with his head at his family. "But, better."

I pull the spoon up from the sauce, and it drips across the linoleum floor as I aim it at him. "I'm borrowing clothes after dinner so I can take you down." Judge me for a dress? He knows better.

He puts his two hands up and grins. "You can borrow clothes, but we both know I'm going to win."

"She's gonna destroy you," his grandmother says.

"See! Nonnina's on my side." I put a free hand on my hip, cleaning drips of sauce from my palm. "Nonnina's on my team."

"Rude! Nonnina has to be on my team because of house rules."

His grandmother belly-laughs, shaking at the celebration plates leaning high against the wall. "Nonnina needs a drink."

Agreed Nonnina. Agreed. She couldn't kick a ball if she tried, but Hawk would never try to steal it from her while she sits, buried under blankets in a fabric chair.

Hawk pours his grandmother a large glass of red wine and places it close to the edge of the table. Her hand shakes as she lifts it, sending the liquid sloshing back and forth. With a large sip, her lips smack apart and she glides the glass to sit atop the floral plastic tablecloth.

The refrigerator door sucks open, and Hawk rummages, pulling dishes out for the table. His mom pulls tinfoil and plastic covers off one at a time, checking the clock every few minutes and muttering under her breath. Two more of Hawk's uncles pour in through the front door, bags with liquor store stamps in hand, and grin like they've already drunk a few bottles on the walk over.

The shorter of the two reaches in front of Nonnina, and her fingers snatch away the plate of rice balls.

"Ma!" he cries. "Not in front of the lady."

Keep the eye-roll in and keep stirring.

The shorter uncle pushes a high stool over for me to sit on. Perfect timing really, as my arm is going to fall off if I keep stirring and standing over this heat.

"Elin!" The taller one comes in, cramming the already-tight kitchen, and kisses my cheeks. "I hear you're a free agent now."

I shoot a glare at Hawk.

"If you can look like that, and cook like that, how come no one's scooped you up?" He snags a green olive and pops it into his mouth. "I know some guys if you want."

I stare at him.

"Don't scare her off with your idiot friends. I like her right here." Nonnina winks at me. She chucks an olive, sending it smacking against his cheek. "See what you made me do, now we have one less olive."

I giggle. This oversized teddy-bear of a grown man makes Hawk's frame seem so small. His uncle wipes the wet mark from his face, walks to Nonnina, and kisses her forehead to apologize.

"Meh, I'm not everyone's cup of tea. A little too feisty."

"Feisty is a requirement in this family." He pats Nonnina's back.

Hawk's face reaches full flush as he grinds a pile of fresh ginger. "She can kick a wicked ball with her instep too."

"Oof." His uncle puts his hands up and contorts his face.

Hawk's mom flaps her arms wide and shoos her brothers from the kitchen.

Yes, please end this awkward interrogation into my dating life before any potential of spillage into the evolution of—there's no real word for what we are. At least they didn't lead with asking what happened with Nate.

The shorter one sends me a wink and a thumbs-up. I glance at Hawk's flushed cheeks and drop the spoon deep into the sauce cauldron. *Shit.*

If I put my hand in there to fish it out, my flesh will boil as part of dinner.

My hands flail to the sides, skating past Hawk and his mother to grab a new spoon. The four of us, plus Curie, in the kitchen is tight, but by no means horrible. After a few minutes we get into a rhythm, circling one another, keeping dinner moving forward.

His mother bangs the side of the pot, still wearing her shining wedding ring like a newlywed, instead of a widow. She snaps behind her and wiggles her fingers. I pull the apron from my shoulders, and pass it back. With a lift of my bell sleeves, speckles of flour from the fresh pasta flutter to the floor.

"In guys! Come on!" The grizzly voice from the living room tries to wrangle the kids.

"Shush. They've got at least another half hour." Mrs. Occhipinti nods her head back and stares down at the empty trays.

Hawk's aunt grunts getting up from her chair, and shoos Hawk and I out of the kitchen so she can help.

"Coming in after the grunt work's done?" Hawk kisses her cheek. "Yell when you need us."

He slides out of the kitchen and nods for me to follow. I grab his leather coat off the couch and slide it on while we stare out the window to watch for a break in the action.

"Race?" I ask.

His fingers linger on the slider, ready to cut through the backyard once the ball crosses the second set of double trees.

"One. Two." He leans forward and blocks the path through the door with his shoulder. "Three!"

Hawk barrels out the door toward the trees, with Curie on his heels, anxious to play, biting at the air in excitement.

I chase after both, but can't catch up to Curie. What am I doing in a dress? I know better, but it's Sunday dinner, which requires dressing in something more than a jersey.

The sides swish up as I sprint to beat Hawk to the ball. His baby cousin passes to me, and I trap it off my chest, dropping it to the ground. With a high flick into the air, the ball bangs off the branch above, redirecting it up-field. A fast look up, and eight sets of eyes are watching the group of us dart up and down the field. Too far in one direction and it'll be atop the pool. Too far in the other direction and the next house over will own it. Hawk flies up my side, sliding the ball from my feet with ease, and sends a quick pass to the five-year-old.

The young girl laughs and trips over the too-big-for-her ball, shoving it up the field. Curie's muscular frame barrels through, and the child falls hard to the ground.

She bursts out laughing. "Ref! Curie fouled! Where's my red?" She flops on the ground, rolling back and forth, caking dirt into her once-white tights.

I crouch beside her.

"Girlfriend, you are one tough cookie," I say. "I love the commitment."

"That was a red!" She jumps up and stomps her foot. "Total foul!"

Curie trots over with the ball, and noses it back to the child.

Hawk jogs over and lifts the child high in the air while she spreads her arms wide.

"I win!" she yells. "I beat Hawk!"

"Grr! No more watching pro sports for you." He lifts her higher and carries her on his back to the house.

The grass crunches under my feet as the rest of us follow suit.

The warm crackle of the lit fire and smell of fresh rolls rumble my stomach. I toss his coat on the bed and race back up the stairs to join everyone at the dinner table. Hawk pulls the young girl's seat out from next to me and pushes her down a place.

"Rude!" she says.

He takes the empty seat. "You can't be trusted after your flop."

Mrs. Occhipinti finishes putting out the last of the standard dishes on the table, and everything in the room is intoxicating. Her strides slow as she places serving tongs in the salad. She leans on the rickety brown chairs and counts the dishes on the table.

She's breathing too heavy. Too much pushing and not enough asking for help. She's as stubborn as Hawk.

I stand up and gesture to the empty wing chair at the head of the table. "Sit. Put me to work."

"I've got it. Two things, I swear." She waves me to sit back in my seat.

I look at Hawk and mouth: "*Help her.*"

She returns with a large tray of wild salmon and scans across the table for a place to rest it.

There's no space on the table for the fish.

"Shove those glasses down?" she asks.

She places the salmon between Hawk's uncle and I. Is *this* what I've been smelling? My mouth waters and I study the ingredients on the tray. It doesn't match the rest of the table.

Fish sure, but not salmon with everything else, and certainly not with cranberry.

I furrow my eyebrows and glance over to his mother, who's busy taking large gulps of water. She's pale and exhausted.

"Don't look at me like that," she says. "Hawk did it."

I admire the fish.

The bigger uncle points to the plate. "Talèèèèèèèèèèèèèèè! If you're gonna make salmon when Elin's here, she's gotta come every Sunday. No more of this once and a while, maybe every other year nonsense." The bigger uncle grabs for a heaping serving of the fresh casarecce pasta for his plate.

My cheeks heat. I've always tried my best to give Hawk his space on Sundays. I know how important his family is to him, and while I know I can come to any dinner without question, these dinners have always felt super intimate. Loud, and intimate. His uncle drops the largest heap of pasta I've ever had on my plate, enough for at least four people.

"She doesn't eat pork." Hawk shoves a bite of roll in his mouth.

The grizzly uncle's mouth drops. "But she was cooking—"

"I'll cook anything for you." I throw him a wink. "Just don't like pork."

His wife pipes in. "He shouldn't be eating all the cheese, but he does. That's not quite the same, but the salmon is gorgeous. You outdid yourself."

Mrs. Occhipinti takes another sip of water and gestures with a big smile to her son. "Hawk made it. I did the last touches when they were all trying to ruin their clothes outside."

Hawk did what? "I'd have been fine with the sides."

"How rude is it if we invite you and don't have food you can eat?" she says.

Hawk's uncle cuts a chunk of the salmon and puts it over the pasta. "She can't have the meatballs or sausage then."

"No. No meatballs, sausage, or sauce. This is seriously—" I stare at the table in a daze. "Thank you."

Hawk flicks my arm under the table. I turn, look at him square in the eyes, and he flicks his eyebrows up.

"*Saluti*," his mother raises her crystal glass to the table.

"*Saluti*." Everyone echoes.

The energy at the table is warm and inviting. The white votive candles flicker in low mercury glass holders atop the pristine white tablecloth. Warm laughter cuts across the table as knives and forks tap against the intricate hand-painted yellow and white stoneware plates.

I take a big bite of salad and fish. Cranberry, ginger, mustard—it's savory and earthy—and damn, he's good.

Chapter Twenty-Eight

"I can't believe I let you take me to a scary movie." I link my arm around Hawk's elbow on the way back to the car. "If anything jumps out, I'm shoving you to protect me."

He glances down at our arms, kisses my cheek, and pulls me closer. His gaze shifts to the car.

I squeeze his arm with mine and cuddle into him. "You're too quiet. Did the movie freak you out?" My stomach gurgles at us. More of the salmon from last weekend would be perfect right now.

"I need to know what we are," Hawk says.

The daring choice of words shoots through my heart. He set the boundaries. We hang out, hook up, and nothing else changes.

"You said friends." I shake my head.

"Did I though?" He puts his hands in his pocket and takes a step back. "It isn't occasional anymore. It hasn't been for a while. We spend nights together, days on days. When I'm not with you, I'm hoping to catch a bit of your scent off my sheets, or the fragrance your soap leaves in the shower. I switched my stupid toothpaste so when I inhale, I can almost taste your kisses during work."

Is he saying—am I passed out on the ground? I pinch my free hand. Nope, and ouch. I'm awake, and this is happening. We're apart on some nights. I check my phone for texts from him when I'm bored and thumb through pictures of us when I need a distraction. This was us before too, though.

"We go hangout, make out, hook up, and when you go out on a date, I sit at home and hope everyone who asks you out is a schmuck." Hawk blinks several times in a row. "But I don't want them to be a schmuck, because I don't want to lose you to a dick."

"You do the same. You're dating the same way I am." I point back and forth between us. "This arrangement was your idea. I agreed because it made sense, and well—" No one else is him.

"It doesn't make sense." He looks down at his feet. "What's the point in hooking up with your best friend, when you only want to be with them. That's more than a best friend. I *love* my best friend, always have. I don't ever want to go back to where I'm left on the sidelines, or riding a bench."

Tears well. The words are right, but also so late. If we try and fail, we lose each other for good. Risking losing him isn't something I'm prepared for. Yet, at some point, and I don't know when, we intertwined in a different way. His eyes are filled with hope. The same hope I've gone back and forth with in my head, over and over, for a decade, assuming it was my imagination, or my heart interpreting false signs. Losing him is too big of a risk. The spinning in my head isn't clearing after the confession that he sees me as more than a best friend, or that the way he uses love is more than how he says he loves Christmas, or sweet maple candies.

"For the first time in over ten years, neither of us is in a relationship with someone else." Hawk's deep voice cracks. "But something happened here. We evolved." He clears his throat.

"That's not fair. This whole conversation isn't fair."

"So, you don't want me?" He looks up, frowning. "You don't want this. You want to keep going out with losers, and I get to see you cry."

Now you want to date me? "I made the mistake of liking you before. And, every time I did, you ended up in a relationship with someone else."

"Ugh!" His eyebrows raise. "You are infuriating, and I want to kiss you. I want to be with you. But—"

"When did we meet Hawk?"

"In college. You were the nerdy high schooler taking college courses. You hung out with what's-his-face."

"The other high school kid in our class. Yeah." What was his name? Mark? John? Keith? Shoot, did he have a name? Focus. "You were still cute then Hawk."

"You brought me a cotton candy milkshake."

"Right. You drove me home from class and kissed me." Which then ended the Mark, John, Keith potential. Not my finest moment.

He runs his hand over his face and shakes his head. "That's ancient history. Besides, I was nineteen and stupid."

"Right. So at seventeen, you noticed me. But then what happened between seventeen and thirty-one? We hung out, and leaned on each other. I fell in deep like with you as a teenager, and in love with you as an adult." The car dips as I lean on the door. "I don't want to be your pick because you've run out of options. I'm not a last resort, or an easy choice."

"That's not fair. I didn't know you then."

"You're sticking with we met in college?"

"Yeah. I'll admit it was weird to know you were in high school. When we weren't in high school anymore, you were in a college relationship. Then I was in a few relationships. We were both constantly in and out of relationships and the timing was always shit."

"Wrong. We first met on a combined class trip to the sushi restaurant. I was a sophomore, and you were a cute senior." My voice cracks as I talk faster. "And before that, two of our friends dated. I knew who you were long before you knew me."

"I would *not* be checking out a sophomore." There's an unsteadiness in his tone, and his words aren't the confident Hawk I know.

My throat is tightening, fighting against the urge to dump all the emotional fear at once. "Right. You see me when it's convenient, because I'm still some seventeen-year-old to you. Or, you need someone to introduce you to friends. I'm the left-over that's fun to hang out with, but not date." Where did this even come from? I should kiss him and jump forward into this. Stop pushing him away. "I need to think. I'm not saying no, but I need to think."

"What is there to think about? You love me back, you admitted it. Our timing is always garbage with each other, but come on, you know you feel it. This is love. This is real."

A sting penetrates my chest. "I love you, but ..."

I broke the third rule of our idiotic agreement long before it was created, and worked hard to bury the reality of us. There's no way to compartmentalize our friendship anymore, because we evolved into more than best friends long before the fire pit. We evolved, yet everything still feels the same except now we kiss. The way I love him isn't different. He's Hawk, and I won't survive the rejection if, or when, he changes his mind.

"There shouldn't be a "but" in "I love you." Look, I thought some gesture like we both get teary in the movies was a smart idea." He lifts his hand toward mine, the hurt stitched in the tightness of his voice and across his face. "I'm sorry. I-I thought we were finally on the same page."

Air smacks from my lungs. I grab his hand and draw him in for a hug. A warm, soft, comforting hug that I don't want to end because I *do* love him.

He leans back and brushes loose hair from my face and lets out a deep sigh. "How about we take two weeks, with no contact, and figure out if this is another misread of chemicals?" His smile quivers as he lifts my chin with his finger.

I nod. Two weeks. I can do two weeks without messaging, or talking to him, or seeing him. We've done this plenty of times before we shifted into a different type of "we" or "us."

I kiss his cheek and close my eyes to stop tears from falling as he takes a step back. Two weeks is going to be awful.

"Man, I should have planned this better." He opens the car door and gestures to the passenger seat. "It's just … I had to put it out there."

"I know, Hawk." He's braver than me. I've choked on those same words so many times.

Two weeks of no Hawk sounds awful.

Chapter Twenty-Nine

THE ORIGINAL PLAN BEFORE last week's break with Hawk was to gather my stuff from Nate's, and then hang out with Hawk to decompress. But now, the bubble of awkward sitting between the last texts we sent to each other yesterday isn't helping me concentrate on the task at hand. He wished me luck today, added a picture of Curie wearing his beard hat, and sent the confirmation information for the van. I said thanks, added a smiley face, and that was it. I stared at my phone for two hours waiting for any type of next message, but nothing came. So much for waiting two weeks to message each other. To be fair, I punched out messages every day to send him and never did. Mainly they said, *I miss you.*

Pack and leave. Feelings and head spins about Hawk must wait while I deal with this other mess. Nate's house smells of menthol and a sweaty gym bag, no different from when I lived here.

"You aren't supposed to be here." I turn as the light in the room shifts, and the damp creak in the wood calls for attention. "Please don't make this difficult."

Nate slicks his hair back, and a fresh scar with surgery staples down the length of his arm stares back at me.

"What happened?" I swallow at the sharp lump seizing real estate in my throat.

"Grocery shopping." He laughs and wipes at his red eyes. "I slipped on the ice and reached for the cart. There was a pop followed by a rip."

My fingers grab at my bicep. Ouch. It's not like I loathe him, though in fairness, he'd deserve it. He's a lost kid who can't grow up, and wants what he wants. I want to not be second to soccer, or the whole world. Doesn't everyone want to be someone's primary, not secondary? In his case, I don't rate enough to exist anywhere near the top of the list. I want a partner who treats me like Hawk. *Damn it Hawk*—not right now.

As much as Nate and I avoided this moment together, cleaning out my stuff is long overdue. The thorn and dread settling in my stomach each time I look for a piece of clothing or a photo, knowing it's here, can finally evaporate. The lump, the tears, all of it can release us from each other as soon as the last box is in the truck. There are no glimmers of hope like last time. The break we took after our first year together proved pointless, because we were so used to being with each other; we never took a true break from hanging out.

"Can you rethink this?" Tears pool in his eyes.

No. He'd erased me before I broke up with him. The pictures of us are long gone, replaced with his teammates, or family. Even his cat is in a heart-shaped frame that once held a picture of us from a baseball game. A tiny moment in time he shuts away with the close of the door.

"I'm not changing my mind." I wipe the tear dangling off his chin with my thumb. "You moved on, and so did I."

His head jerks up and his eyes narrow. "Thad?" He spits fire at the name.

I shake my head. "No, he's a friend. I do have those."

The wood in the doorway splinters under his white knuckles.

"Charming." How on earth did I accumulate so many books? More than half these boxes are super heavy books.

He closes the door behind him and we're in the room together. His back slides down the wall and he pouts with his knees against his cheeks.

If ever I need a tiny reminder of what I wasn't missing, here it is.

The back of his head bangs against the door. "It's only a matter of time before someone from the league asks you out." His lips part and he rubs at his jaw.

I toss the last few things into the plastic box and close the lid. With that arm, he's not going to be much help.

"If not Thad, then is it Hawk? Promise me you aren't thinking about sleeping with that idiot." Nate's stare works to bore a hole in me. "He's been waiting to swoop in forever." The tears stop, and his tone switches to a stern warning. "All he wants is to fuck you, then he'll toss you aside like everyone else. You're his unattainable fuck. Once he has it, he'll have no need for you. The chase is over."

Ignore him. He's being an idiot who knows nothing. "With my stuff out, you'll be able to move on too." If I sniff heavy enough, there's likely evidence someone's already been in his bed.

He can keep the sheets.

A bang on the front door sends my shoulders up past my ears. Shit. Totally forgot.

He gets up and opens the door. "Hawk?" His tone spits the name harsh from his lips. *Jealousy? He's not allowed to be jealous.*

"Liv," I say.

When we booked the moving truck, Hawk begged to come and help me so he could throw raspberries at Nate while we packed. If Liv hadn't stepped in with an offer to help, Hawk would've been here before me with the truck, packing it, singing, and dancing around Nate.

I glance at the lack of new text messages on my screen. Though, with the incident at the movies, maybe he's changed his mind. Subtle and Hawk aren't joinable partners in a sentence.

When I picked up the truck this morning, Hawk had already paid for it, as well as bonuses for straps, boxes, blankets, and tape. He may be upset, but he definitely doesn't want me coming back here. The giant truck took out a branch or two no one will miss as it barely fit to turn around the cul-de-sac. A big van would've sufficed, but the truck screams to the entire neighborhood, I'm leaving.

Trying to back out of the rental lot, I smacked a Mercedes. Thank goodness for insurance and a really understanding owner who gladly took my information.

Nate opens the door, and Liv's standing on the other side of the screen blowing a bubble with a blanket in hand.

"Let's go woman!" She taps Nate on his chest on her way to the spare bedroom. "Thanks prick."

Her membership in the *I Hate Nate Fan Club* is showing its full peacock feathers.

"What'd I do to you?" Nate pulls a box from the room, and hoists it on his chest with a grimace.

"Don't fuck with my keeper." She grabs a bag and chucks it on top of a packed box.

Hers is bigger, heavier, and she knows as well as I do it'll piss him off. She flings her hair back, tucks her chin, and walks effortlessly to the truck. Nate's arm twitches in sync with the grimaces scrolling across his face.

"We can handle this if you want to rest." I nod to the couch.

He shakes his head. "I helped you move in." The box drops with an echoing thud into the back of the truck. "I'll help you move out."

"So gentlemanly." Liv hooks her arm through mine and pulls me back into the house. "What's going?"

"Anything she wants is hers." Nate heaves an exhausted sigh.

The cocky has left the building. He's back to the man I kicked around with on the soccer field after his fiancée left. Deflated. At least this time I know it was his own doing. To think I'd taken his side when she left him, without considering he'd been the ass of the relationship. Fooled by his charm.

Now his charm gets to pound it with a woman over thirty years his senior. That's a lot of well-worn vagina to contend with for someone with such a fragile ego. One little flick and her cards will crumble while he's out flirting with anyone who likes his toothy, falsely innocent smile.

I glance across the house. He can keep it. Keep the couch, the curtains, the chair. I don't need some other woman's juices in the condo, or to picture his testicles rubbing at the fabric as he whacks-off between matches. I need a clean slate.

"This room, minus the desk set. The one box in the kitchen with my plates and glasses, and my table." That's it. For the giant van outside, that's all that's going in.

I look at his eyes as they wander nostalgically around the room. Like he ever came in here other than to grab his checkbook.

Liv and I lift the dresser. If I move again, I'm calling the entire team to come help. I'm pouring sweat, yet freezing at the same time. He never turns the damn heat on in here.

I shove the last box deep into the back of the truck and turn. Nate's standing next to the back gate, his hand covering his mouth, tears pouring down his face.

"All yours." I walk over to wrap my arms around him for a last hug.

Heaps of tears fall on my shirt, and his shoulders quiver as he loses control. "Don't be a smiley face in Hawk's calendar." His hands gently squeeze my back.

The fear of the smiley face is a cheap shot. It's not like I don't know what the symbols on Hawk's calendar mean. I've figured most of it out, but stopped looking at the calendar when he dated Margaret. I didn't want to know if either of them were freaky, nor if I'm rated like poor service in a coffee bar.

I take a step back on the gravel driveway and drop the house key in his breast pocket.

"You're an insecure asshole." He's right though, Hawk doesn't commit.

Hell, Margaret is amazing, and they didn't last. When in the last ten years has he had anything long term? Hawk wouldn't have given me the ultimatum simply to get in my pants. He's not like that with me. My chest tightens with the weight of dread.

The back gate of the truck slams down, and with a swift click of the lock, that's it.

I walk to the driver's seat and hike myself into the truck. Liv leaps into the passenger seat, waving at him with one particular finger through the open window.

"Did he cry like this, and lash out a lot?" she asks.

I nod. The truck throws into reverse, and with too slight of a tap on the pedal takes out the wooden fence at the end of his driveway.

Nate crosses his hands over his stomach, doubling over in a laugh.

I'm good at leaving impressions. Now I'll forever be the ex-girlfriend who took out his fence.

Damn it, Nate's in my head. "Shit. Shit. Shit." I throw the truck into "drive" and hit the gas. We wind up the narrow side street between two lakes, and pull out onto the main road to unload everything at the condo.

CHAPTER THIRTY

NOT A SINGLE TEXT from Hawk since I moved out of Nate's. It's been a week, but I refuse to be the one to cave. The lack of interaction from Hawk proves Nate right.

Tonight is a bad idea. I should text and postpone. Too bad the clear night sky creates an all-too-perfect backdrop.

I glance over at the door, cross my hands atop the table, and correct my posture. Slumped shoulders won't help fake confidence. Junk posture, however, keeps my stomach from rumbling too loudly. I'm starving.

Hawk is on my mind and tonight I'd like to go for ten minutes without wanting to message him. I pull my phone out to zero new messages.

A tap on my shoulder sends me spinning around.

"Hey, am I the only one who wants to dive headfirst into a loaf of bread right now?" Thad asks.

I chuckle. Kismet drew us here tonight, well, kismet and he saw the same baking class flier at the café and called to see if I'd be interested in coming. His voice was sweet and excited on the phone—apparently, he and the owner grew up playing hockey together. Like a gentleman, he asked with three day's notice.

Maybe if Hawk had texted, or called, I'd have said no, but Thad makes sense to hang out with.

"Did I miss anything?" He fingers push his hair back in a single sweep, and then he wraps an apron around his waist.

The numbing guilt in my shoulders dissipates as we set our ingredients out on the table. The bakery's prepared for five other pairs to join the lesson, yet only four of the stations are taken. Warm, fresh baked goodness wafts up, and my stomach gargles in return. I need something to shove in my mouth and chew to distract me.

The instructor walks in, tying his leather apron around his jeans and plaid shirt. His loose blue and purple man-bun fastens his hair back and highlights the contours of his face.

"Welcome to the World of Artisan Bread everyone!" His voice is supportive. I'd have come with Liv if his picture was on the bulletin board at the café with the poster.

I shouldn't be nervous, but it feels weird to be out with Thad. Today's goal is to not quietly ruin this for him. My mess isn't anything he caused. The amount of glass bowls and ingredients on the white quartz countertop is a recipe for klutz disaster. It's comforting to realize the students at other stations have worried faces like mine.

Thad lifts a jar of sesame seeds and glances at the recipe. "This looks complicated." His lips move as he scans the directions. "I'm lost already." He gulps.

The instructor stands in the center of the room, his melodious voice booming out. "Now, no one runs away without giving this a shot." His hand points at the tables and he checks the tiny clipboard he's hidden in the front pocket of his apron.

"I'm going to ruin this bread," Thad says, shaking his head. "I'm a better cook than a baker."

"If you mean stabbing cheese with wooden swords, yes, you are truly a master." I chuckle. "You're not the King of Bread?" He's polite. And so damn sweet for thinking of what I'd like to do.

"I buy from the King of Bread." He nods to the instructor. "It's nice skipping the pitch tonight." A twitch crosses his grin.

Mr. Calm is nervous? I lean in to share the recipe with him, scrolling down what rubber doom I'm about to help create.

The door chimes, and when I glance up my stomach drops. Every nerve in my body fires and I can't stop staring at Hawk and Margaret as they walk to the empty station. Are they on a date, or here as friends? Not that it should matter, it doesn't matter.

Warm fingers settle on my shoulder, and I look over to the sweetness in Thad's eyes. The jolt on my nerves holds fast, yet his fingertips glide down my arm, and send warmth to combat the desire to duck under the table to avoid Hawk.

"This is great!" He waves over Hawk and Margaret. "Are you okay? Your face is pale." Thad gestures to a stool.

"I'm fine." I'm not fine.

Two arms fling around me from behind and tip my feet up off the floor.

"Keep!" Margaret's cheerful voice calls out from behind me. "This is going to be so much fun!"

Thad laughs and extends his arms to offer Margaret a hug. My racing heart no longer seems to know how to beat correctly. I want to go hide in the bathroom for the next several hours. Long enough to make sure everyone leaves, and I can sneak some bread in my coat on the way out the door.

"Oh, this is great!" Margaret claps her hands in front of her chest. "I'm going to ask if that table will switch so we can work together!"

"Great!" I say, smiling through gritted teeth. *Fucking great.*

Margaret skips to the table in front of us and motions in circles with her fingers. I turn to glance at Thad, just in time to witness him and Hawk slapping hands, sideways, like they do on the field. I'd half believe Hawk was fine if he weren't tugging at his ear.

"Wow, so you and Elin?" Hawk rubs at the back of his neck. Wrinkles form on his forehead, and his cheeks twitch. "Makes sense." He nods three times too many.

"I figured we might as well *try* hanging out *off* the pitch." Thad sits on the stool and relaxes his posture, evening the height difference with Hawk.

"Okay, everyone! Let's take our tables." Saved by the instructor. I'd kiss him if it were appropriate.

My phone vibrates on the table. The H for Hawk glows on my screen, and a tiny envelope appears.

Nope. Not checking that right now. I want to click it open. I want to ask him a flood of questions, but I'd also like to not embarrass myself right now. If I click it open and it is anything other than, "I've missed you," getting through bread making will be impossible. The growing tornado of emotions in me is not making breathing easy. The reality is our chance to be together may never come. I rub at the pain in my chest.

Margaret turns, and waves her fingers in my direction.

"Okay, who's ready to make bread?" The instructor holds a beautifully braided loaf up over his head like a trophy. He brings it down and bites a chunk from the end as he throws a thumbs-up.

My mouth goes dry. "Is that what we're making?"

"New plan. I sneak out of the classroom. Buy a loaf from the front, and we switch it at the end of the lesson and pretend it's ours." Thad nods. "Deal?"

"No deal." I'm not leaving if Hawk's not. "Let's make this beautiful disaster."

"What kind did you get?" Margaret's voice not so subtly whispers to us. "We have some kind of cardamom ring bread."

My mouth waters, and I just want to sit in the corner alone and eat everything. "What do we have?"

"Honey whole wheat challah," Thad mouths, shaking his head.

I raise my hand and flick a glance at the instructor.

"Yes. You, you with your hand up," he says joyously and claps his hands together. "You have a question on step one?"

"Our breads aren't the same," I say.

He nods. "Of course not." His hands slide into the front pocket of his apron. "Three and three. We have three different loaves going, so people can trade later."

I glance at the recipe, and Thad's finger is on the bottom instruction. *Be sure to triple the recipe so your classmates can trade with you.*

"Wait. Another question." I raise my hand.

Hawk chuckles in front of me.

"People are going to eat what I make?"

The instructor nods with a big grin. "Yup. So, make it edible." His grin slides to a sly smirk.

"Step 1: Activate the yeast with warm water." Thad's eyebrows furrow and tiny creases form on his forehead.

"We've got this." I grab for the jar of yeast, and a warm cup of water to mix the two together. Two minutes of suspended agony pass and tiny bubbles form on the surface. "Activated!"

"Step 2: Mix with one cup bread flour into a thin batter." He scoops the flour and scrapes a precision perfect cup.

I bite my lower lip and read the next instructions as a puff of flour blooms over Hawk and Margaret. The cloud of powder tickles my nose. The instructor runs to their table and offers dry rags to help wipe down their station. Hawk taps the toe of his boot against the ground. He's not happy. He wants to look slick and smooth in front of everyone, and he's already spilling things.

Margaret turns to me and sticks her tongue out from her flour covered face. I wave her over and wipe the rest from her hair. She even makes being covered in flour not embarrassing.

"Thanks, Keep," Margaret says, and rushes back to her station.

I shrug and measure the honey, vegetable oil, eggs, and salt.

"Hey, may I ask you a personal question?" Thad stares ahead at Hawk, who is busily wrestling another flour bag.

"Personal questions?" I give his arm a soft nudge. "Sure."

"How do you know Hawk?" he asks with a softer tone, and wipes down each tool after I've used it. "I know it's more than soccer, but—"

I drop the measuring cup on the ground with a loud clank. *Subtle.*

"We went to high school and college together." Hawk chimes in. "Elin was a nerdy underclassman in music and chemistry."

"That's great. I don't talk to many people I went to high school with at this point." He wipes the table.

"Phone," Hawk mouths.

I shake my head and flip my phone upside down on the table.

"Okay, beat these in." I pass Thad leveled cups of flour.

I can't make Hawk or Margaret disappear, so this bread needs to be perfect.

Thad folds back the sleeves of his crisp, baby blue button-down shirt to the midpoint of his toned biceps. His muscular arms distract my gaze while he mixes the ingredients.

Stop staring at his hockey arms.

"I'm sorry, I'm hogging the bowl." He extends the bowl to me, and his warmth erases the rest of the room.

"I think it's stiff enough." The instructor's voice cuts in.

I raise my eyebrow at the instructor and turn back to Thad. "Uh, next step?" My voice squeaks out the question as I stifle a laugh.

A handful of flour drifts gently from Thad's well-manicured hands to the cutting board on the table. I bite my lower lip. Halfway through using my goalie arms to punch down the dough, I peek up as a second large puff of flour rises. Hawk and Margaret chuckle, covered for a second time in a fine white dust. I then punch at the dough, popping out every air pocket possible.

Hawk is fun to be around, Margaret's lucky there.

The instructor waltzes over and peeks under the towel.

I press the cloth back down. "No peeking up the skirt."

The instructor laughs and shrugs. "Do you have enough room in this bowl?"

Everything is mapped out. "I think so."

The instructor brushes the back of his fingers against his beard and steps over to the center of the room. "I can see some of you finished with your first steps. Please feel free to come to the back of the room to sample items."

My stomach knots. Socializing is fine, but not with Hawk. Not when each time I see his eyes, the internal tickles I don't want traipse through my body. Not when I'm out with Thad.

Margaret rushes over, tugging me to the small side table covered in fresh cheeses, oils, and gorgeous breads, while bits of flour fall from her hair. I glance over my shoulder to Thad, and my heart rises to my throat. Thad is helping Hawk dust his station, and they're chatting. No amount of straining will help me hear what they're talking about.

"He's cute," Margaret says with a mouth full of brie. "Look at you snagging the man of all men in the league."

He really is. "Mmm, hmm." Keeping focused on the cheeses, anything to not peek back at the two of them, is a struggle. "You and Hawk, huh?"

She grins. "Should I stab one of these pieces of brie for Thad?"

I laugh a little too much. "I think he'd appreciate the purple sword option."

Hawk and Thad join us at the table cutting our conversation short. The beaming happiness from my best friend's face offers reassurance that traces of our friendship may still exist.

"Man, I could use some carbs right about now." Hawk's voice cracks on the last word.

Thad is cute, coy, and totally ruined, thanks to Hawk.

"Check your phone," Hawk hums low next to my ear, and slides my phone into my hand.

I rub at the warm flush that takes over my neck and click the message open.

From Hawk: *Can we go outside to talk?*

A steady exhale releases the constriction in my lungs. Every ounce of me wants to, but this is not the time or place for the conversation we need to have. I can't potentially go outside and end up once again crying on Thad.

To Hawk: *Not right now.*

He shakes his head and looks straight up.

"Do you have any non-soccer Elin stories?" Thad asks Hawk.

Hawk's grin is less than reassuring. "So many. I can give you tips on her likes and dislikes. Anything you want to know—dating history, allergies, embarrassing moments." He wags his eyebrows at me.

Margaret elbows his ribs.

"How about a top one?" Thad asks.

Margaret leans her elbows on the high table. "A nice one."

"That's tricky. I know her well enough to know she hates being embarrassed, so I have to be careful." Hawk clicks his tongue. His gaze falls to mine, and sunshine cuts through his expression.

There's no telling what will fly from his mouth, and the best I can do is swallow to brace myself for whatever comes.

"Summer before senior year. I went with my friends to the quirky musicians' café in town, figuring we could listen to free live music. We get there, and instead of open mic night, there's some prodigy blues piano player." His lips press together while he studies my face.

I fidget with the studs in my ear and glance down at the table.

"The place was filled. This tiny girl in a gray corduroy jacket, and wide leg jeans with a frizzy bun, was going to town on the piano. Three old dudes were playing instruments with her. Turned out they were performing at the arts center later and wanted to jam." He sucks in a deep breath. "She pulled a mic over to her face and this almost siren tone came out, drawing the room in even more. Her forehead was sweat drenched from slamming the keys and heat from the thick crowd, but she practically made the whole building glow. The confidence of this girl—she had one of those smiles where you know the person is in their element. Anyway, that's the first time I saw Wildflower, but we didn't become friends until years later." He shrugs, and grabs for a piece of oat bread.

The air swipes at the bruise on my heart from how we left the movie theater. I don't remember him there.

I glance at Margaret to gauge her response, and I can practically hear the "aww."

"She disappeared faster than Cinderella after her set, and I didn't get a chance to introduce myself." Hawk sips on water.

Margaret tilts her head to the side and gestures at my hands. "And you do what? Why the hell are you risking your talented fingers in goal?"

"I have the best defender in the league to help keep my hands safe." I shake my head and laugh. "And I barely play anymore."

A bell goes off, and an eternity seems to pass. I clap my hands and run to check on our dough—the dough cascading over the top of the glass bowl onto the counter, and pulling the tea towel down with it. This monstrosity is alive, and multiplying at a rate similar to the spread of heaviness taking over my body. Thanks, Hawk.

The instructor comes over, places his elbows on the table, and leans forward with his head in his hands. "How's it going?" he asks, teasing us. "The dough has a great rise."

"The yeast works!" Thad gives two thumbs-up at his old teammate.

How is he still smiling? All I do is mess things up. "We created volcanic challah."

I look at the instructor and pout.

He pouts back. "How many batches did you make?" His tone is patient, and not as teasing as I expected.

Thad and I each hold up three fingers.

"And how many bowls were on the table for rising?" The instructor points to the far corner.

"I thought they were for mixing," I laugh-snort, and tears pool in the corner of my eyes. "Can it be fixed?"

"For an additional three hundred bucks." The instructor smirks. "Kidding. Look at the next step." He pulls the paper in front of us.

"Punch, split, and rise them separately?" Thad's tone is soothing.

"You got it!" The instructor winks and leaves us to fix our dough.

"Don't look so sad, it's only bread." Thad's fingers gently tap the bottom of my chin. "I'd love to hear you play sometime."

The flutters vigorously flapping in my body aren't from him. Each tickle at my nerves calls my attention to Hawk, and fighting myself to not look at him isn't easy. Hawk dropped a bomb in my lap about the café, where we've been hundreds of times together, and is going about his business like the world is normal. How did I not know this story?

"I only do it for fun once in a while at the café now." And not in *years*.

My pulse settles on a more relaxed rhythm, appropriate for pulling apart bread and getting back on track. Thad and I each take a chunk of and break it down three more times until we have nine ropes, ready to fix our mess.

He looks, glances between my hands and his ropes. "Um."

I stop pinching the base of the dough. "You okay?"

"I don't know how to do this." He flops the ropes over one another on the table like a child swinging double-dutch.

"Give me your hands." I pinch the three ropes, placing the bundle center on the table in front of him. With a gentle assist I move his hands, helping them braid over, then under the bread. "See you've got it!"

When our hands cross one another, no little flits or sparks burst in my core.

"Way better." He says in a deep bellow. "We could've cooked my bread snakes."

"True, I hear bread snakes and bread coils are all the rage right now." I pat flour off my apron and grab the next rope to braid it. "You're a trendsetter."

He brushes his thumb across my hand and stares at my face with parted lips. A metal bowl clamors on the floor, shooting a jolt of shock through my body. I glance down at the eggs splattered across the tile. Margaret and Hawk busily gather their supplies and wipe the floor.

Hawk is clearing his throat and won't look in my direction.

Thad grabs a rag and walks over to help clean.

"Thanks, we finished." Hawk waves him off and drops the last egg shell into the metal bowl.

Hawk's grin is enough for me to know he's probably as off-balance as I am. I walk over to the far counter and grab two cups of beer to bring back to the station.

"How's your bread?" I ask Margaret. "Or did it all fall?"

"Hawk turned and bumped into the bowl." She takes a swig of the beer. "Our bread is under the towels, rising like yours." She drops her tone to a whisper. "Is this "friends," or a date?"

I shrug and shake my head.

Hawk grabs Margaret's hand and tugs her back to their workstation.

I lean on my elbows, and glance over at Thad.

"You know, he's a really great guy." He stares up ahead at Hawk. "He's not an asshat like your ex."

"I thought I was the only one who called my ex an asshat."

"Nah, there's a bunch of us." Thad hands me a glass and offers cheers. "To friends."

"To good friends." I toast. At least it's mutual. Or, I'm so blatantly distracted that I've been rude this whole time and need to apologize.

The timer goes off, and I slip the loaves into the oven.

Thad is successful, handsome, smart, and so many things on my list. He's perfect. But we don't click the way that makes my heart want to plow ahead. Not like with Hawk.

Thad flicks a folded paper, and bangs it off the back of Hawk's shoulder. I snicker as Hawk swings around to face us with a raised eyebrow. Thad laughs, and waves them to our station.

"Join us for a drink while it bakes." Thad gestures them over.

"This is my kind of baking," Margaret says as she tugs Hawk to the table.

"Cheers." Hawk tips his cup at each of us and stares at me while taking a long sip.

The catch of our eyes is enough to send sparks from my chest down my arms.

The spark I once figured out how to suppress won't go away. *Damn it, Hawk.*

CHAPTER THIRTY-ONE

SLEEP LAST NIGHT WASN'T an option. Each time I tried, all I saw was the gaze from Hawk straight into my soul while Margaret and Thad were at the table.

My thumb hovers over the text Hawk sent yesterday. He wants to talk. I shake my head at the well of emotion building in my throat, and click the screen dark. Maybe tomorrow, definitely tomorrow.

The cool air helps clear my head. Being in the condo is too much, and air will surely help align my thoughts in the right direction. The key is walking in the opposite direction of Hawk's house, thus limiting the possibility of another run-in today. My shoulders round to combat the gust of wind, but fail to protect my exposed ears.

The shimmer of a daith piercing catches my eye as a woman brushes against me on her walk. My fingers rise to gently brush at the half-sun piercing snuggled safely in the innermost fold of the cartilage in *my* ear. I offer a smile to no one, and glance down while I make my way up the sidewalk. I giggle and blink back tears.

After months of Hawk incessantly asking to get pierced together, he was a jumble of hyper, fun, silly, and stupid. If he was getting his industrial, I was getting my daith. His cocky-self put both feet up in the second chair like he owned the place. Hands behind his head, feet tapping, and a deep grin, while my eyes shot wide at the fat needle.

There was no real reason for me to squirm after nine—ten—piercings. It was only one more, but this one felt different. The piercing said to help ease anxiety was the first one to make me almost crawl from the chair and escape out a window.

Hawk was a champ. He sat in the chair next to me, pointed at his ear, and said to do his first. Now, every time I see an industrial bar in someone's ear, I picture him in the seat with his jaw clenched, pretending to not feel any pain.

When the lanky piercer swiveled his chair to turn and face Hawk with the 14-gauge needle, the blood just about left his face. The last bit of peach disappeared from his skin when the tip of the needle pressed against his ear. His fingers clenched the armrests, and a small twitch grew in the corner of his mouth as tears rolled down his face.

"Courage tears," he called them. Courage tears that took him out of soccer for a few months while it healed. A needed break for both of us from the turf, and well before I'd met Nate. Before I could personally confirm that Hawk has a penis. Despite the stories from teammates, in my head I forced my image of him to be as smooth as a Ken doll. Now I know he's far from smooth, and he's harboring a misplaced unicorn horn eager for constant attention. That his tongue is golden, and his fingers can send a yearning shiver down my spine with a touch softer than air.

The daith was a breeze.

A pop, flinch, and a wink from the piercer, and my new toy to touch or fidget with was in. Did it help my anxiousness? Well, not really, but Hawk says it's my tell. I touch the metal when I'm nervous or anxious.

A chilly breeze winds through the metal in my ears, and I pull my jacket up higher as I open the door to the condo.

His condo. I'm stuck, I signed the lease. Stupid lease was my idea, and I'm locked in.

Writing out checks will be fun. *Hi, remember me, I'm the one you wanted a two-week break from—and I ran the fuck away. Here's your rent.* Month, after month, after month for the next year.

I throw my jacket on the empty dining table, and the metal buttons clack against the wood. If I'm going to be here, more art is going on these walls.

I can do this without texting him for input. Those are things to do with a boyfriend, not a friend. A month ago, had I asked him to help, he'd have said, sure let's go look. We'd have ended up naked in the bed, against the desk, the empty wall in the hallway, or on the floor driving one another to the edge with our hands and mouths. The wall would remain bare.

A deep sigh rolls from my mouth and echoes back. Hang a picture, it's a simple task. I reach into the hall closet and remove a large wrapped picture. I tear open the brown packing paper to expose a large four-by-four wooden frame, and the punch of the imaginary ball against my stomach is almost enough to knock me over.

The piece is a single frame with a series of photos, illustrating from the final buzzer, to a full tackle pileup with my team where I'm buried at the bottom. Our record of one-in-seven, and each of our autographs on a stained napkin with *Go Bumble Bees* sketched across it from the bar. No one knows how we won that one. I'm convinced the ref had a thing for Erika. Either way, the next morning was a blur, and Hawk convinced my aunt to create these extraordinary messes for the entire team. Enough drinks meant we were autographing everything after one victory. Hawk was kindly our designated driver, and helped ensure there were no videos of our stupidity. Every positive memory in recent history I have, he's there. He makes it a point to be there. Not just the positive ones, there have been enough times I've soaked his shirt through with tears from heartbreaks or any other of life's stresses.

What am I doing? I can't put it in the bedroom because then I'll have Rose and the other ladies shouting at me if I ever get a moment of passion. The last thing I need is to picture Margaret cheering me in mid-moment of bliss. "Good job, Keep! Reset!" Seems a bit much.

What am I going to do? To bring someone here after a date is out of the question, because it's a betrayal to Hawk. With a yearlong lease, am I damned to a year of batteries?

Realistically, dates are horrid and Hawk is more fun. I walk the image to the hallway and place it on the floor.

There's a solution.

I pull the handle back, and with a flick of the wrist, bang a nail into the wall. I cringe and look around the empty room. The nail slides through the wall and leaves a pencil sized hole.

Great, now I must cover it. I lift another nail and more gently tap it into a sweat stain the cheap paint holds tight to. The frame of happiness lifts and covers the mess I've made.

With a heavy sigh, I slide down the wall and place my head on my knees. We had an agreement. Why do I feel like absolute garbage and want to text him, or play tic-tac-toe on the phone where it's always a stalemate?

Ugh. Numb. My hands, feet, and brain are worse than when I left Nate. Like someone's been punting balls at me non-stop, and you can see the hexagonal lines bruised into my chest.

None of this was supposed to end in hurt. We. Had. An. Agreement.

An agreement I screwed up by not admitting to him immediately the third rule was never going to work. That I've loved him for longer than he thinks. Bread baking with Thad did not help anything.

I knew after Hawk and I kissed at the firepit there'd be no patching of our relationship which is why I didn't stay. Before that even, he'd always been the person I can't lose in my life. My best friend and biggest cheerleader through everything. I set down the hammer and move to the piano. The keys are cool beneath my fingers. I play and cry onto the keys, there's no shutting off the loneliness of not having my best friend.

CHAPTER THIRTY-TWO

BEERS ALL AROUND FOR another awful, yet wonderful, eight-week season, albeit a week early. A perfect excuse to forget about the pictures to be hung, and to move forward with a table with some of my favorite people. Saturday early bird food and drinks, for a bunch of women in their late twenties to early forties, has its advantages. We can take our time, be loud, and when they talk about sex for hours my face will only be partially the color of a red gummy bear.

Hawk and I tried to draw a line before full-blown intimacy. Reality check, the level of other types of intimacy we have, *had*, is deeper than anything I've experienced before. If I apply the same math to Hawk and I that I used on Nate regarding relationship recovery of the heart and mind, and divide our fifteen years in half—crap. I'm never dating again. Though, we didn't *really* break up. If I don't snap out of my head soon, my teammates will notice, and I don't want to be the one bringing the energy down.

The early darkening of the winter sky is shut outside, beyond the thatched roof of the pub. The enormous stone fireplace offers a perfect location to get all too toasty and snuggly with the team. Celebrating our likely loss this week is premature, but next weekend everyone is too busy. The nice thing about being back at Poseidon's bar is that Liv gets to keep ogling, and I get to stuff my face with delicious homemade fish and chips. The kind where the fry puffs beautifully, and my skin isn't a giant grease ball afterward.

Jeers and chatter scatter across the table. This will be our last game for eight weeks, unless we can pick up a few more players. We're down two now that my extra defender and Erika are each in their second trimester. If Erika had her way, she'd deliver straight on the field, pop up, and keep running.

"Cheers, ladies! To another perfectly *im*perfect season." Amber bubbles fizz to the top as Margaret lifts her pint glass high in the air.

I'm an awful person. She's kind and sweet. I'm the jerk who came between her and Hawk.

"Keep!" Liv throws her hands in the air and giggles loudly.

A crumpled napkin flies across the table straight into my palm. "One! I got one!" I laugh and lean back into the fireplace. The scalding stone burns at my spine, and my body slams forward on the table. "That's hot!"

Snickers across the table remind me I'll not get an ounce of empathy from this team. Poking fun and inappropriate conversations are part of being in this fierce group of women, who will take people down without hesitation.

With them, I can let loose on the field and then kick back. I always have people to support me, no matter what unique decision I make. With them, I'm never alone.

I take a quick sip of soda and shove the steaming, white flaky fish, sprinkled with vinegar, in my mouth.

I need to dig deep and talk to Margaret. She finishes eviscerating a piece of her steak and puts the knife down.

"Margaret. Do you—" Why is this so awkward? My stomach twists, and I'm officially the worst person in the world. What if she likes him?

The table falls silent, and the team eagerly stares at me.

Margaret steals a fork-full of fish from my plate and swallows it with a grin. "What's the deal with you and Hawk?"

My heart thumps backward, hitting my spine, and the room grows sticky hot.

"Come on. I was there last weekend. I saw him acting like an idiot." She takes a swig of beer and gently places the glass back on the table without so much as a clack.

How has it already been a week? An entire week and not a single text from him aside from the one I read at bread baking. The weeks move slower when we don't talk every day, or get into nonsensical debates over silly things. I miss mindless conversation over dinner. Even more so, I miss ending debates on the floor covered in sweat with the smell of hormones and happiness thick in the air.

"You're not mad that we ...?"

"You two had sex?!" Liv yells, covers her mouth, and glances at the surrounding tables with their deadpan stares. She lowers her hand to her lap and nods to the elderly couple, throwing us a thumbs-up.

On the shade scale, my face is a deep maroon.

"Did you?" Margaret bounces in her seat with a too-eager smile.

Heat flushes my cheeks and ears. What is this?

Margaret leans back in her chair. "He's fairly decent in bed. Takes directions well, and adjusts to needs on command." She smacks her fingers against her palm.

What? "Here's my roadblock. Raise your hand if you've made out with Hawk." I raise my fingers above the dark wood table.

Hands fly up, minus two people at the table. I'm an idiot for thinking this was a good idea.

Margaret shakes her head. "Raise your hand if you've slept with Hawk."

She raises her hand, and two other hands go up.

Not helping. I'm no different from them, but I don't know if I could handle Hawk and I not being an *us*.

"He's far from perfect, but we stopped sleeping together or doing anything really right before Christmas." Margaret brushes crumbs off her shirt and the light reflects off her diamond necklace. The amethyst necklace Hawk picked would have looked nice on her. "I knew what I was getting into."

"You still went out with him though," I say.

"There are times it's nice to get a good ride and not much more. He's a guaranteed pleasure badger, working diligently to get the job done." Her dark brown eyes flash wide. "I wanted a distraction, and work is busy. He was convenient, and hung up on someone." She lowers her chin.

I shake my head. "Bread baking?"

"Right! He was over the top because he wanted to do something he could impress *you* with, and suddenly you were right there with Thad. Handsome, sweet, smart, and you haven't jumped on that."

Small beads of sweat drip down my back as the fire flares behind me. Removing my shirt isn't an option with so many people around.

Great. The conversation has devolved to my love life again. "Thad was great. But he doesn't—"

"He doesn't give her the tingles down below." Rose cuts in, nods to the bartender and flicks her fingers.

"Eh." I search for a response, any response. "Our chemistry is non-existent. He's sweet though."

"Oh, gee, is it because you love Hawk?" Margaret asks, teasing me.

I shake my head. "You were on a date with Hawk, and now you're telling me I love him. You make no sense."

She giggles. "I'm not into Hawk for more than friendship. It mortified him when you showed up with Thad, so I played along." Margaret brushes her hair back and stares me down. "Stop using me as an excuse. I would like to climb on top of

Mount Thad and see where that goes." She pumps two hands, pushing his imaginary head low.

I swallow the bitterness and embarrassment resting on my tongue.

Poseidon walks over with a heap of napkins, dropping stacks across the table. He's a brave man to shimmy over to eleven women, at least two of whom would like to know how easily he can command their bodies with his trident. And, if he possesses the ability to cause tidal wave orgasms.

The seat creaks with the shift of my legs. My inner thighs still feel Hawk's fingers spreading across the gap. Not thinking about him isn't as easy as blocking out the last movie we watched together. It's having to ignore the sudden rushes of wanting to call him and feel his skin against mine.

"Hawk's a mess after last weekend." Margaret grabs an olive off the table and pops it in her mouth. "You showed up with Mr. Perfect and it took every ounce of energy to get him to laugh and not run out of the place upset because, in his head, your date was an Olympian in comparison."

This is ridiculous. Hawk can't be mad at me for going on dates. He's the one who created the profile. The one who always encourages me to date.

"Thad wasn't a date." My tongue twitches behind my teeth. "Besides, Hawk's been dating too."

Margaret shakes her head. "Nah. He was pretending. He hasn't been out on a date since before Christmas."

This makes no sense. I shake my head. "What about the pasta burns?" I push my food back and my stomach sinks. My fork clinks against the side of the plate and drops to the top of the napkin.

"I picked his drunk butt up and took him to the hospital." She laughs. "Idiot drank a bottle of red while trying to make pasta for himself and, well, he's not coordinated while drunk."

True, I've seen him stumble into bushes before and pretend it was on purpose. "Why didn't he call me?"

She knocks on the table in front of me. "All he did was mumble about you the whole ride to the hospital. I told dad jokes to help pass the time and to keep him from being a messy puddle when we got to the emergency room. He kept mumbling something about the fire pit and having screwed something up."

The air in the room grows thin and my head is swimming through every close call or second-guessed moment he and I have shared, and then blown off. He said nothing after the fire pit. Then again, it was easier to say nothing.

"Besides, when's the last time you went on a date with someone and didn't go home to hook up with Hawk? Or, have one of your *non-date* dates with him?"

"How do you know any of this?" Think. Think. "Last date I had wasn't a date, date. Especially not with the two of you there." Huh. The last one before that was after Mr. Scarf turned out to be married. That was months ago? Hawk and I hung out almost every night until the movies. I pull a sharp breath to the top of my lungs, refusing to let it out.

"Your vagina has already chosen. No one is going to measure up to the person your vagina and heart want most of all." Liv wags a beer at me.

"Can we leave my vagina out of this?" I whisper, and frantically glance around the room for eavesdroppers.

"In this case, your vagina and your heart are connected." Liv holds the beer to her heart with a big smile. "Team vote?"

The team nods like a choir of meddling grandmothers. This isn't what I want to hear. Denial might be easier if the team couldn't see through me.

"Who here votes Elin and Hawk have make-up-coitus?"

Ugh. That word is so, ugh. "That ship sailed." My eyes drop to my drink.

"No ships have sailed." Liv picks up her napkin, and in bold black is a phone number with the name Steve. Her smile drops to a full teeth grimace.

Such a disappointing name after nicknaming the bartender to be Poseidon. Steve. The excited rush and upright posture at the end of the table curls forward, and I can just about hear the fizzle of interest in Steve.

I can't lose Hawk as my friend despite the awkwardness of him seeing me naked—and all I want to do when I see him is *get* naked. That's not a friendship.

A click on the side button of my phone and there's still no missed calls or messages. In theory, I could text him, but what if he doesn't respond. I side-eye Margaret, and she's busy texting.

"Do you think it'll ever go back?" I ask with an undertone of defeat. "Do you think he even wants me as a friend anymore?"

"Did you ever stop to think maybe he's in the same place as you? Maybe there's a reason he agreed to take it slow? Hawk *loves* sex. But you're never going to be "just sex" for him." Margaret nods with a big smile. "I'll get his ass to a game. *You* have to sort it all out from there." She lifts her glass of water and clacks it against mine. "Introduce me to Thad and we'll call it even. Unless you don't think I'm his type"

"I don't know his type. I can ask."

Hawk won't show up to a game. He's more stubborn than I am, and worse, if Nate's there and Hawk doesn't show, he'll be right. I was a conquest.

"I don't know. I get this vibe from Thad he wants more of a wife and less of a fuck." Erika chimes in.

"I'm out," Margaret says. "I'm not up for serious right now."

I bite at my lower lip, tempering the nerves stomping in my throat.

Our next game is in four days. There's a lot of thinking to do in four days.

Chapter Thirty-Three

Tʜɪs ᴅᴀᴍɴ ᴛᴇᴀᴍ ᴀɢᴀɪɴ. Last time we played them, the game ended in penalty shots and the Bees lost. I'll get lit up by their forward if Margaret doesn't show up soon. I dig my toes into the turf to shake off my nerves. At the very least I'm an idiot, and she's a good teammate and a better friend taking *protect the goalie* to the next level.

Maybe she won't show, or he won't show. She did promise she'd get him here but Saturday was an excruciating four days ago. My arms stretch up to reach the top bar and work to pull the twists in my stomach back into place. The fingers on the glove are too stiff for a perfect grip and I slide off the upper bar, sending me crumpling to the cold blades. Turf shouldn't be cold, but maintaining an ice box field keeps costs down.

I slap my gloves together and stretch out the fingers. New gloves weren't a good idea today. I need comfortable, steady. I need Margaret.

"Shots!" Liv lines up a row of balls and points to me.

My teammates each stand behind a ball and take turns. Three of the five whiz past. Could be worse, could be better.

"Come on, Keep! Head high!" Rose takes a bouncing run, her tight red ponytail bopping before she shoots a high ball at me.

My arms extend, the ball smacks the center of my gloves, and I yank it down to my stomach before landing on a knee and rolling it back to her.

"Yeah! There's my girl!" she yells.

"Mine!" Margaret's voice rings out up the field.

I glance in her direction, and her shining face is a welcome relief. She holds two fingers high and stops the ball with a flexed foot, passing it with whistling force back to Rose. Her quick-footed steps join in defense of the goal, and she waves in the other defender. A little shield of protection against some of the strongest legs and biggest hearts in the league—my team.

"Line up shots!" The other defender calls out. "Stationary play. Shoot from where the ball lands."

Hot chocolate wafts across the field and I glance over to see Ariana sitting happily on the bench with a steaming thermos, ready to cheer us on. I shift my focus to the game ahead and scan the field. *Ten balls, six players taking shots if the defenders turn on me.* Angles are easier to calculate when it's where the ball lands, but my head is kneading dough, toasting marshmallows, and wishing for the cheer section to return. Okay, one person in the cheer section—Hawk. He makes the game more fun with the stupidest of faces to help me relax, or how his fingers gently cup my chin after a game, tilting my head up until I smile with thanks.

The ball whistles past my cheek. I blink hard, and focus on the next. Nothing like flying balls to snap my head from the clouds so I don't end up splayed on the ground from a shot I could've stopped. That ball was a warm-up gift from one of them.

Another shot meanders across the line, slower than a turtle.

I smack my thighs and raise my hands. The midfielder points to the far-left side and I plant my feet on the far-right goal post to practice a dive save. The moment her foot makes contact, my body leaps sideways and stretches long. *Extend the arms, legs, protect the face*—POP! The ball deflects off my gloves. *One down.*

But my moment of triumph disappears fast as all six of my field players barrel toward me. I open my arms wide and nod. They kick in rapid succession, and I miss all but one—saved by some impressive gymnastics.

"I'm not an octopus, people!" The rush of the stop, a successful stop, creates a wonderful high. *Where's Hawk?*

The ref blows a whistle to signal the game will start in ten minutes. Stretching, water, and clearing my head are necessary evils I'm not really into today. At least when the ball whizzes at me, I can focus on the ball and shut out the rest of the world.

With an eye roll, I crawl to the back corner of the net to get ready, and a ball whizzes past my hair, way too close to my face.

"Oh god!" A voice calls out.

"What the ever-loving fuck!" I yell out to the field. "Who does that?"

The familiar chuckle grows louder. *Hawk.*

I ball my fists to keep from shaking, and to keep myself from reaching for him.

My eyes travel from his soft lips to take in his full form. What the hell is he wearing? "Is that Curie's Halloween costume?"

The yellow and black striped bumble bee costume is way too small for Hawk's shoulders, and the tight black, speed skating unitard underneath leaves nothing to the imagination. He's here, and it's taking every ounce of energy I have to not want to wrap my arms under his and let our lips heal where words tend to mess us up. If he gets any closer, he'll feel my heart beating across the grass.

"Every team needs a mascot, I'm here to audition." A trash-bag-turned-stinger drags across the grass with every step he takes.

How do I undo last week? The last three weeks? I kick the ball back to him. My foot is officially a traitor to the rest of my body.

"You've got more in you than that, Keep." He winks, and taps the ball high for an easy stop.

"I'm a little distracted by the stinger." I slap my gloves together and step in front of my goal, closing the space between us. My heart grows lighter. This is flirting, and flirting is good.

He dribbles the ball toward me, and stops mere inches from the penalty line. "Better?"

Yes, if I didn't feel the draw of heat from his body, or have an aching in my gut that he's here to be strictly friends again. To go back to the way things were—I don't want that. I want *him.*

Hawk looks down at the ball, then back at me as I settle in with bent knees and raised hands. This is normal. Normal Hawk. Banter and playfulness.

Shank. The ball cuts to the far wall and rolls down the net.

He walks, head held high, to stand next to me, and the noise of the warm-up on the other side of the field stops. Where's the noise, the echoes of pops, slides, and bangs? The whistles, grunts, chatter, cheers, any of it? This place can't be this quiet.

A thick buzzing of bees draws from the side net. The traitors are blowing with all their might on kazoos, smiling and waving.

"Ooh! Keep!" One of my teammates taunts from the side before she and a few other players bang on the wooden bench, blowing one last elongated buzz on the plastic toys I'll soon burn.

The black net between Margaret and I catches the ball I punt at her before she can put her hands up. She laughs, and her fingers grip the net to peer through with a lineup of other teammates.

"Ever feel like you're being watched?" I ask.

"Ignore them. They're on team Hawk." He points to his heart with his thumb.

"Team Hawk, huh?" I take a step back and instantly regret it, wishing I'd taken two steps forward. "Stealing the entire team now instead of one by one?" Where's the whistle to start?

My chest contorts as tears prickle behind my eyes.

"So I was wondering," we say in unison.

I grin and nod. Three tiny jumps to wake up my legs and disappear these tears is not enough to focus for a game.

"You said you'd need time. But, do you? Why not go for it? This, us." He sits on the field, with his legs criss-crossed, and looks up at me.

"You're going to get plowed by my team." I gesture over to them.

They're busy shaking the net with giant grins.

I shoot Margaret side-eye with a nervous smile. She waves back and gives a thumbs-up. With a few stumbles back, I lean against the right-hand side goal post to control the wobble in my legs.

"As inviting as that offer *isn't*, I want *you*, not your team. Always, you." He places his hands on each knee and sits tall. "I wouldn't turn down being a mascot though." He bites his lower lip and pulls back his grin.

"Just like that?" *Say yes.*

The clock on the wall is no longer ticking down, and the ref makes himself comfortable, leaning back on the net with the bees.

"You know, you kinda suck at soccer," he says. "But damn if you don't put your full heart into everything you do. I love that about you, you put your whole self into people."

He loves me? I nod and blink back the forming tears. This will forever be a surprise.

Hawk stands, takes a few steps forward, and holds each of my hands, staring at my face.

"Hey, Hawk?" I'm used to blocking shots, not taking them. But I constantly scream to the Bees to take all the shots on the pitch and that it's okay if they miss. "Do you maybe want to go on an *actual* date sometime?"

He shakes his head. My heart drops and my arms go numb. Fuck. Fucking fuck. I'm an idiot.

"I don't want *a* date. We've been in this incredible, slow, unconventional but worth every odd moment, type of courtship-to-relationship for the past fifteen years. I want more. No more dates-non-dates. The past few months, where it's been really you and me, I don't need more one-offs to tell me what I already know. What we *both* know." He looks up, and places soft fingers under my chin to tilt my gaze directly to his. "I want you."

Scatters of warmth flutter through my body with a surge of confidence. I place my forehead against his and blink, staring into his lingering, hopeful gaze. With a soft breath, his hands spread across my lower back, pulling me in tight. One of our heads, both—whichever—turn in natural sync, and our lips part before pressing together. His tongue glides, sending heat to unhelpful places in the middle of a soccer pitch.

A long whistle blasts on the far field, and he squeezes me in tighter before releasing my hips.

He licks his bottom lip and runs his finger down my cheek.

I shake my head, and inside, I squeal. "I'm game."

"You've *got* a game." He nods his head to the goal.

I pout. Sex, full-blown sex with Hawk, where inhibition is lost and the months, years, and decade of emotional foreplay throb at my core. I want him, and now I have to get through this game without imagining how many more ways we'll fit together.

He glances over to the side net and back at me. With a swift shift of his legs, he goes down on one knee and a low hum of kazoos begins.

I gesture for him to stand as heat flushes my cheeks. He's busy fiddling with the end of his stinger and tugs out a box.

What the hell is he doing? The lights are hot on my skin, and confused electricity flows across my core. The field is suddenly eight times the size of an outdoor soccer field, but nothing happening is private.

"Marry me." He holds up a ring with a thick flat platinum band, one much too tiny to put over my goalie gloves.

My body freezes, my head swirls, and my mouth has an overflow of saliva it doesn't know how to swallow. With a center cushion cut, a sparkling sapphire stares back at me, and I kneel on the ground to join him, to make us equal. I wish I could read what's going through his head right now. I wish I could turn back time and get a peek at what was going through him the night he first saw me, long before I ever saw him. Before the field trip. Before our friends started dating, and years before we ever even touched a soccer ball together. He noticed me.

Tears flow down my face as words circle through my head, unable to come out.

"I need a word or something here." He grimaces and glances down. "It's too much, isn't it, too public? I went too big?"

"If this is another fake proposal." I grip my hips and work to hold my balance.

"I've *never* fake proposed to you." His tone is steady, calm. "You never said yes. It's never ever been a joke."

The mere presence of the hushed bees adds a supportive calmness to the air.

"Yes, I'll marry you." I blurt out as I raise his chin with my finger to gaze into his hopefulness. "But only if you promise, no matter if I seem embarrassed or uncomfortable, you will never stop being yourself. Be loud, silly, outspoken, and always yourself. I love your loud."

The thunder of rushing feet vibrate across the field, and the team tackles the two of us to the ground with cheers and excitement.

Liv rips the glove off my hand so Hawk can put the ring on my finger. The team circles us, while Hawk and I stare at one another like the idiot teenagers we were when we met.

The ref blows a whistle, and flashes of yellow jerseys disperse on the field.

"Protect this for me?" I hand him the ring to get the glove on.

Hawk takes it, stands, and wipes at his tear-filled eyes. "Don't worry. I'll be here cheering in my favorite corner while you play." He cuts through the gap in the net. With a loud WHOOP and a wave, he settles in to cheer us on. To cheer *me* on.

My head's in the corner with him, with the anticipation of his fingers pressing down my sides, and that—for the first time—we're on the same page.

The page everyone, except us, read, before our timing finally became right.

Margaret flies across the field with the ball cutting in front of the net, and slaps me a side-five before kick-off.

Their team barrels up the field, and I crouch to launch my fully extended body as their striker releases the ball, high off her laces. She shanks, and I hit the grass. Who cares? I laugh and stand up, smiling back to the corner where Hawk holds a turquoise glitter sign.

My Fiancée is the Goalie.

I laugh and cover my mouth.

He points to his heart, then back to me, and flips the sign around.

I Love You for Keeps.

My bottom lip quivers as I pull back a laugh and tamper down the surge of hot excitement spreading rampant through my body. In the path to tonight, to promising to be with him forever, I'd never have guessed everyone we've dated in between was actually the rebound from our first innocent kiss when we were too young to know what we were getting into with one another. The goal has always been simple, to protect my relationship with Hawk. I can't want to turn into the old married couple in the sketch of us by the river, laughing and always putting one another first while our life continues to grow together.

ABOUT THE AUTHOR

Beck Erixson writes about the beautifully awkward world of navigating the journey to true happiness through friendships, love, and family—be it blood, found, or chosen. Her stories enhance the importance of positive interconnection, even when we feel lonely. She lives on the Jersey Shore, and can often be found either writing *by* the river, or *in* it in some way. Her short stories have appeared in *Many Nice Donkeys,* and *Full Mood Mag.*

Like the FMC in Ballsy, she's a former indoor soccer goalie who lived for time on the field with her amazing team.

Connect With Me

Learn about upcoming releases, short stories, and more by visiting her through one of the platforms below.

goodreads.com/author/show/34934710.Beck_Erixson

instagram.com/BeckErixsonAuthor

twitter.com/BErixson

tiktok.com/beckerixsonauthor

www.beckerixson.com

If you enjoyed the story, please consider leaving a review on whichever platform best suits your fancy.

Books by Beck Erixson

Love is Awkward Novels

Feeling Ballsy

Feeling Fiery

Feeling Lively

Additional Books

Just a Fika: Coffee, Connection, and a Matchmaking Ghost Grandmother

Acknowledgements

Elin and Hawk demanded their story be told from day one of placing my fingers against the keyboard. They instantly sucked me into their world of humor, love, nervousness, and support. I fell for them—how they showed one another love, without even thinking about the depth of their actions. The more I wrote, the more excited I was to show love in different ways. Love of family, friendship, and most importantly, love of self.

Please accept the giant love ball below from this appreciative author who didn't know where to start, but kept on pushing thanks to her amazing team.

My writing group, the ones I check messages from daily since #RevPit in 2020, consistently cheered (yelled) to keep going with the beautiful awkwardness of the story. The names in the manuscript may look familiar, but I promise, the characters aren't modeled after them, with the exception of their sheer collective kindness. Thank you, Amelia, Ariana, Janet, Katrina, Kim, Kira, Liv, Melisa, Noreen, and Rose, for enduring endless snippets, providing guidance, and helping me not want to give up on a near daily basis.

Cheers to my Positivity Writing Group, Thursday WriteA-long group with Tiffany, and beta readers. If you haven't had the pleasure of following Mae Bennett on social media yet, do so. She's full of positive energy, is an incredible writer, and absolutely knows the romance genre like a well-seasoned professor.

Dr. Lisa Sisler kicks me on a regular basis to write and believe in my story as much as I believe in hers. She is the epitome of a positive female friendship, and one I wish started much sooner in my life.

My best friends who keep me laughing and always positively scream at me in support of my goals. (You know who you each are. I'll forever love your loud.)

After multiple rounds of edits, and plenty of kicking around a soccer ball with my husband and toddler, I still loved the story and wanted to do it justice which meant working with a Developmental Editor who specialized in Romance. Kristen Weber's wizardry helped confirm there was something fun and special about this story.

Maria Tureaud took on my early writing and helped me figure out my voice. Through her kindness and approach, I never feel like an awful writer—even in the beginning when my writing was truly dreadful. For this manuscript, she worked on loose threads, my cringe-worthy grammar, and pure New Jersey accent spelling, magically washing it away.

No book is complete without a gorgeous cover. Melody Jeffries is a fantastic artist, and happens to be a military spouse.

She took my eight million photos and descriptions to make Hawk and Elin perfect.

Chris, Greta and Svea, you hold my heart always.

Like Elin, I can't say enough positive things about the people who helped make this book happen.

Thank you, dear reader, for coming on this journey of love and friendship with me. Thank you for taking the chance on Elin, Hawk, and myself.

Love,

Beck

If you enjoyed the story, please consider leaving a review on whichever platform best suits your fancy.